HONEY AND ICE

BLACK ROSE and GOLD QUEEN

Copyright © Shannon Mayer, Kelly St. Clare

2024

Black Rose and Gold Queen, The Honey and Ice Series, Book 6

All rights reserved

HiJinks Ink Publishing

All rights reserved. Without limiting the rights under copyright reserved above, no part of this publication may be reproduced, stored in or introduced into a database and retrieval system or transmitted in any form or any means (electronic, mechanical, photocopying or otherwise) without the prior written permission of both the owner of the copyright and the above publishers.

Please do not participate in or encourage the piracy of copyrighted materials in violation of the author's rights. Purchase only authorized editions.

This is a work of fiction. Names, characters, places and incidents are either the product of the author's imagination or are used fictitiously, and any resemblance to actual persons living or dead, business establishments, events or locales is entirely coincidental.

Original illustrations by MB

Mayer, Shannon

St. Clare, Kelly

For all the readers who have stuck with us, this one's for you.

CHAPTER 1

There wouldn't be enough room in a single Fae Court to accommodate all of Underhill's creatures. Worse, how would we get them here?

We had no portal. Our access to Underhill had been cut off, and while I'd been named mistress of that land, I wasn't her. I wasn't my mother.

She was gone, dead, killed by Sigella. *Tea-drinking traitor.*

"Fuck," I whispered under my breath. No matter how we situated the creatures, there was no way they'd fit at the Alaskan Court with Queen Hyacinth, or even split between the Alaskan, Irish, and Louisiana Courts. We needed a solution tonight.

Queen Hyacinth—who'd insisted I call her Cinth since I'd seen her vagina—and my sister, Kallik the Oracle, were leaning over a map of the Earth realm.

We'd convened at the Alaskan court to discuss *possibilities*, of which there was only one.

One none of us wanted to agree to.

All because Underhill, the long-standing home of the fae and all fae creatures was no longer safe. More than that, my home realm was being destroyed by….

My heart clenched. *No*, I wouldn't think about the one doing the destroying.

For the last twenty-nine days, I'd done all I could to avoid thinking of Cormac or Aaden, and the creature they'd become. Andas, he called himself.

If I thought about them too much, then I found myself longing to turn away from those I needed to protect. I found myself *yearning* for something with him that could never be.

A hand settled on my shoulder. "Little sister."

I blinked and turned to Faolan, Kallik's mate and now my brother-in-law. Brother. Family.

As much as I'd lost, the forces governing balance had tried to rectify it by gifting me with replacements. I'd lost my mother, and those forces had given me her power—or a weaker semblance of it. I'd lost Kik, my brother and true family, and those forces had given me Faolan and Kallik and Cinth. Except no one could replace Kik, and no one could fill my mother's boots. Certainly not me.

And, as it turned out, no force in the realms could replace Cormac and Aaden.

"You have an idea," Faolan said to me quietly. "I can

see it in your face." He was the calm one of the group, that was for sure. A good balance for Kallik.

That word—balance—made my guts clench.

Creatures from several realms expected me to take on my mother's job and provide them with that balance, but someday soon they'd figure out I was undeserving of their faith.

"Yes."

His eyes searched mine. "Then you should tell them. You've never held back before, Silver, but this last month that's all you've done."

"How do you know that?" I didn't snap, though, and I didn't push him away. I was fucking exhausted. Tears, grief, and loss had dampened the fire that had burned in my soul my whole life.

"Because in many ways you are a mirror of Kallik, and I know her better than anyone else." He didn't shift his eyes from my face. "Which makes reading you and your emotions significantly easier. Far from perfect, but…easier."

I swallowed hard. We had to move an entire realm of creatures tomorrow. Faolan was right—I had to speak now, or we wouldn't save them all.

Leaving any creature behind to suffer the tyranny of Unbalance as Underhill was destroyed wasn't an option I could live with. The creatures there were family, from Old Man the dragon to the naga to the rainbow flock who'd helped to defeat the sluagh, and everyone between, even the tarbeasts.

I'd been declared their protector, and whether I wanted that title or not, it was my responsibility to fulfill the role as best I could until a worthy replacement could be found.

I turned to the table and steeled myself. "We must let them assimilate as they wish. You cannot contain them."

Silence met my words as Cinth and Kallik faced me, cutting off their conversation about saving a quarter of all the species and leaving the rest in Underhill to become slaves to Andas. Hyacinth was already shaking her head. "I understand how you feel, Silver, but that isn't possible. Human and fae relations are tenuous at best after Rubezahl's attacks. If we unleash these fae creatures on Earth—"

"If we don't do this, a realm of fae beings will die. There isn't enough room, food, or shelter for the creatures of Underhill at any one court. Even if the other courts accepted some of Underhill's creatures, there still isn't enough room for everyone, and I won't leave three-quarters of my people behind to die. The humans will survive. I will instruct the creatures from Underhill to stay as hidden as possible and to attack no human unless in defense."

That would be a large request for creatures who had only ever existed in a kill-or-be-killed world.

"They can't attack at all," Cinth spluttered.

I met her panicked gaze, saying coldly, "This is the way of life and death, Queen Hyacinth, and if humans and fae in the Earth realm have forgotten this, then they will be reminded to their long-term benefit. I will not order any creature to lie down and die. They could have young to protect or a herd. They could also be unable to stop their defensive magics and abilities."

Humans had forgotten they were mere animals in a realm. Earth didn't belong to them, and they—like any other creature—would need to adjust to a change in their habitat. Or perish if adapting was beyond them.

The alterative was killing an earth-equivalent of fae creatures. That made the decision very simple. To me, at least.

Kallik gave me a doubtful look. "You think Old Bastard can stay hidden?"

Old Bastard was the largest of the dragons in Underhill. Other dragons existed, but none of his size. I was fonder of him than most, and he'd also earned rare respect from my mother during her reign.

"Old Man will reside here at the Alaskan Court," I said, certainty coming to me as I spoke. "As will the rawmouths. They'll stay close to where you and Cinth can keep eyes on them."

Hyacinth shook her head again. "The humans will believe we're warring against them. It's the excuse they've been waiting for to try and take our lands and magic. Silver, there are too many of them and their weapons are formidable. There's a reason we haven't pushed for more of a presence in their world."

"Convince them otherwise," I said. "There's no other way."

Kallik's lilac eyes closed, and her essence pulsed as she accessed the unique oracle magic that allowed her to study much of the past, present, and future. "The path has cleared. We must follow Silver, or we will face a worse catastrophe."

"Ah, fuck me with a beetroot tickle," Hyacinth muttered.

Kallik's lips twitched. "That would be an extreme waste of a good beetroot tickle."

I had to agree with her on that point.

Her best friend waved a hand and slumped onto a chair, her skirts fluffing up around her like one of her delicious puff pastries. "You know, sometimes I detest that you made me queen, Kallik. This is not…it was never what I wanted for my life. It was meant to be temporary."

Kallik's smile faded. "I know, my friend, I know."

If Andas—Unbalance—succeeded against us, then Cinth wouldn't need to worry about being Queen of All Fae. Dead fae didn't worry about much at all.

Silence fell as we stared at the map of the world before us. The choice was a simple one, but the consequences wouldn't be. I'd grown up fighting for my life, and if my savage, relentless urge to survive was any indication of how humans might react when their survival was under threat, then we'd face a vicious battle on another front.

"I'll let the human ambassadors know what's happening. I'll tell them this is temporary and the creatures will behave." Hyacinth straightened in her chair, and despite what she'd said, I believed she was the best choice for Queen of All Fae—her diplomacy alone was worth its weight in naga treasure.

This was a temporary situation, but not in the way she'd assumed. Once Andas destroyed Underhill, there would be no home for the creatures of Underhill to return to. Worse, a potential war between the fae and humans would only contribute to his strength.

Andas must be sitting in the scale realm right now, roaring with laughter as we all slid into turmoil and chaos. *Feeding him.*

I walked out of the war room, closing the door behind me. I didn't need to argue more for Underhill and its creatures. Cinth would do as I asked because I was the Mistress of Underhill and Kallik had informed us there was no better path.

Convincing her didn't make me feel any better about what would happen after the creatures of Underhill escaped their home. *My* home.

I strode through the palace, ignoring the other bustling fae, the warrior half-fae, and the subservient full-blooded humans. Escaping to my room was hardly a solace, but the chamber provided a quiet place that I'd hidden in more than once in the last twenty-nine days.

"Oh! I thought you wouldn't be back until much later."

I looked up as Orry, my silver bat friend, floated down from the ceiling, her pale wings spread wide. Behind her was a mess of flowers.

"Orry, what were you doing?" I wasn't sure I wanted to know.

"I was trying to surprise you. I found these flowers that complement your hair in the palace gardens. I was hoping to weave them through a braid?" She landed on my outstretched hand.

"Of course," I said, despite the weight in my gut that wanted nothing more than to be alone.

Orry directed me to sit on the edge of the bed, then fluttered around behind me, her tiny claws dragging through my hair as she swept the long strands into an intricate braid, adding flowers as she went. I'd been born with silver hair that had gone blonde for a time before changing into glimmering silver hair that was as metallic as my mother's golden hair had been. Looking back I could see that my hair had shown the signs of my mother preparing to leave the realms.

"What's going to happen?" she asked quietly. "To Underhill and its creatures?"

"The queen will do as I asked."

"You're going to set them free, aren't you?"

I let out a long, slow breath. Why did this task fall to me? *Mother, why did you leave me alone in this mess?* "How did you know?"

"You've been muttering in your sleep for the last week." Orry finished the braid and crawled onto my shoulder, hugging my neck. I lifted a hand to her tiny body and gently held her.

"Thank you, Orlaith, for being my friend."

"Don't talk like that," she whispered.

"Like what?"

"Like you're going to die. Like you want to."

"That's not the plan." I tried to smile, but my face couldn't seem to remember how. There'd been too much loss. *Mother. Kik. Cormac. Aaden.* My men might be trapped inside Andas, but I knew I'd never see them again. Not as they'd been. Mother had set me an impossible task when she'd ordered me to reach them.

Her words were burned into my memory. *He does carry the souls of the men you love. You have a chance to reach them. Reach them, and they can stop Unbalance.*

Now that the problem of saving the fae creatures from their impending doom had been decided, I had no further reason to delay carrying out her final order to 'reach him'—whatever that meant.

I stood and walked to the open balcony doors.

Alaskan summer was fast fading, and the nights stung with cold as winter snapped at us, eager for its turn. I gripped the balustrade and peered out across the court and Unimak to the ocean beyond. The wind tugged at my senses, bringing the scents of salt, flowers, and magic. A pinprick of white in the night sky swept closer.

"I don't believe you," Orry said, near tears.

I took a breath that didn't fill my lungs. "Andas is

without mature and strong henchmen now. He's on his own, and I've been tasked to defeat him by somehow reaching Cormac and Aaden within him. They must be the source of his power. If I can't beat Unbalance, then he'll kill me and everyone I love. But I know what killing him will take from me. That's why I speak as if I will die. Because I'll either die in spirit and heart if I kill my men, or in body if I can't find the strength to do so."

The white speck in the distance grew larger in size, and wide-spread wings and long legs took form as it grew closer. The being raced toward me, somehow feeling my need even though I'd said nothing.

Was this part of being Underhill's chosen protector?

Orry let go of me and flew forward to bop Peggy on the nose as she landed gracefully on the balcony.

The pegasus was the last of her kind. She'd loved Kik, the last land kelpie, and he'd loved her. At least my friend and brother had known true love before the sluagh killed him.

"Peggy," I murmured.

"Get on. We need to fly. Bat, you stay here." Her command was sharp, and Orry and I both obeyed without question.

As soon as I hopped onto Peggy's back, she launched into the air, her powerful haunches shooting us straight up as her wings caught a current of winter-kissed wind. The sharp cold was a slap in the face as Peggy soared high, so close to the stars that I could have sworn they were within reach. The temperature this high up was freezing. My skin and bones ached as if I'd plunged into the icy end of the purple sea.

"What is it?" My teeth chattered as Peggy leveled out, her wings stretched wide to either side.

"This is the last moment of peace you'll have for a very long time," Peggy whispered. "Once the creatures of Underhill come here, then Unbalance will try to claim Underhill, the very source of fae magic. You stand between us and that future.

I shivered, although not from the cold that wanted to wrap around me again.

"Peace is fleeting," I answered, willing to accept her gift.

"True, and all the sweeter for the moment it touches our hearts." Peggy banked through a cloud and the moisture stuck to my skin, freezing in little ice droplets.

I could have pulled red essence from the stars to warm myself and dispel the ice, but I let the droplets stay. Maybe they'd help freeze my emotions and heartache too.

"Did I call to you?" I asked. "How did you know..."

"That you needed something more than your friend Orlaith could provide? Do you know why Pegasi limit our riders?"

Despite being raised in Underhill, I didn't know the answer. I'd heard of Peggy before Kik had taken me to her, and everyone knew that attempting to ride a

Pegasus was a death wish, but I hadn't realized there was a deeper reason for it. "No."

"Our riders become part of our family, and as part of our family we can sense each other from afar. Almost like homing beacons. More than that, we can sense strong emotions. Your distress called me."

The words poured out of me, up above the world where speaking such things felt safer. "Everything could go wrong, Peggy. Everything *is* going wrong, just the way Andas needs it to. Underhill will be under his power, destroyed for us."

I squeezed my eyes shut and confessed something I hadn't wanted to admit to even myself. "Fae will weaken without a connection to Underhill. They'll lose their magic and, given enough time, they will die. They'll have no option but to do whatever Andas wishes in the end. That's if we can even make a portal big enough for them to come through tomorrow. You've seen the size of Old Man. It's all…destined to fail. I can't see a way through it."

"You have too little faith in yourself, young one." Peggy drifted lower until her legs skimmed the ocean and her wingtips sent up a spray of salt water. "Underhill believed you could face Unbalance and win. You have every creature of Underhill behind you. Even the queen and oracle are following your orders. Do you think a person is given so much respect and trust without having earned it?"

I was a hunter, a savage thing by Earth standards,

and a daughter of Underhill. I had spent my whole life doing Underhill's bidding, as had we all. *I* didn't bid others. I could never be as powerful and confident as my mother had been.

"Peggy, if I fail, I doom every soul that depends on me. Every fae. Every dragon. Every naga."

Peggy pulled up short and landed on a small outcropping of rock. "Dismount."

I slid off her back, and as soon as my feet touched, she spun to face me in the air, her wings barely beating but nonetheless holding her in the air. "You are the chosen one, Silver, Mistress of Underhill. The fae realm shines with your essence. The mantle was passed on to you, and you alone. Young one, you possess all the knowledge and strength needed to meet your destiny with the fearlessness you are renowned for in all realms."

With that, she spun and flew away, leaving me on a rock in the middle of the damn ocean. "Peggy!"

"Regain your heart of fire, Silver," she called over her shoulder, "Remember yourself. Find all you know, for you will need everything to face the coming darkness."

I stared after her retreating form. I hadn't touched my essence, or the magic that connected me to Underhill once in the last twenty-nine days. No one else had noticed.

On that rock I stood, freezing. On that rock, I allowed my suffering to rise and consume me, because my heart deserved to feel everything that I'd battled back for nearly a month. For the first time in my twenty-one years, I couldn't forge on through my pain, so I had to find another way to keep going.

I had to suffer and be unafraid of it. I had to be as fearless in pain as I was against any unknown predator. I had to learn this predator's weaknesses so I might survive.

As the sun slowly rose on the thirtieth day, I was rewarded with my answer.

Suffering was a poison—one that ate at a person over time. And so I'd desensitize to this suffering in the same way I'd sometimes desensitized myself to other poisons. In time, I would suffer without being frozen by it.

I couldn't say what I might do to Unbalance in the end, but I didn't need to worry about that just yet. I had to focus on letting the suffering in little by little in the hope that I could do what was needed when the time came.

I closed my eyes as the surrounding waves swelled up and over the rock, soaking me through, chilling me again. Cold, the darkness was cold. Andas, Unbalance, was also cold.

But the magic of Underhill was light and warm.

Underhill was fire.

I was fire.

A spark grew within me, and I lifted my hands as silver magic coursed through my body, joyous and vibrant after its imprisonment. I'd never seen my essence shine so bright. Fire coursed through my veins, my heart, and my soul. The fire blazed a path around the suffering I'd let in, cordoning the poison off.

I might not be what everyone thought, but I *did* possess the power to do one thing for those I considered family.

The creatures of Underhill needed a portal.

One step at a time, one foot in front of the other down the path.

Silver surged into my fingertips.

"Here we fucking go," I whispered.

CHAPTER 2

I'd known a few beings with the power to open portals.

My mother, who went where she wished.

Kik, the last land kelpie, who'd simply had to lift a foreleg to access realms.

The Oracle, whom I'd never spoken to on the subject. Andas could portal, and Sigella had learned to portal through witnessing me doing so.

Maybe it was different for all of them. All I knew was that as soon as my magic was released, I knew how *I* could create portals.

With every breath of ocean air, I could feel an enormous presence within me that was almost as big as my being.

That presence wasn't just within me, though, it was all around me. I could feel the presence most strongly in the main realms, Earth and Underhill. I could also feel a lesser presence in the scale realm. I pulled a face at the memory of the mass of black ribbons slicing through my legs. Not my favorite realm. I could also feel a tinier presence again in the very smallest of the four realms, the prison realm, that sat within the scale realm and held those fae who'd let too much darkness into their hearts.

This job probably called for finesse, but I didn't feel equipped for finesse. I never felt equipped for much these days.

Fuck it.

I opened a portal to the fae realm and paused for a second to absorb my joy at the sight of purple water on the other side.

I'd start with the ocean creatures.

I threw a lasso of silver toward the biggest presence I sensed—something I'd practiced a few times in recent days. In that, at least, I was prepared.

I hooked a rawmouth, and the huge water fae didn't need any encouragement to speed toward me.

A great eye filled the portal I'd opened.

"Hi Bawth," his voice came.

Hi, Boss.

I dipped my head. "Rawmouth. Summon your kind. It's time to leave Underhill for ruin."

"Forr ruinnn, bawth?" he said sadly.

"For ruin," I repeated. "Do it now. Do not delay."

There was another who would not like my presence here, nor my intention to steal his future slaves.

I felt the surge of nearing rawmouths. Holding the portal to Underhill, I opened a second portal to a lake on Unimak that I hoped would be large enough to hold the rawmouths.

"Ready bawth," he said.

I nodded and opened both portals wide. The drain on my essence wasn't significant, but the job had only just begun. "Come now."

The rawmouths dove into the cold sea before me, covering me in a seemingly endless wave of water that I breathed through without fear of death. They rose in a second dive to pass through the second portal to the lake.

I waited until the last fin had passed into relative safety, then closed the portal to Unimak.

Now came the harder task. Andas hadn't noticed me yet, and I couldn't risk alerting him by sending a pulse of my magic through the purple ocean. I lashed out the teensiest wisp of my magic and then cast a net when I located my target.

Like the rawmouth, she came willingly with my magic.

Soon a tiny cloud hovered in the portal to Underhill.

She didn't speak, but glowed silver happiness at the sight of me.

I took note of the twin suns' positions in the sky behind her.

"Little one," I said to her. "You and your family must

spread a message to the other creatures of Underhill for me. You must do this as quickly and quietly as you can lest darker forces suspect what is afoot. All land creatures must gather at Dragonsmount without delay. Any not there as the suns set will be left in peril."

The tiny cloud began to rain.

"Yes," I said. "I wish it had not come to this. I will help you along."

I released the tiny cloud back to where I'd found her in the cloud forest where Peggy had lived until recent times.

Then I cracked my damn knuckles.

"That was one of the many bad habits I deplored in you," someone said from my right.

I bared my teeth and whirled on the tea-drinking traitor who'd killed my mother—who'd killed the mother of all creatures. "Sigella."

She waved a hand in the air. "Yes, yes, you want to kill me."

"You killed my mother."

"I killed your mother to spare her from a horrific end, as you know."

Fury built in me, and yet…"I don't have time for this now, Sigella."

"Why do you think I chose this exact moment to leave Underhill? I have no desire to die, now that I'm free."

"Go be free then," I told her. "I will have nothing more to do with you."

I faced the portal again, then reached my little finger through to dip it in the purple water. I drew it back, then squinted at my wet finger. "I know you are there, ones that connect the purple ocean and all its creatures." Except for the rawmouths. They didn't listen to anyone who couldn't beat them—which is why I'd dealt with them first.

Microscopic flecks glowed purple on my finger. The slightly acidic plankton pulsed in response to my magic and touch. It struck me how often the fates of realms so often depended on the smallest beings. "The ocean fae need your help," I told the plankton. "You must carry a message to all to evacuate to this portal into the Earth realm. They must be here before the suns set. Do not speak this message to any dark creature, do you hear me?"

The creatures pulsed, burning my skin, which healed as quickly as it was injured.

I dipped my finger through the portal again and released them. Through my window into Underhill, I watched as the purple ocean lit up in a wave until the glow of the bright-purple plankton extended farther than my eyes could see.

"Very clever," Sigella said. "Though you were always good at surviving. Towering amount of annoying, vile habits aside, I couldn't have asked for a better prison."

"You talk a lot for someone who murdered my mother and the mother of all creatures."

I threw her a glare and caught the shrug of her shoulders.

"I meant what I said," I repeated. "I will have nothing more to do with you."

"No one, not even you, will dictate my life," she replied.

I smiled. "You have wanted freedom for so long, Sigella. What a shame if word were to spread of how you killed the revered and beloved Underhill. You would be hunted and pursued for the rest of time."

She didn't answer.

"Nothing to say now?" I asked.

"I have belief in your determination to do good."

I'd always had belief in that side of myself. I might be savage by Earth standards, but I wasn't cruel. I loved all creatures, and respect for their role in balance had been carved into me nearly from birth. "You would like me to forgive you as easily as you appear to have forgiven yourself."

"What I did was a mercy."

"What you did was too hasty," I informed her in a calm voice I didn't recognize. Perhaps I was already desensitizing to suffering, because in the past, the fury I felt would've had me clawing for Sigella's ruffled throat.

Sigella's focus bored into my face. "You believe there was time to do something?"

"The right to try should have been mine, and you stole it from me. I think you've gone so long without having to answer to anyone that it didn't occur to you to consider anyone other than yourself."

She scoffed. "How many times have I saved your life?"

"To save your prison," I said scathingly. "To preserve your new freedom."

There was a slight sourness to the words which told me they weren't entirely true. I tilted my head, watching as the tidal wave of purple shifted, heading toward the portal. Soon, the ocean creatures would gather. Andas couldn't fail to notice that. What happened then?

"What will you do when Unbalance arrives?" Sigella asked.

I looked at her. "Maybe you could shoot an arrow into him too."

"Gladly."

I wanted to shout and scream at Sigella. I wanted to hurt her. Yet these parts of me were balanced by one annoying and persistent truth that I couldn't quite deny.

I sighed heavily. "I can admit that mother might have suffered a horrible fate if Andas had succeeded in taking her."

The ancient fae blinked.

"I will never know if Andas would have succeeded though. Perhaps I would have found a way to thwart him. And so I cannot forgive you for stealing the possibility of more time with her from me," I told Sigella in the next breath. How different this battle against Unbalance would have been if we'd had my mother and her knowledge and experience on our side. "Begone, Sigella. I am done with you and your fucking teacups."

She didn't budge, but fae of all shapes and sizes were visible in the tidal wave careening ever closer to my portal.

The time for hiding was over.

I flung the portal wider than my mind could fathom. Perhaps the whole of Alaska could fit within the confines, I knew not. I just knew that some unlucky human fishermen were about to get the shock of their lives, along with any marine life in Earth's oceans.

The tidal wave split to either side of me, hopefully collecting Sigella in its torrent, and as I held the portal of gigantic proportions open, thousands upon thousands of fae beings surged passed me, carried by the powerful swell of their own making and encased in water.

They looked at me for the split second they could, and I looked at them. I saw their fins and barbs, their gills, their teeth. I saw their colors like rainbow streaks against the purple canvas. I felt their awe and their fear and their hope. They stored that hope within me.

Me, of all people.

Water pounded, and new tidal waves formed from the arrival of so many fae in one place, as much as I'd tried to spread the portal. Some of the fae would be crushed in the mass of bodies. Humans and other animals might die in the resulting tidal waves too.

The rush was slowing. The suns were just a sliver on the horizon of Underhill through the portal.

There was a tap on my shoulder, and I glanced at Sigella.

Her voice was impossible to hear, but I read her lips.

"He is coming."

I nodded, shrinking the portal rapidly as the last creatures threw themselves into the Earth realm. I shrunk it to the size of my body, then opened a second, larger portal.

Andas appeared, and I threw the larger portal at him, promptly closing the entrance to Underhill afterward.

Sigella whistled. "Nice move. Where did the second portal go?"

"The waterhole in the prison realm. I'm hoping someone shat in there recently."

She laughed, but said afterward, "That won't hold him."

"No shit, Sigella."

I turned to face a literal sea of fae, hundreds of thousands that I could see and millions that I couldn't. "Listen well. The daughter of Underhill has brought you to the Earth realm for a time. Stay hidden. Anyone who attacks the humans unprovoked will have me to deal with. We are guests here, and you would be wise to remember it. Spread out. Be safe."

The suns had set in Underhill, and I didn't have the luxury of a longer warning. Not if I wanted to save their earthbound counterparts. I'd dragged these fae from their homes into this foreign world, and now I would leave them, cruelly, to learn and survive as best they could.

Sweat beaded on my brow, and though my legs wanted to fold, I was surprised not to feel more of a drain after such a feat.

"Where to next?" Sigella shouted over the crashing waves as fae escaped in every direction to hide.

I portaled away.

There was a barren part of Unimak I'd noticed, where the court fae didn't tend to go. Kallik and Faolan lived closest to it. I was sure they'd have something to say about their new neighbors, but so be it.

Barren land underfoot, I opened a portal to Dragonsmount and stepped into Underhill this time.

"Old Man," I said. "You're first."

"I know of humans," he replied from the depths of his hole. "I know they will fear me, and they are slaves to their fear. They will war against fae because of my presence. I cannot go, Mistress of Underhill."

I didn't have time for this. "You will go because you are too powerful for me to let you fall into the hands of Unbalance."

There was quiet. "Wisdom that I see no path around."

"No," I told him. "And so go Old Man, and we will fight what wars we must together."

There were no more arguments from him. I threw the portal wide, and the magnificent dragon slid from his huge den in the mountainside, dislodging razor-sharp shingles with his gliding exit, which was a mere whisper considering his size.

"Impressive." The voice reverberated through the land and through my body. It plucked at the suffering in my heart.

I glanced over my shoulder and found Andas hovering in the sky. He sat upon a steed of skulls that I recalled the sluagh riding. The steed had found a fitting new master.

"Andas," I called back. "Has anyone told you how similar your name sounds to 'Anus'?"

"Childish remarks are beneath you, Underhill."

I'd grown up with a land kelpie whose language was more colorful than a rainbow flock. A childish comment or two could sure help a person feel better.

I closed the portal after Old Man. "Been busy?"

"But of course," he said. "Have you missed me?"

"You? No. Cormac and Aaden, yes."

"You still live under the illusion that they're within me. They *are* me, you fool. They are merged to become me, and they no longer exist as individuals."

Yet my mother had said I could reach my men and

undo the darkness of Unbalance. "They are within you, and I hope they know how much I miss them. What we had was taken too soon, yet I know that they were for me, and I was for them. I hold the beauty of that in my heart even as I mourn that we didn't have more time together."

I could hardly put a word to what had bound the three of us together, and yet I knew they were a part of me just like my arms were my arms and my brain was my brain.

Andas grinned. "You've spent the last month crying over them, haven't you? You, the chosen of Underhill, a savage creature raised in the cold belly of the fae realm, brought to tears like a little girl over two men who barely tolerated you."

Suffering was a poison.

I absorbed the blow of his words because they *were* a blow. They clawed at my fears. Cormac and I had only just found common ground shortly before the tree of life had killed him—or his body, at least. After the tree had injected Cormac's soul into Aaden, Aaden had 'barely tolerated' me for the most part too.

And yet they were mine just as my arms were my arms and my brain was my brain.

I let myself feel the suffering invoked by his words, but I didn't let that stop me from opening a portal to the barren area on Unimak. I pushed the opening between realms to the proportions of a country once more.

"Creatures of Underhill, it is time to leave this place."

They didn't hesitate, the fastest of them blurring through the portal ahead of the others. The sky was filled with as much of a stampede as there was on the surface—and beneath it.

Andas's laughter was terrible, more terrible still because I could hear Cormac's low rumble and Aaden's lighter humor within it. "You think I'll allow you to take my subjects?"

"Subjects is a loose term for what you mean to do with them." I readied myself for his attack, knowing already that Andas was stronger than me.

His steed trotted through the sky toward me, and the moonlights caught at the angles of the cracked skulls that formed it. "I need my subjects just as you need yours. You're no different from me."

"With me, they might live and prosper. What life do you offer them, Unbalance?"

"I offer them the life that makes me powerful. With power, I am better able to do what I am made for."

Oddly, his words made sense to me. "I understand you."

There was a pulse in the air between us. A flicker in his eyes and a tightening in my chest.

I *did* understand him, if not the darkness that was his reason for being. But I comprehended the undeniable drive to fulfil his purpose. I felt that too. We just so happened to have completely opposite purposes, and there was nothing that could be done about that.

"And so we will fight now," he said.

I gathered my magic in great gulping waves, but daggers of burgundy essence sang through the air. One lodged in the skulled steed, and its scream ricocheted through Dragonsmount. Andas was flung from the steed's back, and I whipped out my silver power to grip his middle, then hurtled him into the deepest part of the dragon's mountain den.

I wasted no time collapsing the mountain on him.

Another part of Underhill destroyed, and this time I was the one who'd done it.

I wiped sweat away, realizing then that the drain of maintaining the portal had driven me to my knees. "Move," I commanded the creatures with in a roar.

There were so many of them left.

Polished, buckled heels came into view as I blinked through sweat.

"*You* threw the daggers?" I grunted at Sigella.

"You're welcome."

She walked past me across the shingles and then through thin air as Andas burst from the collapsed mountain with a menacing bellow.

"Calm yourself, Unbalance. Goodness, she's but a bumbling child. Don't tell me she's gotten the best of you."

Andas turned black eyes on her. "Sigella, you are freed."

"As you knew."

"Of course. You gave this child of Underhill the key to defeating my sluagh, if memory serves."

Sigella released more burgundy magic, and a table and two chairs appeared. "I killed Underhill also. You know better than to weigh unbalance on one act alone."

Andas shot me a look, then glanced down at the disappearing fae below. Around half had made it through. "You seek to delay me."

"And I am worth delaying things for, or you would not otherwise still be speaking with me. Tea?"

Andas focused on her, and in his black eyes I saw the calculation that Cormac and Aaden had never possessed apart. Combined, they'd created an ancient being—or become the vessel for one, if mother were to be believed.

Sigella sat at the table and a teapot and two teacups appeared.

My body started to shake as the tarbeasts stampeded their way to earth. The alicorns were behind them. I propped myself up on my hands, unable to keep my head raised any longer.

I listened instead.

"You expect me to believe that you deal truthfully," Andas sneered.

"Everything can be seen in two lights at least. I helped Silver kill your sluagh. And now you are without any soldiers of darkness. Perhaps I was creating a job opportunity for myself."

"I am not without any soldiers of darkness," he answered. "But two are in their infancy again."

Two are in their infancy. He was either referring to himself as the only mature henchmen or there was a third I hadn't known about. *Damn it.* I'd assumed that Andas was the final one.

"Infants aren't much use. If Silver is a child of Underhill, she herself has seasoned henchmen."

Henchmen. I'd never thought of my friends that way.

"A bat who'd prefer to braid hair, and—oh, wait, I believe my sluagh killed the land kelpie."

I shut my eyes against a wave of grief, resting my forehead against the jagged shingles. The ground shook with the movement of the fae creatures. That would need to be my assurance of their passage.

Sigella snorted. "Good riddance, but you must know that the previous Underhill replaced him before I killed her."

There was a heavy pause. "Who has replaced him?"

"Won't you sit down to tea?" Steel entered Sigella's voice.

"If you were interested in joining me, then you wouldn't stand between me and securing my subjects below."

"I will keep my options open until my decision is made, and you know I'm powerful enough to stand in the way for long enough for them all to depart anyway." She paused. "You also know that whether they are here or on Earth, you will have them eventually."

"Yes," he said. "But the notion of waiting is bothersome…You forget that just as Silver is mistress of balance, I am master of unbalance. I see your path, and it does not join mine. You have come to trick me, and I shall take your life for it."

There was a clink of a teacup against a saucer.

"You should have chosen to drink tea, Andas. A bit of lemon balm might've calmed you."

I couldn't keep this up for much longer. I was almost drunk with the spending of my power.

Out of nowhere, paths burst from under my hands in a criss-crossing maze. *My magic.* What had I done to summon it forth? Or had it exploded of its own accord? This was the magic of Underhill—the magic my mother had possessed, and I had no idea how to begin unwinding the maze of pathways.

But even I could sense who the paths belonged to.

Three shone bright silver and ran parallel to the path that I could sense was mine. Another of the paths was connected to Orry in the earth realm. One belonged to Peggy, and her path wove around another that had withered—the one that had been Kik's.

The third path led directly to Sigella.

I groaned. A warning indeed. Sigella was one of my fucking henchmen. My magic was warning me that she had to live.

Black exploded as Andas surged forward in attack.

Sigella flung up a wall of burgundy but was belted down the collapsed mountainside in a blur. She didn't stand a chance, and she'd known that.

She'd done it anyway.

And I still hated her for killing my mother before I had a chance to save her.

The ground continued to rumble, and the mass of creatures thundering through my portal blurred in and out of focus. I couldn't tell how many remained. Less than one-third, maybe.

Yet now I found myself in the same position as Andas, weighing the worth of a henchman against the lives of those who trusted me to save them. I could only save one or the other.

The path to Sigella's broken form below shone silver.

I followed her path into the future, seeing how my path almost appeared to lean against hers for support at points. Her purpose was to strengthen me. I would need her help…if I could let myself do so.

My gaze fixed on Kik's withered path. That would be Sigella's fate if I didn't act. What was more, if I had three henchmen, then I could assume that Andas might have a third helper too. *Great.*

"Thank you," I whispered to my magic as the tangle of paths faded from my sight.

There would be death today, but it wasn't Sigella's. Such was her importance that the demand of balance was a horrific one. An unimaginable one.

Her path must continue, while another one—belonging to thousands—would not.

Suffering.

How much of it could I bear?

I gathered my remaining power, closing the gigantic portal. "I'm sorry," I said hoarsely.

I heard their screams as the portal disappeared. I heard their confusion as I shot myself toward Sigella like a bullet. Andas would soon enslave them to darkness, and from this moment, they would believe that their chosen Underhill had abandoned them to save her own skin.

Latching onto Sigella's ankle, I opened a smaller portal ahead of us, feeling Andas's power try to snatch at me.

He hadn't expected me to leave anyone behind. Because Silver wouldn't have.

But I didn't know who I was anymore, and as I passed through the portal into the unknown beyond, I didn't know much of anything at all.

CHAPTER 3

Suffering wasn't new to me, but on this level, on this magnitude, the sensation was like being crushed under Old Man, and I was surprised none of my bones shattered under the weight of what I'd just done.

The choice I'd made was the type of decision my *mother* might have made. Then again, she would've had the power to battle Andas *and* keep the portal open.

My breath came in great gulps as I released Sigella's ankle and rolled to my knees, the small portal shutting behind us.

Sigella stood beside me.

I gulped for air, fighting the pain and guilt…because I could *feel* them dying. I could feel their fear as they ran from Andas. "I thought your body was broken."

"Sometimes the predator is too powerful for the prey to do anything other than play dead," she replied.

I screamed and curled in a ball as the pain of thousands hit me wave after wave. There was no reprieve. I couldn't find the surface to take a breath.

"You must close yourself off, Silver. Those fae belong to him now. Close yourself off before they break you." Sigella's words snapped my chin up so I could stare at her.

"They are not his." I bared my teeth, even though the ache in my bones and heart confirmed she was right. I'd lost some of my family to Unbalance. I'd sacrificed them. But if I fought for them now, I could spare them darkness for a while longer. Maybe I could save them still.

Sigella sighed. "Cut them off."

Trembling, I staggered upright and peered around. I'd instinctively brought us to the Irish court, where I'd first come earthside. We'd arrived outside the cave where I'd fought Unbalance's first henchman, the child thief, alongside Cormac and Aaden. Here I'd lost my amber-eyed wolf. Here I'd started to lose my green-eyed, kind-hearted Aaden.

"Why did you bring us here?" Sigella asked. "A place of so much pain for you?"

"Pain births pain, I suppose." I closed my eyes and saw thousands of tiny filaments that tied me to the creatures I'd left behind, floating through the air like whipping spider silk. I raised my hand and drew power from the world around me, unleashing a burst of flame that turned the filaments to ash, cutting the lost creatures free from me.

I don't know what I expected, but the backlash that hit me was not it. A thousand souls crying out at once, screaming for a mother and protector. The force of their pain slapped me in the face, and I was catapulted along the rocky ground until a fallen tree stopped me short.

Shaking on the ground, the tree at my back, I let their fear and confusion and panic run through me, water down a hill, and slowly, slowly their screams faded.

But I'd never—not in all my days, however many I had left—forget what I'd just felt, or what I'd done to inspire it.

Sigella walked over and crouched beside me. "Good."

"Good isn't the word I'd use." I pushed back to my feet, my body aching like I'd wrestled with tarbeasts.

Sigella shrugged. "It is what it is. You cannot save them all, nor will you ever be able to. Unbalance will always exist, taking the lives of those just out of your reach."

"I've let them go, but he hasn't destroyed Underhill…not yet anyway." I'd certainly feel that.

I ran a hand over my silver braid and looked around as Sigella's question returned to me. Without the screaming of the lost fae battering me, I had better perspective, and I had to agree with her that my instinct to come here was strange to say the least. *Pain birthspain.*

Something about this place had called me back in a moment of blind instinct. I'd never regretted following my instincts, though, and *always* regretted when I didn't.

I picked my way over rocks toward the cave opening. "Something is in here."

"You don't say. The question is what?" Sigella drawled, a half step behind.

What was it about difficult souls being drawn to me? Sigella, Kik, even Orry and Peggy at times. They were meant to be my henchmen. They must've missed the part about obeying my orders without sarcastic retorts and poor attitudes. They weren't at all like Andas's henchman. More like...helpmates.

Helpmates. They were family...and family didn't follow orders. More like the opposite, which meant I wouldn't be controlling them any time soon.

"I can feel a spark of laughter in you," Sigella said.

I kept my eyes forward, searching for something in the cave..."I realized that you are family, in a strange way. That's why we butt heads like ramming goats."

I'd reduced her act of murdering my mother to us 'butting heads,' and that was almost normal on the scale of my messed-up existence.

Her laughter echoed as we stepped into the cave. "Far more than you know, Silver. Far more than you know."

I held up my palm and pulled on the heat of the sun to create a flame in it as darkness slipped around us. At my feet, I saw a starburst of threads...no, not threads, roots. They burst from where I stood, climbing over the ground's surface.

"What are those?" I whispered, staring down at the vibrating cords.

"The roots of the tree of life," Sigella said. As if that were common knowledge.

I slammed to a stop, and Sigella stepped aside.

"The tree of life is made of death," I blurted.

"Well, that's a tad dramatic, don't you think?" She lifted her hand and helped me to light the space. We'd stopped at the top of a slope that opened to a vista below–the cavern where I'd fought the child thief.

Cormac had died right there. How many times had I replayed that moment in my head? If I'd been faster... If I'd taken the hornless unicorn's warning about sacrifice more seriously...If I'd done any number of things differently, then Cormac would be alive and Aaden wouldn't have changed. Unbalance might've taken centuries longer to find a strong enough vessel to hold him.

"The cave has changed since I was last here," I told her.

"This place is alive. You know that better than anyone. Why would the cave remain the same?"

I stepped closer to the edge and peered over. At the

bottom of the cavern, in the very center of the floor, was an unexpected sight.

"A sapling," I breathed.

I leaped from the top of the cavern, landing in a crouch twenty feet from the sapling. The young tree was perfect green with tiny white flowers bursting along the fragile, slender branches. Veins ran under the nearly transparent bark. Veins of darkness? "This sapling is a new beginning. But there's something wrong with it. There's darkness in it."

Sigella hissed from the top of the slope. "We're not alone."

I spun and pulled a blade free from my thigh sheath in one smooth motion.

A man stepped from the shadows deeper within the cavern. Fae. He held up both hands, palms facing me. "Peace, young friend, I felt the draw of the tree. I've watched it for some time, thinking of how I might move it to the Irish Court where its mother once resided." His voice was a slow drawl, and I couldn't place the accent. He sounded similar to Cormac and Aaden, but not quite.

Sigella held the high ground behind me. "Not one more step, or we'll kill you."

He froze between one step and the next, his foot hovering in the air. "May I take a step back, or is your stepping ultimatum just for those I take toward you? I'd prefer not to balance in the middle, you see. I might have had a bit of drink this morning and find myself a tad wobbly." He winked at Sigella, hiccupping as he did.

As if that would work on her.

So the fae was drunk, which was an impressive feat on his own. Fae couldn't easily get that way.

She snorted. "A charmer then. Take three steps back and turn slowly with your hands raised above your head."

He did as she asked, reversing three steps from me and the tree and then slowly turned back around and raised his hands. "Satisfied?"

"Hardly," she said.

Funny. The male fae's eyes were locked on Sigella, and he seemed to have forgotten that I was even here. The curve to his mouth suggested that he'd like to know her better, and I could only imagine the things Kik would say about that pairing. Probably something about the man's weak neck and the tangles in his long, black mane. Though he'd approve of the fae's drunkenness. A soft pang brushed my heart as I thought of my mentor and best friend, followed by a tidal wave of grief.

I snapped my fingers, drawing his attention back to me. "What's your name?"

He tilted his head. "Keefe. And you are?"

"Of no mind to you," Sigella snapped. "You need to leave this place, it's not for you."

He laughed at her, and I tensed, expecting her to blast him all the way to Alaska.

He said, "If this place is not for me, then what makes you think it's for you? Beautiful goddess or not, this is a sacred place meant only for Underhill herself."

Sigella spluttered...fucking *spluttered*, as if he'd flustered her with the goddess compliment. Could that be? I wasn't sure, but I wouldn't have expected a woman whom a man had trapped in a harp, then in another's body and mind, to be affected by such flattery.

Then again, relationships were not a strong suit of mine.

The tiny sapling wasn't done with me though. Fragile limbs veined in darkness shot toward the three of us at a speed my eyes couldn't follow and my reflexes couldn't dodge. Thin branches wrapped around me like a rain snake, pinning my arms to my sides. My ribs cracked, and my breath stuttered, but it was the tiny thorns digging into my flesh that were the kicker. Deeper and deeper they went, pulsing.

A voice echoed through the chamber, rising and falling in time with the tree's heartbeat.

I lead you to where you must go.

Could the others hear it too?

The voice didn't belong to my mother, but a woman much older. It struck me that the impulse to come here hadn't been my own after all—ancient deities, goddesses long departed the realms, had summoned me. Unless I was wrong, I was speaking to a goddess, maybe even Gaia herself.

"Where?" I asked.

To the realm where all must be decided. To the realm of power between worlds.

Sigella called to me, her voice as close to panic as I'd ever heard it.

"I must fight for the scale realm?" My heart settled into the rhythm of the thorns' pulsing, and I felt a rush of power as they synced. This entity was pumping me full of the tree's magic, both light and dark. The tree wasn't trying to kill me, not as it had done Cormac, nor did I feel any other entity trying to take me over as had happened with Aaden. But I wasn't meant for darkness. What did she mean by it?

The sapling was strengthening me, and not just with the power of light I'd grown up with in mother's presence.

To create balance, the voice said.

In a blink, the rock walls in the cave were gone, replaced with black ribbons.

I knew well enough what ribbons meant. I was inside the scale realm. I tensed for the ribbons' slicing attack before realizing that my body was still within the cave.

He cannot see you here with darkness in your essence, the voice said. *Do what you must, mistress of balance. Do what you must.*

She'd camouflaged me.

"For how long?" I called, but the ancient voice didn't answer.

"I thought I'd be more sober for this moment."

I spun around to find Keefe leaning against the black ribbons of the cave wall.

"What the fuck are you doing here?" I stared at him, and it was my turn to splutter.

"What are any of us doing in this Unbalance-ridden place?"

I spun to see Sigella at my other side. "You two got pulled through as well. I don't understand."

"What is this place?" Keefe waved a hand in the air. "Care to explain?"

"It would take far more time and effort to teach you than you're worthy of considering your limited cognitive abilities," Sigella sneered.

He shrugged and looked at me. "Short version, young one?"

"This realm is vital, and we need to take it back from the bad guy," I said.

"Do we know how?" He tugged at his short goatee. "As in, do you have a plan?"

"There's no *we*," Sigella cut in.

I agreed with her. I had a plan, but no, I wasn't about to fill a drunk fae in on it.

Sigella slowly walked around the sapling that was still rooted at the center of the cave. "This sapling is the heart of all realms. It's the new tree of life."

I nodded. "I heard her voice."

Her eyes shot to mine. "You don't mean Underhill, do you?"

"No. The ancient mother. Gaia. She said that we, *I*,

need to fight for balance again. Starting with the scale realm." The question was how? Andas was stronger than me. He'd already taken over this place. The evidence was all around me. These ribbons used to shine with every color imaginable, each ribbon denoting a living creature of balance. And now so many had been enslaved to Andas, blackened by evil and unbalance.

I shot Keefe a look and told Sigella in an undertone, "What if we could lock him out? I can't lock him out of Underhill, but perhaps…"

Sigella's eyebrows rose. "How?"

I paced the cave around the small tree, considering the question as the predator I was, deep down. My emotional turmoil tied to Andas, combined with the swiftness with which I'd lost my mother, Kik, and my men had left me reeling and numbed to my senses. But I knew how to fight. I just had to remember.

What did I have that Andas might want? Besides my defeat. What was his weakness, his motivation? What did he *need* to survive?

A thought began to form, and as it formed, fire burned brighter in my heart. Was Hope showing its face to me once more? Like a trickster that came and went, Hope was one day faithful and the next fleeing. Maybe this time she'd stick around a while longer and lay the foundations for peace.

"Andas wants *me*," I said. "But I need his eyes elsewhere while I strip the scale realm of darkness."

Sigella's eyebrows shot straight to her hairline. "And just how do you plan to do that?"

"Who?" Keefe grunted, hiccupping after. "Sorry, just trying to keep up with you ladies. Wait, do you mean the bad guy? Is he really called Anus?"

My grin caught me off guard, but at Sigella's scowl, I tucked it away again.

Keefe shrugged. "Look, I didn't ask to be here. Maybe the tree knew you'd need extra help. Right? So what can I do?"

"Why would *you* help us?" Sigella narrowed her eyes. "What is in it for you?"

"To help a beautiful woman is a gift in and of itself, I need nothing more." He scooped up her hand and kissed the back.

She flung her hand away and glared. "I think not."

"Wait." I moved between them. "You two can go to the prison realm."

"W-what did you say?" Sigella dragged her focus away to lock eyes with me.

"To draw him away," I explained. The fact that I needed to explain showed just how much drunken Keefe was affecting her. I couldn't have foretold this in a millennia. The possibility that she would embark on a century-long rampage to castrate male fae would've occurred to me sooner.

I looked at the little tree at my feet. "I start here, digging out the darkness from the roots of this sapling. This is the heart. If there isn't any darkness in the heart, then Andas's hold will weaken elsewhere. It will loosen his grip in the scale realm."

Sigella grimaced. "You won't remain hidden from him. Not indefinitely."

She didn't know about the camouflage Gaia had given me, but she was right. The darkness in me was already slipping away.

Andas would notice me eventually, but that didn't mean he would hunt me. Both of us knew the time wasn't right for a one-on-one battle. Andas had to focus on strengthening his foothold so his darkness could reign unchallenged for hundreds of years. I had to focus on…scrambling to prevent that.

"I'll protect her," Keefe said, and we both turned to him.

He grinned. "I mean, you don't want me here, right?"

"And I don't want you with me." Sigella stepped back. Keefe shrugged his lanky shoulders. I enjoyed the contrast between them. One prim and proper without a hair out of place, and the other kind of grubby and uncaring—though with an undeniable charm, as Sigella had discovered.

"I get the feeling you aren't the boss here, beautiful. But I'll let you boss me around any time you wish. You can try to fix me, if you like. Women like hopeless projects like that." He bowed in her direction as he waggled his eyebrows.

She snorted and turned her back, but I caught a hint of high color in her cheeks.

"I will go, and I will allow him to follow me." Sigella reached out and snatched a long strand of silver hair from my head. She moved so fast, I barely felt the twinge as she plucked the strand free.

With a twist of her wrist, she summoned a teacup and pot from the ether, the pot steaming already. Dropping my hair into the boiling water, she muttered something about stupid men, stupid hopeless projects, and stupid charm, then filled her cup with the tea and drank it down. She snapped her head back to swallow despite the obvious heat of the hairy brew.

"An hour is all you have," she said as her body changed to mirror mine. Her hair slid into a metallic glimmer that extended down her back. Her eyes became silver, too, and piercing to an unsettling degree. She shone and dazzled, and the muscular lines of her lean body convinced me that she could take on the world and then some.

That was…me.

I was all those things to other people. They looked at me and saw power and capability. They saw a woman who couldn't be toppled. They saw someone to depend on and pledge their loyalty and lives to.

Shock gripped me at the sight of myself. Could I really be those things? Could it be that everyone wasn't making a huge mistake appointing me as Underhill and trusting me to save them?

"I was just going to suggest we switched clothing," I managed to say.

She snorted. "I know."

I wanted henchmen with better attitudes.

Without another word, Sigella hurried through the ribbon cave toward the entrance, and Keefe followed along.

Which left me alone with the tree of life. I put my shock in a box for later. "I should pull you up by the roots." This tree had caused me so much pain and confusion.

But then the world, human and fae, would die, the voice said.

I knelt and cupped my hands around the sapling. Drawing magic from the cave and trees and air for miles around, I wove the essences in my hands and gently used them to pry at the veins of darkness on the fragile branches. The darkness was deep, though, woven through every layer of the branches and trunk and every leaf.

But this was how I needed to take the scale realm back, away from Unbalance, no matter how impossible it seemed.

"Gently," I whispered, stroking my fingers along the edges of the leaves, drawing the darkness to the surface, then flicking it aside. The tree shivered, and at first I thought I'd made progress.

I was ten minutes in when the first twig snapped under my ministrations. The cave shuddered, and I felt the horror of the broken limb in my arm as if I'd broken my own bone.

I fell to my side, breathing hard.

You are doing this wrong, the voice said.

No shit. "Help me do it right then, show me." Just once, I wanted help from someone who wasn't a cryptic ancient asshole.

You must create balance.

The twig in my hand turned to dust, coating my fingers in greasy black ash. I peered at the little sapling. "How?"

The slightest scuff of a boot on the hard-packed earth warned me, but I wasn't quick enough. A hand went to the back of my neck and tightened, holding me still on my knees.

He could break my neck, of that I had no doubt, and that thought alone kept me frozen.

His touch was familiar, as if he were Cormac or Aaden in truth. Part of me wanted to turn my head and rub my cheek against his forearm. Part of me wanted to give up everyone and just go along with his wicked plans because, with all these odds stacked against me, that was likely how things would end anyway.

"I wondered where you might hide, my silver bird. Did you really think she'd fool me?"

"Sigella *did* fool you," I answered.

He snorted. "She and that fool of a fae…they went to the prison realm."

"Yes."

"Where you'd sent me." The laughter in his voice wasn't lost on me.

Fuck. I hadn't expected him to linger there. I'd expected him to return to Underhill to hunt down the remaining fae in Underhill without delay. An assumption on my part, and a foolish one. He'd simply hunted my sacrificed creatures from his perfect view of the tally of good and evil in the scale realm. Far easier.

Silver, you fool.

He crouched and placed his mouth against the back of my ear, and I shivered at his hot breath against my skin.

"You knew I'd find you, Silver," Unbalance told me. "I think you very much wanted me to find you here. To cage you and show you how delicious being tamed could be."

He was right, in part, and I was too far gone in this mess to feel ashamed of that.

His words pulled at me. They whispered at me to give in and lean on him. I turned my cheek so I could feel the comfort of his skin and then bit down hard on his forearm.

Andas howled and let go, but he was stronger than that, really. He'd chosen to let me go. And…I wasn't sure he was even aware of making that choice. I released a shaking breath.

He stumbled away, touching the bite, cursing under his breath.

Andas didn't realize Cormac and Aaden were

keeping him from harming me. That was the only explanation that made sense.

For the first time I felt that reaching my men might really be possible.

They were still looking out for me, working together within this evil being, and that gave me more strength than the sapling had earlier. A sureness and power returned to me.

He glared across the room. "Don't look at me like that, silver bird."

"Like what?" I asked, sliding sideways, keeping him at a distance as if he were a ruby-red on a double eclipse. I tried not to notice the sharp lines of his face, or the fall of his dark hair. Andas was dressed in black from his long coat to his boots, and he was impossibly perfect, even for a fae. Cormac and Aaden had been devastatingly handsome by themselves, let alone combined in one body.

"As if those fools are still in me. They are not."

I covered my lack of focus with a smile, laying out the next steps of my plan in my mind. "No? Then why do they keep you from harming me?"

He threw back his head and laughed. This was the only opportunity I'd get.

I made my move and bolted for the exit. Scrambling through the tunnels, driven along by my power, I ran out of the cave, Andas right behind me.

He tackled me, and we went down to the shingled ground in a heap, our bodies flush. At the speed with which we rolled down the rocky slope, my senses should have been blinded with the blur, but I was so keenly attuned to Cormac and Aaden that I noted the obvious desire he had for me as his length pressed between my legs. I felt the heat of his skin through our layers of clothing. I drowned in the wild blackness of his eyes and froze at the way his mouth hovered over my own.

I had a flashback of tackling Aaden, of holding Cormac, of being pressed between the two men. Of the taste of their kisses. My eyelids fluttered. I wanted Andas because wanting him was the only way I could reach the two other parts of me.

Do not give in. Balance must be achieved, Gaia boomed for my ears alone.

I slammed my magic into his solar plexus, sending him flying straight into the sky. Black ribbons exploded everywhere, reminding me of where we were. They wove such a tight fabric that there was nothing else around us but writhing blackness.

It was all the reminder I needed that Unbalance had claimed this realm.

He landed about a hundred feet from me, light on his feet. "Ready to bow down to me, Mistress of Underhill?"

Fury shot through me at his mocking tone. "I won't give up."

Andas darted toward me and I flipped my hand, driving the earth up in a burst of soil that...floated around us. The scale realm was no longer holding together.

He tossed a rock toward my head, and when I ducked he tried to tackle me again.

I dropped flat onto my belly, and he sailed right over me. I kicked back, catching him in the ribs, feeling the crack of bone under my blow. I wouldn't feel bad about hurting him. We both knew the way this would go, whether now or in the end.

He grabbed my ankles and dragged me toward him. His magic pinned me to the ground, holding me exactly where he wanted me.

"I will not," I screamed as he crawled up and over me.

"Oh, I'd never take you that way," he whispered as he ran a finger down the side of my face. "There's more power to be had from your submission and self-loathing. But before we are done, you will beg me to touch you, Silver. You will beg to have me between your legs."

I shivered, his words scaring me more than anything else could have, because…because I couldn't share much at all with Aaden and Cormac now, but Andas bore the perfect union of their features, and sharing intimacy with him would feel enough like sharing it with them.

"You'll be the one to beg, for me to let you go," I growled at him.

He smirked. "I doubt that very much."

Around us, the world of the scale realm shivered. The air shook and danced and the black ribbons danced with it. Andas leapt to his feet. His magic slid off me instead of killing me, and I scrambled away, pushing distance between us.

He whipped around, rage etching into his face. "What have you done?"

There wasn't time to answer, the scale realm exploded; heat and cold, color and light, and darkness...so much darkness. I was thrown and only realized I'd been bodily thrown from the scale realm when I once again landed outside the cave where I'd fought the child thief.

I was back on Earth.

Sigella and Keefe stumbled toward me from the cave entrance.

"What happened?" I took in their dishevelled states, the marks on their skin, and the blood dripping from small wounds.

"He..." Sigella looked at Keefe. "This drunken fae closed the scale realm."

I whipped around to focus on the strange fae man who'd shown up just when we'd needed him. I was supposed to have henchmen...but as far as I'd seen, my henchmen were Orry, Peggy, and Sigella. There had been no silver path belonging to Keefe running parallel to mine in the criss-cross maze of my future as Underhill. What part did he play in this?

"You closed…the scale realm?" I asked. This fae had somehow done what I couldn't.

He shrugged. "I don't know. It just came to me, and honestly, I am not even sure how I did it."

That was a bit of bullshit right there. But I'd learn the truth in time.

Sigella didn't budge her gaze from him. "We combined our magic, Silver. We lost control of what was happening, so I can't say how we managed to shut the realm, but the realm is closed off—maybe for good. Unbalance can no longer travel there to watch and intercept our every move. He's lost a huge advantage."

"And I still can't access it either, I assume." I could no longer sense the realm, which seemed answer enough.

Sigella finally looked at me. "Not what we'd planned, but this might keep things safer for a little while. We'll be able to move around without him watching our every step."

That was a win.

I'd take it for the time being. I drew magic from my surroundings to heal my scrapes and bruises, then took a deep breath. "Right. On to the next disaster."

CHAPTER 4

I squinted at Queen Hyacinth, having just made it inside the glitter-sickening explosion they called an entrance to the palace.

"When you said rawmouths, I expected *two*. Not a flock of them." She paused and pursed her lips. "Family? Herd?"

"Pod," I supplied.

She seized the word with spirit. "*Pod.* The lake you put them in wasn't nearly big enough. Distributing them through our other lakes required twenty fae *per* rawmouth. They tried to eat our people at every turn. If it weren't for that flying city that you call a dragon reminding them that you'd ordered no attacks, then we'd have dead fae on our hands."

That would be their faults for trying to move a rawmouth, in my opinion.

"Be grateful you only had to transport rawmouths

this week," I interrupted her. "Or ordered it so." I'd had plenty more to deal with, from sacrificing thousands of fae to save Sigella's life to a face-to-face confrontation with Andas.

"A week? I'm only complaining about a day."

I paused. "Only a day has passed here?"

"Yes, why?"

"Because an entire week usually passes here when I spend one day in Underhill."

The queen focused on me. "The realms are...equalizing or something?"

Equalizing. That might be the perfect word for it. "Equalizing as unbalance grows stronger." Would it then reverse? Would one day on Earth become a week in Underhill? I couldn't say—and yet the lack of time difference between the realms was a small relief. "So you're only complaining about one day?"

Cinth sniffed, tilting her chin, which made her ample bosom jiggle and highlighted the burns on her cheek. "I got my hands dirty, don't you worry about that. I've been curious about cooking rawmouth after you returned covered in their stench that time. I let them know as much, and they decided to play ball."

I frowned. "They did? That would be a sight."

The queen sighed. "To be helpful, that's what I mean."

She should just say what she meant then. While I'd decided to adopt earthspeak, I refused to use words that weren't actually the right words. Maybe using earthspeak had started as defiance to my mother, but I could see that speaking this way would build bridges between fae on Underhill and Earth.

"Is everyone settling in?"

"Settling in?" she screeched. "I'm dodging calls from the president, sultans, ambassadors, you fucking name it. Our only saving grace is that they have no idea of the scale of fae you've let in. By the time human authorities had arrived at the Alaskan Triangle, most of the creatures you'd let through had scattered. The humans only have snippets of satellite footage to go off of. But they'll find out, Silver. *Please* tell me this is temporary."

That Andas would shut down the fae realm had seemed a certainty before, but I could still feel its magic within me. "Most likely, yes," I hedged.

I strode past her as she half-screamed, "Most likely?!"

Luckily, I walked faster than the queen and quickly lost her in the halls. I needed time to think about my next step. There were so many factors to consider.

My helpmates. I should gather my helpmates. Four brains were better than one.

I considered gathering Sigella, Peggy, and Orry in the same room, then grimaced. Perhaps I could hold individual meetings with them. Peggy blamed Sigella for Kik's death, so she and Sigella would probably lock in a battle to the death. Orry was a sly one, though, I could see her strangling them with their own hair to emerge the victor.

My weary grin dropped as I kicked open the door to my bed chamber.

A woman stood on the balcony, smoothing her hands over a silver dress that draped over her many curves. Red hair massed over her shoulders, lit from behind by Earth's setting sun. Her blue eyes demanded attention, and all-in-all, I thought that this alluring, powerful fae might be the most beautiful woman I'd ever seen.

"Orlaith?" I hushed. "Is that you? How?"

She smiled nervously. "I didn't know whether you'd recognize me in this."

My bat-turned-two-legged-fae gestured at her body as I might leather trousers. "I saw you once before, when our magics first touched."

I tossed my cloud bow on the bed, followed by the quiver, careful not to touch the iron tips dipped in Gavala root. "Did you make any harmful deals to get your body back, Orlaith?"

The nickname Orry didn't quite fit this woman. She might have smiled nervously just now, but in this form, I could tell the gesture was designed to make *me* feel powerful. I knew enough of my friend's past to have figured out that she'd been the mastermind of some kind of criminal circuit, which she'd referred to as 'being good at networking.' These little studied gestures had worked to make her powerful in life, just as Old Man's fire made him powerful. The subtle manipulations didn't concern me. I'd get used to Orlaith in this form in time.

"No," she shook her head quickly, just like she had as a bat. I tucked away a smile.

"If we need to work some impossible magic to break a curse, let me know now."

Orlaith blinked. "I'm telling the truth, Silver. I woke up like this, and I've been trying to figure out why ever since. H-how?"

She combed her fingers through her long hair, and I gathered that she'd actually been doing *that* since waking in her old body.

My mother had trapped Orlaith in a bat form and sent her to the prison realm long ago for actions that aligned too closely with the darkness of unbalance. She'd then asked Orry's father to deliver his gold daughter bat to me hours after I was taken from Underhill. A bat hadn't seemed like much of a weapon at the time, but Orlaith had proven herself time and again. She was still standing, after all, and both the child thief and the sluagh had fallen. Size didn't always equate to power.

I unstrapped my dagger holsters. "The scale realm was shut down and the prison realm was inside of it, so that's shut too. I'm guessing that had something to do with your change."

Pausing to tap into my magic, I studied the threads around the woman, both ahead of her and immediately behind her, and nodded afterward. "Yes, that's correct."

I peered down. *Naga shit.* I had dirt all over me, along with tiny rocks in every bodily crevice I'd known of—and some I hadn't. This would be the perfect camouflage to spear a grunga lizard for dinner, but as it was, perhaps I'd take a bath.

Orlaith closed the gap and took both of my hands in hers. "You're gonna need to back up on that one. What in Underhill's name happened to your braid? That was my best work yet."

"Wrestled with Andas." To say the least.

Her blue eyes widened to saucers. Everything in her posture and expression told me to confide in and trust her. Humans could take a lesson on survival from this woman. Still, the change from when she'd been a bat was pronounced and I would need to get used to it.

"Were you guys naked?" she demanded.

"Not this time."

"Not this time! What do you mean?"

I strode to the adjoining bath chamber and used the plumbing system to deliver water from somewhere into the bath. I hadn't figured that one out yet. "A male fae made Sigella blush."

Orlaith sucked in a breath as she followed me. "No. Wait, you were going to murder Sigella in cold blood. What happened? But tell me how she blushed first. No, wait, you were telling me about naked wrestling with Andas. That's what I'd like to hear about first."

I decided against adding the soap that bubbled up and masked my scent and set to unlacing my leather vest. I rolled down my trousers afterward, then kicked them aside. "Do you like having hair again?"

"Every time I'm set on getting answers out of you, you ask a really good question to distract me," she said mournfully. "I love, love, love it. Going to the prisoner realm was not great, you know, but losing my hair hit me right between the legs. I mean, in many ways the prison realm wasn't that different from what my life had been. I just wasn't the CEO for a while—you know, the apex predator, so I really had to work on myself."

I stepped down in the bath. "You were a criminal mastermind, Orlaith. You can say it."

I glanced back to watch as she pressed her lips together.

She released a breath. "I have my body back and the prison realm is shut. Okay, fine. I, Orlaith, was a criminal mastermind. But I had the purest intentions when I started pimping. Just a select few of the most stunning women around."

The fae touched her chest, and I noticed a silver ink pattern there. Raindrops. I had a feeling that Orlaith had a habit of revealing her real thoughts with subconscious touches. They were her tells more than any expression on her face. "The markings on your chest, what are they?"

"Rain, hail, or shine," she answered, sweeping a hand down her front. "If you were lucky, you'd see the rain. If you were lucky and rich, you'd see the hail." She rested a hand low on her stomach. "Lucky, rich, *and* powerful, then you'd see the shine. They used to be black, but I guess the silver is your influence on me. I named my business after them anyway. Then I realized most of our clients were too stupid to appreciate a beautiful, meaningful brothel name, so it became Harlots for Rain, Hail, or Shine. A few decades later, everyone called it Harlots For, which pissed me off a little, and then men kept merging the words together because of the way they muttered it under their breaths to their friends so their wives wouldn't hear. After fifty years, my business was called Hore. So in case you ever wondered where the word 'whore' came from, it was all me. You're welcome."

I considered that, and wasn't sure whether to feel grateful to her or not. Still, there were worse legacies to leave behind. "You ran your criminal operations through Rain, Hail, or Shine then."

"Criminal operations, such strong wording." She laughed, then swept her silver gown aside to dangle her porcelain, unscarred legs in the enormous bath.

She hadn't answered my question.

Orlaith sighed. "Silver, what do you suppose happened to my father?"

I lifted my head. "Your father was still in the prison realm. I didn't even think to ask about him."

"He was one of thousands in there," she reprimanded. "They might've been prisoners, but they were fae too."

A drifting feeling came over me then, as if I were deep in the purple ocean with no idea which way to swim. When had I become so tunnel-visioned that I could simply forget thousands of fae.

Maybe around the time I'd sacrificed several more thousand. This is why I needed my bat pimp. She'd help ground me when the enormity of my decisions made me lose touch with reality. Though perhaps I shouldn't rely on an ex-criminal mastermind as my moral compass…"I'll find out. About your father and the others. I should already know, and I'm sorry that I didn't bother to find out before now."

Orlaith shrugged a shoulder. "You can be forgiven the occasional oversight, Silver. You have a lot on your plate." Her gaze drifted to my hair. "What do you say? Would it be weird for me to still do your hair when you're in the bath?"

There was a crackle in the air.

I had a dagger of silver magic at the ready when Sigella appeared. I swallowed the magic back up. "Where's your man?" I asked.

"I don't have a man."

"Not yet."

Her prim and proper form disappeared, and her savage, grimy, tattered alter ego flashed toward me, sharp teeth bared. In a flash, the tea-drinking version of Sigella was back. I hadn't seen her savage alter ego in a while, and I'd assumed her darker side had disappeared when I'd freed her.

"Not *at all*."

I smirked in reply. "That's why you had him turn and then move back three steps. Because you're not interested at all."

Sigella straightened her back. "As to that. It's good to view the goods. You young ones could learn a lot from me."

"I liked to crack a whip at their heels and get them dancing around," Orlaith said.

Sigella glanced at her for the first time. "You... are?"

"Orry the bat." She stood and curtsied, and her silver dress tightened in just the right places to hint at her curves and...shine.

"Ah, from closing the prison realm."

I cut the ancient being a look. "What of the occupants of the prison realm? Where did they go?"

"They were squeezed out. Either to Underhill or Earth."

Squeezed out. I raised my eyebrows, then decided to move on to the larger issue. Thousands of unbalanced fae could be running rampant around Earth. I blinked into my magic, mentally waving aside the lattice of threads arising from all the fae on Unimak. I could see the enormous cocoons of magic that formed Old Man and the rawmouths dotted around the island. The feeling of millions of threads beyond them was a heady and overwhelming sensation. I could feel my power over them. I could feel my duty to them.

But I couldn't sense anything other than vibrant silver threads from fae creatures. Nothing like what a fae from the prison realm would feel like—a mixture of black and silver magics.

I opened my eyes. "They're not on Earth."

"Then Unbalance has them," Sigella said conversationally.

Orlaith gasped. "Father." She hugged her body and sank to the ground.

I wasn't sure how to react to the news on a larger scale. An entire realm of prisoners in Andas's power was nearly as bad as having them wreaking havoc on Earth. "I'm sorry, Orlaith. I'm so sorry."

Her father had been in the prison realm and was probably already lost. It was too late to help him. I'd tried to burn darkness from fae in the past, only to accidentally kill them. A fae possessing darkness couldn't be saved, or at least I hadn't figured out the means. They had to save themselves. No doubt that was why mother or her predecessors had formed the prison realm in the first place. Only under the right circumstances, as Orry had discovered, would a fae feel inclined to 'work on herself.'

Tears slipped over her porcelain skin. "There's nothing you can do?"

"I could try to search for him—"

"Snap out of it," Sigella snarled at her. "Underhill doesn't have time to carry out sentimental little missions for you. You lost a parent. Get in line."

And this is why I'd decided to hold individual meetings. I'd recently lost a parent—one I could barely depend on, who'd put me through hell in a bid to make me resilient enough for my future. If I missed her after that steaming pile of turd called my childhood, then Orlaith must be torn into shreds over the loss of her father, whom she'd loved very much, and who had, by all accounts, loved her very much.

Orlaith cried, and I dunked myself a few times, then climbed out of the bath, dripping water over the stone floor.

I pulled on my magic to dry my body, then crouched to wrap my arms around her. "I wish things had been different. I didn't stop to think of the consequences for you, and I should have. You're my dear friend."

Sigella scoffed. "You didn't even know the prison realm would shut."

"Y-you consider me a d-dear friend?" Blue eyes peeked at me from between her hands.

There was a calculated edge to them that reminded me of the way Kik used to look at me when assessing how much to insult my mother before she'd set the tarbeasts on him.

This was Orry though, so I rubbed her arm. "I do."

I left her and strode into the bed chamber.

Sigella trailed after me. "Just because you dip yourself in water, it doesn't mean you've bathed."

They were one and the same to me, but I didn't bother responding.

Orlaith followed us, wiping her pale face. She didn't speak as she made her way to the small breakfast table by the window and sat.

A pull of silver magic tugged me toward the balcony. I withheld a groan when the beating of wings signalled the arrival of Peggy. She landed on the balcony and stuck her head in through the door.

She and Sigella locked gazes.

"Here we go," I muttered.

"Pegatheoria," Sigella said politely.

Peggy dipped her beautiful white head. "Lady Sigella."

Their civility didn't fool me for a second. Both were scoping out the other's power.

I cleared my throat. "While you're all here then. We need to figure out how to reach Cormac and Aaden through Unbalance to weaken him and drive him back into the smallest presence possible. We don't have a scale realm to use against him, but he doesn't have it either. He's stronger than me for now. Probably for centuries if I live that long. And he has the power to shut down Underhill and kill or control all fae through the loss of their connection to Underhill. What ideas do we have?"

The three fae stared at me.

"Use your body," Orlaith said.

"Your magic can reach them," said Sigella.

"Unbalance is a predator like any other." Peggy put in last. "Use your intelligence in such things against him."

My body, my power, or my mind. Talk about conflicting advice.

Sigella's mouth twisted in a wry grin as she took the seat opposite Orlaith, leaving me to perch on the bed, still naked.

Peggy shook her gleaming mane, and her deep, amber eyes reminded me of Cormac. "Your outlook has changed. You'd dismissed your mother's orders. What changed?"

My mind returned to the moment Andas showed me mercy. He could've killed me, but he hadn't. He *couldn't*. "I believe that Cormac and Aaden wield some power over Unbalance from within him. Andas had a chance to kill or seriously hurt me earlier and didn't take it. Couldn't take it, I suspect. But reaching them seems impossible. Besides, to do that, I would need to spend time in Andas's company, and that's a great risk considering the power imbalance."

"What does your magic tell you?" Sigella said, already pouring tea from who-knows-where. She shoved a cup to Orlaith, who—rightly so—sniffed the contents.

"Nothing. I can't see any way forward in this, which

leads me again to suspect that reaching them is impossible."

"Is there some—"

Peggy was cut off at a knock on the door.

"Enter," I called.

Sigella lowered her teacup as Keefe entered.

The male fae appeared confused. He'd taken off his hat to wring it in both hands. "Mistress, forgive the intrusion. I was called here."

He didn't seem uncomfortable with my nudity, and that was a mark in his favor. "By who?"

"Your magic."

As had often been the case with Keefe in the short time I'd known him, I got the sense he knew far more than he let on. And yet he'd closed a realm with Sigella's help that had strengthened me in the battle against Unbalance. "You're sober."

"Unfortunately, mistress. And hopefully that's short-lived, if you get my drift." He threw me a charming smile, but then his eyes darted to where Sigella sat. He did peer at Orlaith for a time, but his focus promptly returned to Sigella.

Smart man.

"Keefe," I said. "I have a problem for you to solve. There is a man, he is made up of two other men. The first man is a gatekeeper of sorts, and I must get past him to reach the two men within. How do you propose I do so without hurting them?"

The fae whistled and hooked his thumbs in his belt.

"That's a doozy, Mistress. Can't say I've come across that in life. You can't see ahead?"

"I can, but not in this."

He tapped his temple and winked. "There's another who's rather good at glimpsing the future. The Oracle is a servant to Underhill. Use her as the tool she is."

"I wonder how my sister would react to being called a tool."

He blanched, but another knock at the door interrupted the impromptu meeting of my helpmates and Keefe.

"What is it?" I snapped as Keefe swung open the door and executed a mocking bow to the administrative fae in the hall.

"Humans have arrived. They came in a fleet of aircraft," the fae stuttered. "Queen Hyacinth is requesting that you attend her urgently."

At least I got a bath. Sort of.

I strode to the door.

"Clothes," Sigella called.

I paused to jerk my clothing to me with magic.

"No. Clean them first. Use your magic. It will only take a second! Surely you won't…" Sigella blurted, then moaned low when I yanked on the filthy garments. "I can't believe I used to live in you."

I'd intended to clean them, but I'd happily stay dirty to mess with her. That was just the kind of person I was.

I walked past the wide-eyed fae in the hall. "Where is she?"

"Throne room," he shouted after me, then said frantically into his mouthpiece, "Mistress of Underhill incoming. Code ten-two-eighty. Did you hear me? Code ten-two-eighty!"

CHAPTER 5

I forced myself not to run toward the throne room. The urge to do so was strong, but the people—fae and human alike—who lined the halls were already filled with terror.

The stench practically rolled off them. Thick like a fog of fear that they couldn't help but expel when faced with creatures from Underhill. Mind you, more than a few people pinched their noses as I strode by, so perhaps it was my own stench they were reacting to.

That was entirely possible.

"What do you think is happening?" Orlaith caught up to me, trying to braid my hair as we walked.

"Butting of heads," I muttered. "Humans don't want to share this massive world with the fae. This won't surprise anyone."

A couple of humans blushed beet red when my words reached them, but they couldn't deny it. The human world was, by all accounts, a selfish one. The question only was what had they already done, and to which creatures of Underhill had they done it to?

"If we're not in a rush, you could stop, and I could finish this braid," Orlaith said. Her finger slipped and all of her work came loose. "Damn it! The whole thing came apart."

"Leave her be," Sigella snapped, and Orlaith was yanked from my side. "She doesn't need us for this battle."

I felt intent on those who awaited my arrival, and I could sense the situation waiting for me as clearly as if I could already see it with my eyes. Sigella was right. This was my fight, not theirs.

The humans had decided to wait for me to arrive before they did anything drastic to defend themselves against the amassed fae creatures. They'd never heard of me before the fae queen's mention of me today. They wanted to see what other enemies they might possess. They'd also never seen anything like the creatures they'd witnessed, and their instincts–if they still possessed them–warned them to act with caution.

One of Cinth's royal ladies-in-waiting came bustling toward me as I neared the throne room, her grass green eyes wild and her cheeks in high color. She waved her hands in the air in a flurry of nonsense. "Hurry! They're going to kill them! Queen Hyacinth won't want that."

"Who's killing who?" I snapped.

"The half-serpent creatures are going to kill the humans," she sobbed.

I managed not to roll my eyes at her hysterics. "The naga will wait for me to make the call on whether the humans live or die."

The green-eyed lady-in-waiting gasped and clutched at her chest.

She'd come to hurry me along, but had only further delayed me. I lifted my hand and set her firmly aside with a burst of magic.

Rolling my shoulders, I braced myself to push past the crowd of soldiers at the entrance to the throne room. But they parted for me without order, their armor and weapons clinking as they allowed me to glimpse the scene below.

And what a scene it was.

Queen Hyacinth stood before her throne. Her dress of deep fuchsia hugged her curves, and the thick gold band belted around her middle accentuated her ample bosom. A delicate crown nestled perfectly in her coiled hair—Orlaith would be extra unhappy about the state of mine next to that expert voluminous and sleek... thing. The queen's face was tight, her gaze locked on the action in the middle of the room.

On her left was her mate, Ronan, and on her right hunched the stooped and hooded figure of the Oracle. My sister, Kallik. Just behind Kallik was Faolan, poised in the shadows with his weapons at the ready.

"Mistress of Underhill, we have human visitors, and

they're being threatened. You need to deal with these fae," Queen Hyacinth said. "The naga will not listen to reason."

Of that I had no doubt. But if the naga were pissed, there was a cause.

"Nesssst mate."

My eyes swept to the king of the Naga at the center of the room. He'd wrapped his serpentine upper body around a human male dressed in a stiff and unyielding garment with sharp, angled lapels. The king was surrounded by his many queens and the greater nest of naga, but a thick band of uniformed humans surrounded the naga, their weapons raised. At least one hundred.

The naga swayed in unison, their once gold, but now silver coins tinkling and singing with their movements. More than a few fae and humans swayed with them, their eyes glazed.

But not all had succumbed to the trance magic of these creatures. The naga were outnumbered, and their magic had been spread thin to cover the volume of creatures in the room.

The human at the mercy of the naga king had his eyes half closed, and I couldn't tell if lack of air or trance magic had caused that. The man wasn't thrashing about in fear, by any means. He stood quietly, as if he too were waiting for me.

Or maybe he was keenly aware these moments could be his last.

I tipped my head to the king. "What is the meaning of this, King of the Naga? Why do you hold this man so close to death? I ordered no attacks. I ordered no fighting with the humans."

He hissed low. "Thisssss human…took naga coins. Sssstole them."

I blinked, more than a little surprised. Naga coins were nearly impossible to steal. I looked closer at the human. He didn't seem extraordinary at first glance. Brown hair fell over gray eyes. The pallor of his skin made me wonder if he often saw the sun, and the softness of his body implied he wasn't accustomed to chasing his food or running after predators. He certainly didn't look to be the sort who could successfully steal coins from naga.

"Where and how did you manage to steal from the naga?" I asked him.

"I didn't touch anything," he spluttered. "I didn't take anything either!"

He was very adamant about that.

"The king needs to let Canada's ambassador go— immediately," Hyacinth snarled. "This will not help the negotiations, not one bit. There's no proof of any theft, he's had a fae with him every step of the way to this throne room."

I held up a hand. "Wait."

The naga let me pass through their outer circle, bowing to me as I went, which pulled a rumbling murmur from the crowd. The chiming of the naga's silver coins sent a second rumble through the crowd, but this was more of a sigh. A few human bodies dropped to the ground, asleep.

"What's happening?" blustered another, similarly suited human male. His white hair could have implied wisdom, but…"Why are we waiting on a girl to make decisions when you are a queen, or so you say, *Queen* Hyacinth? You said the ruler of the fae realm was coming." His words, his tone, his disrespect…they were all too much.

I snapped a hand outward, drawing power from the world around me, not singling out a particular color or strand, faster than I'd ever drawn on my magic before. Flicking my fingers, I bound him up and lifted him from the ground.

He squawked like a chicken strung up by its legs—no words, just high-pitched squawking. I wove my magic into his throat to keep him from speaking anything other than grunts or more squawks. That way, everyone would know how stupid he really was. The other humans didn't move to help him, and instead backed away, establishing distance between themselves and their companion.

"Do not disrespect our queen," I told them. "Ever. Or you will face me, you fool of a human." I'd spoken the words, but my voice sounded deeper and more sonorous. The words resonated through the room and silenced the muttering of both the humans and fae.

Holding the disrespectful one in the air, I approached the thief.

I could feel something hanging in the air, different than my magic and different than the connection to the creatures of Underhill and the fae. I wanted to touch this new thing, so I lowered my right hand, stretching my fingers toward the unseen force, which wove itself around my legs like a large cat.

A quick glance through my magic showed me a strange glimmer of rippling movement as though a shimmering piece of transparent fabric stretched between me and the thief of all people. It seemed to pronounce that this was a moment that mattered.

Balance. You must find true balance. For this collection of realms is shattering. Gaia's voice whispered up through my feet, settling me and guiding me.

Balance wasn't easy to maintain, but wasn't balance a lot like justice? Didn't they go together?

I raised my left hand in front of the thief's face. "Speak the truth and I'll let you live. Lie, and I will make an example of what happens to those who think the fae weak. The choice is yours."

His eyes narrowed, and the future paths that rolled around him were indiscernible for the time being. Would he speak the truth? I could sense the silver coins hidden inside an inner pocket of his outfit. They called to me. In his eyes, I saw contempt. His nose wrinkled, and I smiled at him—not a happy smile. The possible paths hadn't cleared, but I did feel like I could win either way.

"I'm not a thief." He spoke the lie with as much conviction as anyone could, I supposed.

That didn't make it any less of a lie.

"Silver, we believe our ambassadors from the human realm, of course. They are not to be harmed," Cinth pleaded with me.

Perhaps this ambassador thought his strange suit would protect him. Or did he think his human friends would come to his aid? He wished to take advantage of the fae and get away with it. He'd rather use his power against them than spend time learning to respect them.

"The hidden place under your right armpit has seven silver coins that you stole from the naga on your way into the throne room. While I'm impressed that your clothing has such a sly hiding place, I am deeply saddened that you chose to rely on your power and status to shield you from accountability."

"He sssssstole from a youngling," the naga king said. "Kicked her assside and took her necklacccce."

"Silver, you must stop this," Queen Hyacinth said in a tight voice. "We are friends with humans, most especially to those *just south* of our island. We do not accuse them of stealing."

I heard her. She wanted to get along with her neighbors. Mostly because they had large weapons and not much sense.

I glanced over my shoulder at her. "But do we not hold thieves accountable, Queen Hyacinth? I do. This ambassador has chosen not to hand the coins back. If he had, we might have admired his strength and cunning in stealing naga coins. That is not a task for the weak. Instead, this man intends to keep the coins. He intends to display them to his friends and colleagues as the first spoils of a war they intend to win."

Hyacinth shook her head ever so subtly, and fear radiated from her. But it was Kallik I looked to, because like me, she could see the swirling paths.

"Only you can choose the path, Mistress of Underhill." Kallik tipped her robed head to me.

Cinth spun to stare at her friend. "You can't be serious."

A slow clap of hands drew all eyes to the far right of the room. A man stepped through the gathered crowd, and they parted for him too. He wore black from head to foot. His boots came to his knees, his dark hair was pulled back, and the sharp lines of his face were far too familiar to me.

Unbalance himself.

I withheld a groan. *Great.*

"You mean to kill him, Silver?" Andas cocked his head, and when I looked around, I saw that everyone had stilled, and not because they were terrified of the monster who'd strolled into their midst as casually as a summer breeze blowing through.

No, they were *frozen* by the power he'd wrapped around them to keep them immobile. I focused on the magic he'd woven through the space. I hadn't even sensed him doing that. But the eyes, ears, and mouths of everyone in the space were blocked from making or hearing sound, and of seeing or doing anything.

"I mean to hold him accountable." I moved opposite Andas, weaving through the crowd to keep my sights on him.

"Interesting," he hummed, and the sound reverberated through the air, caressing its way down my arms, making the hair on them stand up.

"Why would that interest you?" I asked.

If Andas was here, then this had to be a pivotal moment for him too.

"Well…it's what I want. Killing him will start the war with the humans. A war that will create chaos and unbalance and feed my power and reign for a very, very long time. Those humans hold amazing, pitiful grudges, better even than the most selfish and weak of fae." He flashed a smile, and I caught a gut-wrenching glimmer of Cormac in the gesture.

"Killing him could start a war, but you warn me of that because you'd like me to choose the opposite." The path where I let the thief live was darker yet, I sensed, seeing a glimmer of it. In that future, fae were enslaved to humans and placed in zoos, even turned into pets. That pathway didn't have an end point in sight, whereas a war between humans and fae did, and if I'd learned one thing in recent months, it was that the impossible was never impossible. I could figure out a way to stop a war from happening.

"You lose this round either way. I wanted to witness your defeat." he said after a pause that let me know I'd guessed his ploy right. He wasn't happy about it, but war would suit him just fine.

"Sending a message to the humans is the right course," I said. "They can't be allowed to believe fae are unworthy of respect or a place in this world. I will not allow fae to become *pets*."

He laughed. "Truly, I should have set my sights on you sooner. That is not what your mother would have said."

I frowned. "She would have protected—"

"She kept the fae enslaved to the rules the humans created for them. Her fear kept her in a place where there was no escaping the humans' control." He shrugged. "That you disagree is intriguing to me."

That was the second time I'd made him curious. Go me. "So you're here to gloat."

He was very close now. His circling had narrowed the distance between us. "That's what I told myself. And yet, I wonder if I came to see you make the same choice I would. How often do Balance and Unbalance agree?"

There was a solidarity in his words that called to a lonely part of myself.

Did he feel that loneliness too? We were apex predators. No one in the realms would ever possess the magic we possessed, or the burdens and power. Only I could understand him. Only he could understand me.

He held out his hand to me.

I stepped back. "Why are you not attacking me?"

"Because you're about to set the world on a course of action that I desire, does that not deserve a cease fire? You feel the truth of my words. Let us pause to admire this unison that cannot be experienced more than once a millennia."

He moved like lightning to grab my hand and pull me into his arms. His mouth pressed lightly to mine. "I find myself enjoying this game we play."

"Game?" I spluttered, and then his lips crushed against mine. Or did I crush mine to his?

I forgot that I was afraid of him.

I forgot that we were fighting on opposite sides.

Spring rain, ice in the winter, spice and sweet, fire and wild wind…all were wrapped into the taste of him. Both Cormac and Aaden were in this kiss, and I could never get enough of them.

I kissed Andas, and he groaned. His hands slid up to cup the back of my head, fingers digging through my hair, holding me tightly against his powerful frame. He wanted me, and as much as I wanted to believe that longing went one way, I also wanted him because he was Cormac and Aaden.

I bit his lower lip and tasted blood. He growled and

returned the favor, and the sharp sting of teeth made me yelp and pull back, breathing hard.

His eyes were a mixture of green, gold, and black. Two souls I loved, blended with the darkness of Unbalance.

"Do not give up," he whispered so quietly I was not sure I heard him right.

Then his hands were sliding down my arms, trailing heat and promises as he put distance between us. The world began to speed up. His eyes flickered, the colors swirling, and then they were completely dark again. "In case you decide to change your mind."

He pulled a short dagger from his hip and offered me the handle. As if he hadn't heard the four words he'd just spoken.

I exhaled slowly.

He didn't know. Cormac and Aaden had just taken over, and Andas was none the wiser.

Hope seized my chest, and when I blinked, Andas was gone. The human and fae ambassadors started to fidget and rustle as they shook off his magic.

The dagger weighed heavy in my hand, and I peered down at the weapon, noting how one side of the blade was silver while the other side was black. Light and dark, wrapped in a single weapon.

"Silver, don't," Cinth screamed.

There was a surge toward me, soldiers, fae, and human alike. The naga circle swayed in earnest, putting most people back into a trance in a matter of seconds.

"You're a thief, ambassador." I looked at the ambassador from Canada and spotted the darkness in him that had driven him to this choice—a darkness he'd invited in by making corrupt decisions again and again. I'd imagine that Unbalance had merely needed to pluck a few strings to make this human steal the naga coins, because I had no doubt Unbalance was behind this.

"I'm here to do my master's bidding," the ambassador said, confirming my suspicions. "And then I will be given riches untold and a prestigious position by his side. My master knows you are not a murderer. You will not kill me today."

As a human, he shouldn't have been able to break the naga king's hold or pull a weapon without me being able to stop him, but magic burst against me, weighing my limbs as if I'd been stuffed into a bog pit up to my neck.

The ambassador yanked a long thin knife from under his strange suit and slashed it across the Naga king's arm. On the back-handed swing, he buried the blade into the king's neck.

I screamed a wordless howl as pain ripped through my body—my connection to the naga lit with grief and fury. Whatever power Unbalance had used to freeze me—and I was sure this, too, had been him—released. I lunged and drove my new dagger into the thief's heart, twisting the blade as I buried it deep.

He smiled at me. "My master thanks you. For this and the kiss."

His body slumped to the floor, his lifeblood pouring from the wound, and his chest quickly stilled.

The naga king demanded my attention. He was fading quickly.

I dropped to my knees and poured my magic into his wound. My magic slid off, hovering uselessly as blood pooled around us. *What?*

I tried again, and when my magic failed to connect with his essence, I grabbed the thin knife from the thief's limp hand and studied it. *Darkness. Impenetrable.*

Andas had poured a great deal of power into this. But his was only the top layer infusing the weapon.

"Many darknesssesss have formed thissss," a queen sobbed behind me.

I lowered the knife. "Yes."

She was right. This weapon was ancient beyond measure and tended by more than one Unbalance in its existence.

I couldn't help him with magic.

"I need a human healer," I roared.

The throne room was in chaos. Bodies careened, feet thundered, and yelling echoed in all directions.

I crouched beside the Naga king, and he fumbled for my hand. "No healersssss. It isssss time. Thissss musssst be."

"No, no, it's not." I pressed a hand against his wound. This was the naga who'd invited me into his nest when I'd only ever taunted and toyed with his people. He'd given me a family when I'd had none. He'd made it possible for me to free Sigella. The naga had lost so much recently. I couldn't bear for them to lose their beloved king. "It's not your time. There are healers here."

"You defend the nesssssst, Silver one. You fight the darknesssss. Naga bessssside you. All creaturessss bessssside you." He fumbled with something at his side. Cormac's sword.

My heart leaped into my throat. "I gave that to you."

"You take now. Need sssssword. Nessssst mate."

I took the weapon but laid it down so I could keep a hand on his wound.

"Stay with our family," I begged him despite the heavy knowledge in my heart and mind.

"Time," he whispered, nuzzling into the shaking caresses of his queens. The other naga circled around, swaying, singing softly between hissed sobs.

Hessuwa, hessuwa, davishula lisseni ap aw worine, mianana hik la, reginata.

The king's slitted eyes stared past me, a shadow sliding through them as his light slipped away, gone from the world. I knew death, I'd seen it enough times, but it didn't lessen the shock of seeing the king die.

Gentle nudges urged me to my feet. The other naga. I looked around to see that the room had been mostly cleared out.

Hyacinth sat on her throne, face pale. Kallik lingered beside her.

"This is…this is the worst thing that could have happened," Cinth breathed out. "I can't do this. I can't do whatever *this* is."

"This was meant to happen," Kallik told her. "The other alternative was far worse, and Unbalance gave her no choice in the end."

"Silver?" Orlaith's voice turned me around and the naga let her through as if she were an extension of me. Maybe, as one of my helpmates, she was. "What were they singing? The song was beautiful."

I closed my eyes and swayed with them. "They said, 'We remember, we remember, death is not the end for our nest mate, his soul lives on.'"

"No one speaks Naga," Kallik said.

"Nessssst matesssss do." The naga spoke as one as they bent to pick up their fallen king, carrying him away.

I faced Hyacinth. I expected rage, but all I saw was sadness and pain and regret that she'd ever agreed to become queen in her best friend's stead.

"This is the war you've been seeing, isn't it?" Her question was directed at Kallik.

My sister sighed and nodded. "Yes. I thought it was years away, but this was the start. Unbalance has won a great victory today."

And I'd never seen him happier. Happy enough to kiss his adversary.

Cinth paled, then focused on me. "But you'll save us now. Balance will find a way to end it."

Kallik looked at me, too, from the depths of her deep, black hood, but didn't say a word.

Like me, she saw just how much trouble lay ahead.

CHAPTER 6

I kicked my feet in the freezing blue water of the largest lake on Unimak. A baby rawmouth circled beneath my legs, and as I cast her a warning look, her mother circled her away from the mistake of biting Underhill's toes off.

Across the lake, visible in the near darkness by the glint of their coins, naga swayed in time to their haunting song. Old Man watched the funeral from his mountain-top perch, and most of the rawmouths had congregated close to the shore by the naga for another reason entirely.

The naga's song soared to wailing tones and then cut off abruptly. Two of the queens lifted the king's crown from his head, and a young naga male with barely any tarnish to his scales approached. He seemed impossibly young, no more than a boy. Yet the naga had to have a king.

When the queens set the crown on the small boy's serpentine head, they pushed their magic into the metal and shrunk the crown to fit. The boy walked to stand beside the dead king's head and waited there as his naga tribe approached to take a heart piece—a treasured item—from their previous ruler. The group of queens approached their late king first—some picking strings of silver coins, while others picked amulets or gleaming gems. Then the remaining princess and princes of the tribe collected their pieces, from eldest to youngest. The new king's task would be to earn those heart pieces back in time. When he'd regained all, then he would know his tribe adored him, and his tribe would believe in their king without fail.

I'd become Underhill at twenty-one, and still I'd felt much too young for the responsibility.

I couldn't imagine what the young naga felt in this moment. Perhaps his youthful mind would protect him from understanding the enormity of ruling.

Standing, I portaled to join the naga.

Swaying with them, I approached the young king. He flicked out his tongue to taste the air at my approach, and though his instincts must have told him to bow, he straightened his scaled upper body and met my gaze.

I smiled. "You will do, master king. I will help you. I am your family."

There was a tremble in his body that he tried to hide by shifting on the spot. "Thank you, nessst mate."

"For your coronation, I bring you a gift," I told him.

Awed whispers hissed behind me. *A gift from Underhill.*

Whether I deserved the title or not, I'd accepted that I'd be Underhill for a time. Their awe didn't resonate with me, though I understood a gift from me would be treasured indeed. "I cannot say that you will not meet adversity, young king. I cannot say that people won't try to hurt you. But," I said, "you will not meet the same end of your last beloved king."

I looked to the dead ruler at my left and sent my magic forth. I'd watched enough naga coronations to remember what happened next. Naga, along with most creatures in Underhill, understood that a dead body was just a dead body. Naga liked to keep the skulls of their kings, but I'd add my own twist to that rite.

I pulled the late king's skull from his head, leaving his flesh and brain behind, as intact as I could manage. I encased the skull in my magic, and soon it glowed a brilliant silver—though the metal itself was something other than silver.

I pulled the king's shiniest scales from where his torso met his legs and arranged them in a band on either side of the skull. Bending to pick up pebbles from the shore, I used magic to liquify them, then finished my piece.

A cooling blast over the gift set it, and gasps rang out over the lake.

I leaned down to the new boy king and fastened the

thick, banded collar around his neck. The skull rested at the nape of his neck and faced outward, and the late king's scales that I'd set in the rock of his funeral site protected the young naga's throat.

I told the boy, "He will watch your back and your neck."

The young king touched the neck plate. "No one will know whichhh is my real faccce. A disssguissse. Thank you, neessst mate."

Mimicry. I hadn't thought of that, but he was right, and I enjoyed the insight into how he viewed the world and his survivalist role in it. I had a feeling the naga had picked their next king wisely.

The tribe gathered to look at the king's first treasure, and some of the younger naga handed over their heart pieces right then and there.

I stood with the queens as the boy king lifted the remains of the last ruler.

The songs had been sung, and the dance had been danced. The new king set the ruler into the water.

He stood at the shore as the rawmouths surged forward, eager to be first to snatch a bite of their promised meal. Not many could stomach naga without the ability to cook the meat properly. Rawmouths could, even if this meal might make their mouths especially raw.

The king's body was dragged down, and the waves of water cleared to reveal the new king still standing in the same spot.

Old Man roared flame high into the air over the lake, and the naga sighed and swayed, and I felt their hope renew. Underhill had presented their new king with a treasure, and the oldest dragon had given his blessing too. Many queens and kings came and went without either.

I said to the king, "I don't wish for your tribe to become a target for any vengeful ambassadors. It would be better to leave this place, but I know of another, where the ground is loose enough for a new nest. I believe you won't be hunted, and in return, you would be doing me a service of guarding this space."

"Sssspeak it, nesst mate. You will not guide us assstray," said the king after a glance at the eldest queens, who would advise him until he was old enough to reign alone.

I opened a portal to the sapling in Ireland. "This way."

I stepped through the portal to arrive at the cave's entrance. The tribe filed through the portal behind me, and in the brief lull—the first I'd had since Unbalance had driven the Canadian ambassador to kill the naga king, I thought about the new weight on my left hip.

Cormac's sword returned to me.

And why? The naga king had given the blade back to me on his dying breaths. He hadn't spent those moments uttering goodbyes to his people. He'd returned the blade to me. I wouldn't disrespect his wisdom by ignoring the significance of what he'd done. Cormac's sword had to mean something.

"Thissss is the placccce?" the new king asked.

I didn't turn from the cave. "It is."

"There issss darknesssss here. Nesssting here cannot be."

The ground wasn't right? They must be able to sense something about it that I couldn't. I turned to apologize, only to find the tribe had spread out and the naga were flicking their tongues along the shingled ground.

"Would not take muchhhh to fix darknesssss in ground," a naga queen hissed to the king.

He nodded. "Not muchhhh."

I blinked. "What would fix it?"

"Just a mother'sss touchhh," the queen answered. "And we have a mothhher."

Me?

I almost pressed a hand against my chest in surprise.

"Darkness veinssss from in cave," another queen said.

"There's a sapling inside. The tree of life. It's sick."

Their mournful sighs filled the air.

The new king walked up to join me, turning his serpent head toward me. "Moossst important that the mothhher touchhhessss."

I'd tried before, and yet, the naga seemed so certain

about what the ground needed. "Who is the best at sourcing new ground among you?"

The new king pointed out a younger queen, then pointed to himself. "We will joinnn you. Wait here, nesst mates. Sssoon, I returnnn."

I walked inside the cave and felt the heaviness of my steps.

"Thisss placcce hurtsss your heart," said the young queen.

I glanced at her. One thing I loved about naga? They knew that all beings were born with wisdom, and only knowledge could be gained in life. They assigned leadership to the wisest among them, regardless of age. "Yes, nest mate. I lost part of my heart here."

"If you had lossst your heart here, darknesss would have a claim on you," she disagreed.

"You're right," I said after a beat. "Part of my heart is adrift."

"Then you musssst tie it to yoursssself again," said the new king.

If only it were so simple.

We reached the sapling, and the two naga swayed mournfully, gazing at the dark veins in the young tree.

"This is the source?" I asked them.

The young queen nodded. "Darkness poisssonsss from thisss sssource."

I'd tried to force out the darkness without success. I'd also failed to force the darkness out of living beings. I was missing something and figuring that out felt crucial, but I hadn't dared to linger here when Andas could still access the scale realm and see my every move. "You spoke of a mother's touch. What did that mean?"

The new king tilted his head to display his glowing neck piece. "You touchhhed this."

I'd encased the items with my essence and magic. "That will extract the darkness?"

"No sssuch thing," said the queen. "Darknesss can only be balanccced."

Gaia had told me as much, but with the information the naga had provided, the meaning clicked into place. "I must give the sapling more light to balance the darkness within it. The answer isn't to burn out the darkness, just to tip the scales in my favor."

A grin broke out on my face that was echoed on the faces of my nest mates.

I hovered my hands over the sapling before it could stab me or strangle me, or both of the above. I pulled from my surroundings in a dragging gulp, then released my magic. This time, I didn't direct my essence toward the dark veins at all. Instead, I coated the leaves with silver. I coated them in a thick layer of my magic. Then I moved to the fragile branches, wrapping them in the same blanket. The trunk too. The roots next. I slid completely into my magical sight, walking across the ground to trace the roots beneath the soil and touch them with silver, from root tip to trunk. Over and over I did this until not a single tiny hair of a root was without the sheath of my essence.

I lifted my head and blinked a few times to clear the threads of magic from my sight.

"The ground is loosssse," whispered the naga king. "The ground isss worthy of a nesst. The sssapling has been sssaved."

My knees shook at the sheer expenditure of magic I'd released—I would've died five times over trying to carry out such a task the first time I'd come to this cave. I could see what the naga king meant though. The angry, clawing roots had smoothed along the surface and now sparkled with silver, through which the dark veins were barely visible. The sapling had tripled in size already and the trunk was thicker too.

"Thank you," I told the king and young queen. "You've both done the realms a service today."

"Where nnnext, nessst mate?" the king asked.

I wish I knew. Without Underhill, I'd lost my anchor, and there was a feeling of being adrift that was a first for me. All of Underhill's creatures must feel this way now, or perhaps I felt it more keenly with two parts of my heart floating around in Andas. "I will be at the Alaskan court for the time being, dealing with any…teething issues between the fae and humans. I will task Peggy and Sigella to check in with you regularly. I hope this nest brings you peace for a time. Guard it from those you can. Abandon it from those you can't fight. No nest is worth your lives."

The king dipped his head, and the young queen brushed her scales against me in goodbye.

I portaled away to the Alaskan palace and burst into my room.

Orlaith stood on the balcony in whispered conversation with Keefe.

I ground to a halt. "Am I interrupting something?"

They leaped apart, and Orlaith hurried closer. "No, no. Just getting to know each other better."

A LIE, but I didn't call her out. Why were they together?

Keefe had smoothed his expression of any emotion by the time he entered the room after her. "Mistress of Underhill."

I dipped my head at the mysterious fae—and then took a dive into his pathways. There was no sense to be made of the mess. Maybe if I had more time, I could pick apart all of his possible futures to figure out his game. As it was, the paths all seemed to turn into the same outcome—a meeting between me and Andas. In some of the futures, I faced Unbalance in the fae realm. Some of them on Earth, and some in this very room. But in every future, Keefe had turned his paths so they led to that exact point.

"And what do you see?" he asked me.

I focused on him again. "I see that you hold power over your fate."

Keefe winked. "A man can dream."

I didn't say more. This man meant something. Was he here to help me? I couldn't be sure just yet. I also couldn't blast him to the most desolate pit in Earth until I knew.

Keefe executed a flourishing bow, then hooked his thumbs in his belt and swaggered to the door. "Goodnight, fair ladies."

The door closed, and I took in Orlaith's blush.

"I wouldn't get involved if not for the tension this tryst could create between you and Sigella," I said to her.

"There won't be any problems with Sigella," she answered, not meeting my gaze.

There was a hint of subterfuge behind her words, but overall she seemed to have meant what she'd said. And while I could interrogate her for answers, her demeanor made it clear that more questions weren't welcome.

She'd always been truthful, and she'd always been true, so I decided I'd leave her to come clean in her own time. "So be it. I believe you."

If anything, that made her blush deepen. She walked over to sit at the small breakfast table. "Shit hit the fan, huh?"

I'd seen some of these fans in the palace. I imagined shit hitting one of them and exploding in every direction. The visual was an accurate one, even if the words weren't as direct as I preferred. "Yes, shit hit the fan.

The naga king has been laid to rest, and a new one crowned."

"They don't waste time."

"In Underhill, it isn't wise to waste time. You never know when one moment might be your last."

"And Cormac's sword?" she asked. "The naga king gave it back to you. That means something right?"

She was asking a flurry of questions to take my mind off her and Keefe.

I flopped back onto the bed, weapons, grime, blood, and all. "There can be great power in items like this. Sigella was trapped in Lugh's harp for centuries." Faolan had given me his ancestor's shield, too, which had protected me from a bone from the sluagh's corset.

"Tell me you realize there's more to Cormac's sword than meets the eye," pressed my silver-dressed helpmate.

"He was very attached to it," I told her. "You're right. The naga king wouldn't have returned it if it wasn't vital to do so. I must learn more about the sword."

Orlaith burst upward. "Good. It's settled. A trip to the Irish court. Oh, I've longed to see the Ríchashaoir's botchy face when I show up in my body again."

From past comments, I understood that Orlaith was more intimately acquainted with the leader of the Irish court than most. She'd said something about complaining about his size and then hinted at a long story. At the time, I hadn't wanted to ask her more, and I still didn't really want to, if truth be told. The

Ríchashaoir's size or lack thereof could remain a mystery to me.

"Yes, we'll go to the Irish court." I pulled on the cord that summoned the human staff. I'd leave a message for the queen.

Orlaith had erupted in a flurry of packing. I was quite curious about where she'd procured so many silver garments and accessories in such a short timeframe. And two trunks. One appeared to be for her, and there was a second, *smaller* trunk that she was tossing leather trousers and vests into, presumably for me. "So you think the key to reaching Cormac and Aaden is in the sword somehow?"

The sword itself? No. But perhaps something attached to the sword. A memory or the history or the others who'd wielded it. "I think there's only one key to besting a predator, Orlaith. Observing them." *That* was the problem. I could only chase so much information before I'd need to go to the source.

"If only we could put Andas in a glass ball, right?" she said, then sighed.

If only. Because I could say one thing with certainty. I wouldn't learn much more about beating Unbalance from afar.

Orlaith slowed in her packing flurry. Without turning to me, she sighed. "I need to tell you something."

About Keefe? "Of course."

"I heard something at dinner, but I don't want to tell you."

I blinked as a wisp of black caught my eye. The next instant the wisp was gone. But I was certain I'd seen it in Orlaith. My mouth dried.

I'd just seen darkness in my friend. Just a flash of it. I pressed my lips into a firm line, realizing that I'd greatly underestimated how vulnerable she must be after receiving her body back. "Why don't you wish to tell me?"

She threw a shimmering garment onto the bed. "Because you'll charge off and get hurt."

A wisp of black. Darkness again. Was she lying about not wishing to tell me or the part about not wanting me to get hurt? "You must do whatever you believe is best."

She turned then and her look was quizzical. "I don't know what's best though. You're Underhill. I'm just… *was* a bat."

"And I loved you then, and I love you now," I told her. "I don't care what form you hold, Orlaith."

She studied her hands. "I always longed for my body back."

"Then what's the matter?"

"I hated your mother for a while," she answered. "And now, I see her wisdom and can only mourn that it is gone."

I've never heard Orlaith speak like this. Morose.

Regretful. "You are what you are, and you are my dear friend."

Her head snapped up, but her stare was unfocused, though aimed in my direction. "I am who I am." She blinked a few times. "I must tell you."

Another wisp of black. "Then I will listen."

And then I'd figure out how Andas was preying on her.

"A few fae are visiting from the Irish Court," she half-blurted. "They were discussing some rumors about a sorceress who has taken up residence in a lake close to their court. I didn't think much of it with all the creatures who've come through recently, but then they mentioned the name of the lake."

I quirked a brow, more focused on watching for the appearance of darkness in her.

"The Lake of Jealousy," she said.

That stole my focus. "That's…coincidental." Both of us knew by now there was no such thing as coincidence. "What's the sorceress doing?"

"The subject changed, but their tones when speaking of her didn't imply anything good."

Shit. "She could be Andas's third henchman." I dragged a hand over my face.

Orlaith wrung her hands together. "That's what I was worried about, but I had to tell you because if we're going to defeat Andas, then we need to make sure he's at his weakest."

I frowned. Her words weren't entirely true. Neither

were they entirely false. She'd never lied so artfully as a bat, and if she'd lied at all, then she'd admitted the truth in the next breath. Orlaith needed my help. I'd need to safeguard her from this darkness while she found her footing in her body again. "We will travel to the Irish Court. I'll investigate the sword and ask the Irish leader more about these rumors."

"The Ríchashaoir," she scoffed, and the darkness appeared again, and this time it stayed. "He's useless. I doubt he'll know anything about the sorceress."

The smear on her essence made my heart stop in a way it wouldn't when faced with a thousand foe. I said quietly, "What would you have me do, Orlaith?"

She blurted, "You need to go to the lake. If it's a henchman, then we'll take her out." She smacked her fist into her other palm. "She'll rue the day you crossed her path."

Orlaith hadn't wanted to tell me about the sorceress for fear I'd charge off and get hurt, but now she wanted exactly that. Darkness was trying its best to sink its teeth into her. But did darkness want me to go to the lake, or to stay away? Which was really Orlaith?

I crossed to her and took her hands in mine. "With you by my side, she will rue the day we crossed her path."

Orlaith dropped her gaze and slipped her hands from mine. "Y-yes."

I lowered my voice as if trying to hypnotise a bell skink. "Are you well, Orry?"

She didn't meet my gaze. "I'm not a bat anymore, Silver, of course I'm well. Perhaps it happened sooner than anticipated or planned by your mother, but here I am. Be happy for me?"

But she still didn't meet my gaze. "If you're happy, then I'm happy," I said.

"Good then! Now, let me pack. We better get going."

"I'll return to collect you once I find Sigella."

"Oh, look! I'm done. I'll come with you to find her, shall I?" Orlaith shoved a half-packed bag at me, grabbing the second which was nearly empty. Her cheeks were flushed, and the wisp of black I'd seen in her had taken up a tiny residence within her essence.

She hadn't been done with packing. Orlaith didn't want me to speak to Sigella alone.

All I felt was sadness. And panic. Andas couldn't have Orry too. He couldn't take everyone I loved.

I held out my hand to the beautiful fae. "Let's go then."

CHAPTER 7

"I'm sorry," Sigella drawled from beside me. "Are your portals malfunctioning or did you feel like a hike?"

We crouched in front of the Ríchashaoir's castle—well, not quite in front. I'd portaled us in a mile from the gates, into the surrounding forest. Orlaith was quiet on my other side as I gazed through the trees at the castle. She hadn't uttered a word since Sigella joined us.

"I'm deliberating," I admitted. "Orlaith overhead something about a lake near here. Andas's third henchman might be there."

But that wasn't really the issue. The issue was that Orlaith was acting strangely.

Sigella stepped in front of me and blocked my view of the castle. "All the more reason to figure out why the naga king left you Cormac's sword. You may need it to defeat the henchman."

I couldn't fault her logic. In the battle against Unbalance, that was my next clear move. Yet darkness was trying to take root in Orlaith, and I had to help her. But I was Underhill and my duty wasn't to her.

So should I enter the castle and investigate the sword, or go to the Lake of Jealousy and get to the bottom of Orlaith's darkness?

"We left Keefe and Peggy behind, too, are you going to tell us why?" Sigella asked. The ancient fae was suspicious of our behavior, and with good reason. Orlaith never went this long without speaking.

"I can portal them here if we need them." I frowned. The words were true, and as I spoke them, a thread of magic pulsed within me—my connection to Peggy. I was sure that I could locate Keefe if I focused enough too.

"We should go in," Orlaith whispered.

The words were so opposite to those she'd uttered an hour ago that I turned bodily to face her. "What?"

She swallowed. "The sword is more important. We should go in."

I heard no subterfuge in her words. This was Orlaith. And yet I could see darkness in her still. Darkness she was trying to fight by the looks of the battle on her face.

Sigella sucked in a breath, and I flashed her a warning look.

She'd just seen it too.

"Sigella is right," Orlaith hissed as though in pain. "You may need the sword to help you fight the henchman." She doubled over slightly. "Go into the castle."

The darkness in her strengthened, and I flinched, only just managing to stop myself from grabbing her.

I'd run through any number of possibilities in my mind. I'd considered a desperate attempt to burn the darkness out of her. I'd never succeeded with that, but perhaps my new power would reveal something I hadn't noticed in the past. I'd also considered the opposite—adding my magic into Orlaith to further outweigh the darkness in her, similar to how I'd layered magic onto the tree of life. But I'd done that to the *tree of life*, an entity more powerful than I could fathom. A normal fae couldn't just hold the power of Underhill. The most likely result from doing that is that Orlaith would explode in every direction.

No. I had a terrible and sinking feeling that only Orlaith could beat it back. That all I could do was support her. But there had to be some other way to help her. There was *always* another way, and I couldn't rest until I knew the answer one way or another.

"I'm going to the lake," I replied.

Sigella was taking her turn to be quiet.

"No," Orlaith snapped. "We need to go to the castle."

And yet when I'd declared my choice, the darkness in her had lessened. She may suddenly want me to investigate the sword, but the evil presence in her wanted me at the lake. If I didn't choose that, it would root more deeply in my friend.

More than that, I had to find answers. Answers that were selfish and would no doubt carry serious consequences for the realm. Yet Orlaith meant too much to me *not* to do this.

"Orry," I said. "Look at me."

The look she gave me was half glare, and I ignored it.

"An hour ago you were certain I had to go to the lake, and now you're certain I shouldn't. I've asked you already, but I'll ask again. Are you well?"

"Yes, I'm well. A woman can change her mind. That's all," she said in a scathing tone.

A tone that wasn't her. Maybe I'd only known her as a bat, but I *did* know her. That voice belonged to a darker creature.

She was put in the prison realm.

I silenced the quiet voice in my mind, refusing to give it any room. This was Andas's work—just like how he'd taken over that human ambassador. I *would* stop him from controlling Orlaith, but perhaps the best thing was that he remain unaware that I knew what he was up to. For now.

I smiled. "Which is what I'm doing. I won't be long. In the meantime, I want you to start digging up what you can on Cormac's sword."

She opened her mouth.

"You'll need to let me know what the Ríchashaoir

says when he sees you've returned." I winked for good measure.

Orlaith's red hair was perfectly coiled and twisted, and she'd left a few strands loose to catch the breeze. Having dressed to accentuate her curves and highlight the perfect glow of her porcelain skin, she was a devastating beauty. Her eyes called to me most of all in this moment, and almost erased all else.

Innocent, guileless blue, glittering with…slight malice.

Malice that wasn't her.

"You're leaving me behind." She narrowed her gaze. "Let me guess, Sigella is going with you?"

Sigella stepped closer to her. "Your role is not to question Underhill. Your role is to help her and do as she says. If she is asking this of you, then it is for a reason, you stupid twit."

The glitter of malice intensified, and the air tightened as if Orlaith might attack.

I cleared my throat, and Orlaith blinked, leaning away from Sigella again.

She glanced at me, then curtsied. "Whatever Underhill commands."

In a whirl of silver fabric, Orlaith spun and marched from the treeline. Her hurt slashed through me, and I made to step after her, but Sigella whipped out a hand to grip my arm.

Very quietly, she said, "Silver, can't you sense the darkness in her?"

I watched Orlaith storm toward the castle. "I can. It appeared an hour ago and has already strengthened in her."

"She wanted you to go to the lake?"

"Initially, yes."

"Then that tells you everything you need to know."

But it didn't. That darkness told me that Orlaith needed my help—that her sentence imprisoned in bat form had ended too soon, and Orlaith was struggling to keep the darkness of her past life from claiming her again. "I'm not about to abandon her to Andas when she needs me most. She's been there for me more times than I can count."

"Perhaps that's why Keefe has joined us," Sigella said. "To replace her. Balance doesn't care about your feelings, Silver. Balance will drive a dagger through your heart thousands of times and then a thousand times more. If Orlaith's time with you is done, then nothing you do will change that."

A shiver ran through me. "Your theories are premature. I understand the ruthlessness of balance all too well, and I am no stranger to painful choices or painful indecision. She is still within my grasp. If she was beyond my reach, then she wouldn't care so much about experiencing that darkness."

Sigella sighed. "So you'll go to the lake for answers."

"Just like I walked into danger to free you," I replied. "Keep up if you can."

I broke into a run, and Sigella soon caught up and

matched the length of my bounding leaps toward the Lake of Jealousy.

On the way, I wove spell after spell, drawing warmth and power to me before tucking the reserves deep within my body. The pallor of the available essences on Earth sent a pang of longing for Underhill through me. Earth had provided fae with a refuge in times of danger, yet we were not meant for this place, really. Here, we couldn't thrive. Here, magic didn't fill our chests and steal our breath with its fullness as it had in my vibrant childhood home.

We ran in relative silence for nearly an hour.

"You know this will likely be a trap," Sigella stated.

I gave her a sidelong glance. "Yes." Andas was behind the darkness in Orry, and that meant he was behind her original insistence that I come to this lake. Andas was either sending me to be slaughtered by his last henchman, or he'd come to do the job himself.

"If he succeeds? It's not too late to return to the castle."

I answered her more honestly than I'd answered myself with the same question. "If I am to learn about him, then perhaps he is meant to succeed."

She scoffed. "You think he'll keep you alive and close and just spill his secrets? Fool!"

No, I didn't think that. I'd answered on a whim—on a deep suspicion that I hadn't realized had been growing within me.

I could feel Sigella building up to a lecture. I cut her

off. "Orlaith has always told me I should just bed him. Perhaps that's the answer."

She snorted. "Now you plan to seduce Unbalance? We're doomed. Have you ever bedded another?"

"Had sex? No, but if a three-legged teekek can figure it out, then so can I."

How did we get onto this subject? I had a feeling I was to blame.

Sigella grabbed my arm and yanked me to a halt. "Do not for one second think that you can love them through this, Silver. Or even fuck Andas through this. He's a *villain*. He is made to be so by the enormous forces of this universe. You're our only hope, and if you fall into the trap of believing he can be cured by your kisses and what's between your legs, then you're a bigger fool than even I realized. You'd be as big of a fool as *me*. Too many women believe if they love hard enough or deep enough a man will become everything they hope and dream he'll be. Life and love don't work that way, and you know enough of my past to understand I know what I speak of."

I pushed her hand off my arm. "I don't believe I can change Andas. That's not what I'm trying to do. I was repeating Orlaith's thought, not mine."

Yet how many times had I yearned to give in to Andas?

"I hope so," she said shortly. "For everyone's sake."

I didn't answer. That would teach me for trying to distract Sigella with a subject change.

My surroundings registered. "We're nearly there."

Sigella narrowed her eyes but didn't say anything further about me seducing Andas.

The sparse trees cleared, and pebbles crushed underfoot as the Lake of Jealousy came into view.

The lake was still and so calm the surface looked more like ice. I quelled a shiver at the memory of how cold the water had been, though I couldn't be sure whether that was due to other memories attached to this place. I'd kissed Cormac and Aaden here. I'd stood crushed between them as we'd finally submitted to that pounding power of our fated bond. This was where destiny had bitten into us and swirled deep around and within us.

"There is something here. Something dark." The power present was so large that balance was nearly forcing me to the water to deal with it.

For good or for ill, this was where I needed to be.

Sigella spoke low. "I sense it also, but it's…hidden too."

I dipped my head. "If it's not a henchman, then I still need to deal with a dark creature of this magnitude. Hide," I said to her. "No matter what happens, do not try to save me. I mean it."

She grabbed me by both arms. "Are you sure of this, Silver? We can still choose a different path."

I felt the pressure of balance around me as if there were a scale under my ribs. "I came here for answers to save Orlaith, but I'm meant to work balance here, too, Sigella. This is right."

Hopefully for both reasons. I refused to leave Orry to battle Andas's power alone.

Sigella drew me into a hug and kissed my forehead, and I was too shocked by the display of affection to react. "Go carefully. The water in the lake is sick with darkness."

She let me go and backed away into the trees, waving her hand over her footprints to erase them until no trace of her remained. She disappeared from sight, and her magic muted a few moments later.

I could feel her watching, and that would have to be enough.

I walked to the lake's edge and tried to wade into the water. My foot encountered firm resistance. Not an attack, but a barrier. A magical buffer existed over the lake that wouldn't permit me to enter the water. Was it cast over the surface like icing on a cake or infused in the water itself like tea?

I needed to try a slice to find out.

Unsheathing my dagger, I stabbed at the surface and yelled when my arm and the dagger bounced off the barrier.

Sigella's soft laughter reached my ears, but I tilted my head and ignored her, a slight frown marring my brows.

I drew out Cormac's sword and held it in both hands, staring down at the blade. *Why not?* Wasn't

Cormac currently trapped inside of Unbalance? If the creature in the lake was a henchman of Unbalance, there was a certain sense in the idea that I could only enter with the sword of my wolf, who was now trapped within Unbalance.

The naga king had pressed this blade back into my hands with his dying breath. He'd known I would need this weapon.

In a whoosh of singing metal, I sunk the sword through the barrier and into the water until it lodged in the pebbled lakebed below. The magic in the barrier shied away from the sword, almost screaming in its haste to do so.

Whatever the nature of this creature's dark power, there was no doubt that its magic detested the sword. Which was good and bad. Good, because I possessed the creature's weakness in my hands. Bad, because the creature likely wouldn't face me if I attacked with the sword.

When I pulled the sword free, the hole in the lake's barrier remained and didn't close over. Slowly I reached through the hole and waved my hand through the water. My movement under the surface wasn't impeded.

Perfect.

Looked like an entrance to me.

Then there was the matter of the sword. I couldn't enter with it. But I'd need the weapon eventually.

I also needed an exit.

Gripping the pommel, I hurled the blade to the middle of the lake.

There was a soft plunk as the weapon pierced the surface, then a last flash of steel. Barely a ripple reached the shore after the sword disappeared.

The ground beneath my feet trembled though. Someone had noticed.

"That's because you fuckers always pick the darkest and coldest place to live," I muttered.

I rolled my shoulders and dove through the hole I'd created and into the cold water. The icy jealousy seeped through my boots and pants as it attempted to reach my heart and mind. The envy-inducing power of the lake was intact, and it quickly snaked over me.

I trailed my fingers through the water, and icy rage washed over my skin. Unlike the first time I'd come here, I could feel the push of the lake's magic. I could feel how it wanted me to conjure visions of Andas with a harem of naked women. The lake whispered that Cormac and Aaden had enjoyed their time away from me. The water wished me to believe that my men were choosing to stay buried in Andas because they'd never truly loved me.

But those spells I'd woven on our walk here? They were buffering me against the lake's power and preserving my magic too.

I swam deeper, and I let out a hiss as jealousy stabbed at me from a hundred different directions. This was fucking awful. Worse than the first time because my heart ached so badly, but at least I was powerful enough to function through the lake's attack.

The cold was worse than I remembered, but I gritted my teeth.

If Kik had been with me, he'd have told me to stop being a pussy. While I'd always thought of cats as ferocious, he'd seemed to believe them weak.

Sigella had been right earlier. The water here was sick, and I held my breath, though I could have breathed the lake in and survived as all fae could. Today, that seemed like a bad idea. The weight and press of the unnatural cold was like a living thing.

The creature causing this was close. I could feel it in the surroundings watching me and monitoring my progress…waiting for the water to weaken me.

I had to get to the sword before this darkness broke through my buffers.

I pulsed my magic outward and found my exit point. Above and to my right. That meant the sword was below.

Nothing for it. I swam for the bottom of the lake.

The resistance was immediate. My movements became harder the deeper I swam. I struggled to cut through the vise-like grip of the liquid as I pushed deeper. No creature lurked in sight, and yet, closer to the creature, I could sense this force was old. Very old. More like Gaia.

I squinted ahead at a faint glimmer. Was that the sword?

Cold daggers sliced through my skin, and bubbles poured from my mouth at the suddenness of the creature's attack. It didn't want me to reach the sword.

Icy bands of magic tightened around my chest, squeezing me tightly and driving an icy chill into the marrow of my bones. Tiny, sharp pinpricks stabbed through the icy bands and into my skin.

Shit.

Guarded as I was by all my woven spells, the poison didn't kill me in seconds, but it worked quicker than I could spin a spell to burn it out of me. What the hell was this thing?

I cried out as poison seared through my veins and essence, and screamed bubbles escaped my mouth as I pushed hard to reach the lakebed. I had to get to the bottom. Cormac's sword had sliced through this creature's power like butter. Perhaps throwing it wasn't my best idea, but this creature never would have attacked otherwise.

There is always someone stronger, someone older, little one. Remember this moment.

Gaia's voice wasn't soothing. She'd picked a shitty moment to warn me.

Whatever had a hold on me didn't ease an inch, and the poison in my system had started wrapping its way around my heart, around my lungs and muscles.

My eyes opened wide when my fingers brushed the pommel of the sword. Hardly believing I'd found it again, I gasped and grabbed hold of the blade. I wasn't capable of more. My body was unresponsive to my urges to swim and fight. To use the blade to stab.

Sigella was right, I was a fool.

I'd been incapacitated well and truly.

A warm hand curled around my wrist, and an explosion of light gave me my first view of what had attacked me as I was ripped from the water and high into the air.

Power rippled out from the creature in waves. It had the appearance of a massive ventipus, only bigger and with glowing red eyes. And it had a hold on me too.

I was yanked downward again, and a distant part of my mind understood that I was being dragged to the creature's mouth. From here, I could see its rows upon rows of teeth. This was a creature of darkness, of malevolence—one that even Underhill had never tried to take on.

The kraken.

"Help me fight it!" A male voice roared through the dark. Was he kidding? I was literally poisoned and nearly dead.

Couldn't a woman die in peace?

Then again, I wasn't entirely sure what peace was, only that it was a fleeting thing.

I pushed what power I had left toward the man who had hold of me—because what did it matter now if I gave him my strength?

The reserves I'd tucked away slammed into him.

Our power tangled, light and dark, and he raised his hand as he conjured a spear made of pure power. He hurled it at the kraken.

The monster bellowed and flailed, and I felt the crushing weight on my body ease. That hardly mattered. I could already feel my life force slipping away.

The hand that had a hold of me yanked me upward as the last of the tentacles slid off my body. I was limp in body and mind, unable to do anything but grip the sword, and only that because my hand had frozen around the pommel.

Stars sparkled around me in the darkness, and I was sure I saw Kik, my old friend. I smiled at him and said softly, "Come back for me, Kik. Take me with you."

"Don't you dare!" A voice bellowed as power slammed into me.

There was no daring left in me. I could go now. There was no point in fighting the poison that the monster had shoved into me. Maybe the battle could be fought by someone else. "I lost them."

The words slid out of me.

Lost Cormac. Lost Aaden.

"No. No you didn't. Powers be damned, it would be easier if you had."

Power, so much power rippled around us, and I should have feared what was happening, but I was warm now, and I could see my friend in the darkness, so I had nothing to fear. I didn't need to fear the rough hands that gently held me either.

I'd meant something to them after all. He'd said as much—*Andas.*

Lips pressed to mine, and I felt the heat of them distantly.

They are still here, Silver. Live for them. Live for me.

I couldn't recall who the man referred to. I couldn't recall who he was, though I enjoyed his warmth.

Live, he'd said.

I just had to live.

CHAPTER 8

"Kik," I moaned. I felt like a tarbeast's asshole after it had eaten too much whip flax. Worse even.

A sigh. "Kik's not here. His death was regrettable. As much as I hated him, I knew you loved him."

I opened my eyes a crack. Because that sure as hell had sounded like Andas.

It *was* Andas.

"You," I croaked, not able to budge anything aside from my vocal cords and eyelids.

Andas jerked on the hard rock he'd perched on and whipped to look at me. He swallowed once. "You're awake this time. You've muttered Kik's name more than once…"

And clearly he'd been answering. Had I just heard him say that he regretted Kik's death because *I'd* loved him?

I stared at Unbalance.

A soft breeze lifted his dark hair and the unlaced neck of his light tunic. He'd brought me somewhere warm, and I could hear the crash of waves and take in the scent of the sweet and salty ocean air. I couldn't feel the grittiness of sand on the exposed skin of my arms, but a soft leather that smelled entirely of Aaden and Cormac. *Andas's long coat.*

I closed my eyes in a bid to connect how I'd come to be on this beach, laid out on my enemy's jacket while he whispered lover's words to me.

"Kraken," he grunted.

The lovers' words were gone?

Ah, yes. The kraken. Technically, a kraken wasn't as bad to fight as a rawmouth, but that was because the kraken's numbing magic was so diluted in an ocean. As long as you never entered their cave lairs, you'd be fine. But in a lake?

I'd protected myself against the jealous magic of the lake, and my layers of spells had helped somewhat repel the kraken's power, but I hadn't even sensed it coming through the cold of the water and the narrowed direction of my thoughts. I'd been too rigid in my plan.

"You've taken my kraken," I said to Unbalance. Because surely this was the kraken from Underhill.

He hummed. "Yes. He didn't get through your portal in time. He didn't want to numb the other creatures and prevent their escape."

My chest squeezed. He'd sacrificed himself. And now look at what he'd become. "You sent him through afterward then. A little trap?"

"A little trap, yes. I sent a few whispers to the Alaskan Court about a sorceress. I knew you would find it impossible not to investigate. I didn't expect you to throw my—*his*—sword into the fucking middle of the lake."

I shrugged a shoulder. "You win some, you lose some. I was trying to lure the creature out, and with how the sword worked against its power, it would have retreated if I'd kept the weapon on me."

"Exactly," he said from between clenched teeth.

Andas seemed upset that he couldn't anticipate my every move. I could've sworn his exhale shook.

"What's the state of your body?" he asked roughly.

I cracked open my eyes again. "You don't want to ask how I am, yet you do. That must be confusing." His jaw tightened, and my lips found the energy to smirk. *Look at me go.* "I'm incapacitated, Andas. You have me. Unbalance will rule unchecked for centuries and maybe millennia. You've won. All you need to do is kill me."

I couldn't have stopped him. Unless Sigella showed up to drown him in tea, I was on my own. My magic wasn't answering me, so I couldn't check where any of them were, but Sigella must've seen Andas drag me from peril. She was smart enough to wonder what I was thinking.

"Why didn't you let the kraken kill me?" I asked him aloud.

I tried to shift my shoulders and grimaced.

He leaned down to help me but stopped himself, curling his hands to fists instead. "I had not yet decided whether to replace you. That is all."

There was a whisper in my mind, though, something he'd said in what I'd expected to be my last moments. What was it?

I played along. "You'd rather stick with the kelpie you know."

He frowned. "The devil I know? Yes, that is what I must decide. Forces in the greater universe will always ensure there is both Unbalance and Balance in this collection of realms. Another Balance will exist the moment you are gone. I would need to find this Balance—which would be difficult since your henchmen would use their powers to hide her until the time when the scales might be tipped. So why go to that trouble when I have tipped the scales in my favor already, and now that I have you trapped?" He took a deep breath. "Another Balance would not be you."

I blinked. Then again. "You don't want to kill me."

He clenched his jaw again. "I haven't decided. It's time to move."

Andas stood abruptly, then bent down to scoop up me and his jacket. There was a weight in my hand, and I tightened my grip around the pommel of Cormac's sword, surprised that I still held it. He hadn't tried to take it from me.

I exhaled, my head lolling against his chest. I had the perfect view of the strong angle of his jaw and cheekbones. He had Cormac's skin tone, and grime still covered him from the fight against the kraken. That warmed my blood. My men hadn't been afraid to get their hands dirty, and I found that attractive considering I could barely recall a time when my hands hadn't been that way.

He opened a portal that reeked of sulphur and stepped us through.

A tropical oasis, with a waterfall pounding to my left. Andas sat me up against a moss-covered boulder, then lashed out a spear of his magic at a wriggling creature.

The long, thin Earth creature thrashed around for a time before going still, and conversation halted as Andas set to the task of skinning the animal and setting it over a patch of his black fire.

My mind was caught between two states, the sluggishness of near-death and frantic whirling from the bizarreness of this situation.

Andas had saved me from the kraken and his own trap. Andas…was about to feed me. Nurse me back to health. All because he 'hadn't decided whether to replace me.'

I had an inkling that Unbalanced felt…unbalanced. Perhaps I'd intended to trap *him*, but here I was. With him unsettled, I couldn't have asked for a better chance to learn about him.

"Why did we just move locations?" I unlocked my fingers from the pommel of Cormac's sword as I asked the question.

Andas focused on the blade. "I couldn't pry the weapon from your hand. Even a whisper away from death, you held it fast." He lifted his gaze to mine. "Why?"

I could choose not to give him the truth, but there would be no learning about this fae without a little give. "Because it's Cormac's."

Because the naga king had pressed it into my hands in his last moments.

"It *was* Cormac's," said Andas. "He's gone."

The whispering in my mind strengthened, and my brows drew together. "That's not true. You asked me to live for them." I didn't speak the rest because shock gripped my throat as the full memory swam back to me. Unbalance had asked me to live for them *and* him.

"And the ploy worked," he sneered. "How pathetic you are. The tiniest speck of hope can motivate you to claw back from death itself."

"Then there was no point," I replied. Picking up the blade, I set it against my throat.

His roar filled the waterfall oasis. Birds rocketed into the sky, and the surrounding forest exploded in a flurry of startled animals.

Without breaking our locked gazes—mine calm and his panicked—I lowered the sword to the ground again.

Fury lit Andas's black-eyed gaze, reminiscent of Cormac's temper. He opened a portal and stepped through, leaving only the acrid scent of sulphur behind.

I pursed my lips and glanced around. My magic was null for the time being—likely for several days. That meant no portals. "Where the hell am I?"

I could tell this was the earth realm. Beyond that, nothing.

My stomach rumbled, erasing my need to know my location.

I crawled to where the skinned creature was cooking. It looked a lot like the slithering creatures in Underhill that were edible. "Better raw."

Just like Aaden to overcook something that could be enjoyed cold and bloody. I twisted off a chunk of the flesh and tore off a small bite that I could chew in my weakened state.

I licked my fingers afterward. *Not bad.* I went back for seconds. Andas shouldn't have left if he'd wanted half the food.

Instead of crawling back to the rock, I slanted sideways to land in a clump of grass growing beside the pool. The spray of the water was refreshing against the humid temperature.

He'd kissed me.

He'd begged me to live for him.

He'd done something to bring me back from the verge of death. What had he done?

I shifted, then groaned. Not a minute more went by before I tried again. Grimace. Groan. Curse. Moan.

"Fuck." I curled into a ball against the screaming ache in my body, then I glared at the water. Cold instead of warm, but it would help, clothes and all.

I heaved my body closer, then rolled with pitiful slowness until I could dangle my hand in the water. My fingertips brushed shingles. *Shallow.* I had a healthy respect for the dangers and unpredictability of water. Andas had also roared any creatures away before he'd left.

How good of him.

I heaved off the bank and landed in the water on my back. Air whooshed from my lungs as I discovered just how shallow it was.

"Ah," I sighed as the cool liquid ran over my body, sweeping away some of the aching sensation.

I gazed up at the sun, barely visible through the thick tropical canopy. I wasn't sure I'd enjoyed this much quiet since—

Sulphur.

"And now you're trying to drown yourself," snapped Andas.

I shifted my gaze to find him looming over me. "Still having a tantrum, Cormac?"

There was a flicker of amber in his gaze.

"There *is* no Cormac." He entered the water, all the better to loom over me, I supposed.

"Then why are *you* having a tantrum?"

He crouched by my head. "Remind me why I didn't kill you."

I closed my eyes. The sight of him was too much for my heart in this state. "Because you're in denial. You don't want to exist this way, apart from me, at odds with me, in danger from me, and in danger of your creatures killing me. You don't want to be without me either. So do you choose eternal torture? Or do you choose eternal loneliness?"

He was quiet.

So was I.

I'd felt the hopelessness of that choice since the moment Andas had appeared with my men trapped inside of him. I'd wondered how I'd ever find the strength to kill them.

"They are inside of you," I whispered. "They *are*."

"They are, but they are me."

I opened my eyes and shouted in his face. "Then tell me how I see them!"

He gripped me by the shoulders and pulled me to sitting, kneeling in the water to bring our faces nose-to-nose.

"Tell me," I screamed. I was hurt, in heart and body. I'd probably been dead for a while. I. Was. Done. I hit his shoulder with all the strength of a newborn alicorn. "Tell me!"

His breath was ragged. "See for yourself."

He dragged me closer to set my lips against his. I no longer had the strength to deny how much I'd craved his touch in the past weeks. I moved my lips against his, wishing I could press against his mouth more firmly to gain the access I wanted.

Andas broke off the kiss, then gripped my hair to tilt my head back and expose my neck. Black eyes bored into mine before his power hit me. Without my magic, I was defenseless against the onslaught. I screamed, my eyes tightening but never leaving his as I was filled with his black essence.

Darkness filled my body and mind, and I thrashed against the attack.

"Stop panicking," Andas said.

The calmness of his tone touched my frantic mind and soothed me enough for me to realize his magic wasn't hurting me. Another's essence filling me should have felt foreign, but there was a soothing coolness to his presence within me.

There was a—

I sucked in a breath, then took a closer look at the magic flooding me

"You see at last what I am," Andas said in a low voice.

I'd never bothered to peer into the black of Andas's magic. Every creature knew darkness was something to avoid, unless they'd already chosen to embrace

Unbalance. But now that his magic wove through me, I could *feel* it.

There was amber. There was green. Black encased them both, doing its best to press the essences together into one.

And failing.

I swallowed. "You're—"

"You see that they are me." He laughed, cold and dull. "You see that I am them, and that they are me. They are here, but they are not as they were. They will never be as they were."

I didn't see that at all.

I'd seen two magics swirling inside of black. Two separate magics.

Andas was breathing hard, still maintaining his tight grip on my hair. His gaze lowered to my lips, then raised again. "Why won't you forget them? Why won't you accept that they are changed, that they are me?"

Why wouldn't I accept it?

Because it wasn't true. There was a rift in Andas that I wasn't sure *he* even saw. Aaden and Cormac *were* separate within him. They'd refused to merge into one —just as they'd resisted doing anything together in life.

My smile was genuine, even if it had nothing to do with what Andas was saying.

Andas loosened his grip and rested his forehead against mine. "You only smile like that when you're about to kill something."

I had no idea what the hell this messed-up thing

was between us. I didn't want Andas, but my body didn't seem to mind whether I was crushed between Aaden and Cormac or crushed by the master of darkness.

I gripped his tunic tightly, then lowered *my* gaze to his lips.

His breath stalled, and if I'd been the type of creature that purred, my chest would be rumbling with it. He wanted me. I didn't have magic, but there was a different kind of power in this.

And I'd wield any weapon at my disposal against him—and enjoy it for good measure.

I flicked out my tongue and traced his bottom lip, enjoying the way his body froze.

There was a rift in Andas.

Driving a wedge into that rift to widen it seemed appropriate.

CHAPTER 9

It was my only choice, that's what I told myself, though if I was being honest, Orlaith had been right. I wanted whatever contact I could have with Cormac and Aaden, even if that contact was through Andas.

My breath and his mingled as we knelt there, so close, touching tongue to lip, fingertips to wrist, knee to thigh—like ignition points for the bolts of electricity racing between us and tingling across my skin. I traced my hand down his bare arm, watching the tiny jumps of his muscles and the uncontrollable twitching of my fingers. Like touching one of the little clouds in Underhill when it was storming—the contact wouldn't kill you, but you'd feel more alive than you had in days.

"Stop it." He growled and stepped away, cutting off the current that had danced between us.

I blinked and stared at him. "Why? It wasn't hurting either of us."

He shook his head, and flashes of gold and green rippled through the darkness of his eyes. My men were drawn to my touch, as I was to them. I just had to keep…doing what I was doing.

A wave of bone-deep fatigue caught me off guard, and I wobbled, stars and darkness coating my vision as I toppled toward him.

"You don't fool me. Catch yourself," he snapped.

What did he mean? That wasn't my first concern as I fell to the side, the world tumbling with me, trees and sky twisting in the wrong direction entirely.

The lurch of my gut made me feel as if I'd fall *through* the earth instead of landing hard. What a strange, unsettling feeling. Had I fallen through the top layer of Earth?

Yelling, someone was yelling, calling my name. *Muffled.* I liked the voice.

A hard slap smarted across my cheek, once, twice, before I lifted a hand to stall a third slap. "Mm fine." Shit, was that my voice? My words were as slurred as if I'd been drinking poppy juices from the plain creeks.

"I'm not here to keep you from killing yourself!" Andas roared in my face, though the look on his face wasn't fury, or anger, or even indifference. He was fearful.

I swallowed and tried to sit, but the world wobbled again, and I fell back so Andas was left supporting me.

This worked for me. Robbed of power as I was, I knew what I had to say to open that rift within him further. "My powers are drained, and I'm as weak as I'll ever be, Andas. If you're going to kill me, now's the time to do it."

My head lolled, and I looked up into his face, seeing the colors swirl in his eyes. His lips pressed together. Unbalance was torn.

"We leave this place," he said. "Now."

As if I hadn't just offered my life to him again.

He slipped an arm under my legs and the other behind my back, then stood. He took three quick strides, and I smelled sulphur as he opened a portal. But my sights were set over his shoulder. The trees surrounding the waterfall had been lush when we'd arrived, but now they were dying. Birds lay lifeless on the ground, and the soil itself was blackening as if with disease.

What *was* that?

A flash of bright light, and we were through the portal and somewhere new on Earth. Why wasn't he taking me to Underhill? I'd thought for sure that was where he'd try to keep me captive.

Cold cracked into me and against my skin, as if it were a living thing seeking entrance into me. I scanned the new place he'd brought us. Deep snow. And we were high in the mountains. From the high plateau, I could see the land was flat for miles in either direction until it burst upward into enormous peaks to the east and west. There didn't appear to be another living being anywhere near us.

Andas set me down in the snow. "I imagine you can't hurt yourself falling here at least."

My teeth were chattering, and the snow soaked through my tunic. "I can't pull magic to myself right now. Why not Underhill? You rule there now, do you not?"

"You think I'd take you there, and give you what *you* want? No, whatever this is, you'll have an agenda and a plan to escape. I won't take you where you want to be." Andas held his hands out, his power roaring around us like a thunderstorm. "I will keep you captive here. For a time, while I decide whether killing you suits me best."

I don't know who he thought he was convincing.

Mountain rock shot from the ground, curling in on itself to form a foundation, then walls, curved doors, rooftops, a portcullis, and stone battlements. A castle high in the mountains. The amount of power Andas possessed still staggered me, and I'd grown up with Underhill for a mother. I couldn't have built a castle like this when at full power—and I doubted whether I could have built a stone hut right now, magically *or* physically.

Without missing a beat, as if it had cost him nothing to raise the castle into being, he strode back to me, scooped me up, and carried me in through the front gates. They fell shut behind us with a resounding clatter of stone on stone.

He didn't set me down but continued to carry me up a tight flight of stairs and down a long walkway.

Rift.

If he intended to leave me here, I needed to make the most of each moment with him. I couldn't remember what Sigella had told me about seduction, but I'd grown up watching Kik whore around. I had nothing else to pull from. "So, we just stay here until you decide to kill me or fuck me?"

Andas stopped and stared down, our eyes locking. "You say that like they're mutually exclusive."

My brows rose. "You mean like Petr Mantis?" They were the only animal I knew of who preferred to reproduce with a recently dead partner.

He rolled his eyes. "Not literally dead."

"I don't like when people speak words and the meaning is different."

Andas's brows slammed together, and he hissed, "I could fuck you one hundred times and care nothing for you. I'd use you and discard you, Mistress of Underhill, and then I'd ensure everyone knew it. I might even bed you just to see if Balance is anything more than the miserable fuck I expect she'd be. You think fucking me will bring Cormac and Aaden back, and I'd enjoy every moment of watching you try your hardest, only to see it fail."

He laughed, his mouth showing off Cormac's dimples. The curve of Aaden's lips.

I might not know how to seduce, but I knew not to

back down ever. "Fucking me would break you, Andas. That's what you're afraid of. You wouldn't survive touching that much of my skin. You'd be my creature from the first touch. So you're right to hide your fear behind all those words designed to hurt me. Which they don't, by the way. Because I would fuck you as hard as I could, but only because that's how I imagine I'd like it."

I could almost hear Sigella and Orlaith groan. That wasn't a particularly sexy thing to say, I was sure, but it was the truth. Something about our connection made me feel certain that sex with Andas would be... catastrophic. For him more than me, or perhaps that was wishful thinking.

His smile and laughter cut short. His throat worked before Andas said low, "You can be sure, Silver, that if I ever bed you, there will be nothing soft about it."

He kicked into a room, then tossed me onto the huge bed inside. Not only had he manifested this castle, he'd furnished it too.

I looked at him. "Promise? And there will be no *bedding* between us, Andas. Only fucking."

I'd never seen him breathe harder. He looked furious. "I'll kill you in the morning."

I frowned when he slammed the door shut.

"Why in the morning? Why not now?" I shouted after him, then smirked.

Part of me enjoyed getting under his skin. Without the distraction of him, the ache of my body registered full force. I looked around, wonder creeping in.

My fantasies of entering Andas's cage hadn't included this bed, covered in thick blankets. It definitely hadn't included a table weighed down with food or the steaming hot bath in the corner with plush towels laid out on a stool beside it. Did he keep this castle design in his head or something? I would've gone for a tree hut personally.

I sniffed my armpit and grimaced. I was on the ripe side of ripe. My gut told me I needed to drag Andas to me in order to push the rift within wider. Smelling better seemed like a good step toward achieving that. But the question was, would cracking apart the rift between Aaden and Cormac do as I hoped?

The questions and fears of what could be rolled through me as I set to the arduous task of stripping.

I crawled across the room and half rolled into the perfectly hot bath. "So good." Nothing had *ever* felt this good.

As I scrubbed my hair and body, for a short time I let my mind float in nothing. How would life be if I had nothing much to think about? Some people must live like this, with no worries and/or realm-sized worries to puzzle over. They'd just soak in the hot water and feel peaceful and…bored.

I shot up, water sloshing everywhere. "Gaia!"

Scrambling out of the bath, then slipping, I landed on my knees on the cold stone floor.

I pressed my palms to the stone. "Gaia, can you hear me?"

Silence for a moment, then a whisper of warmth curling around me.

I can always hear you.

Always? Or just since I'd become the caretaker of Balance? "There's a rift in Andas. What should I do with it?"

Her answer took some time. *The sword of the wolf is the key. Use it.*

Her warmth slid from me, leaving me cold and dripping on the floor. I didn't mind. I bowed my body, touching my forehead to the stone. Even if I didn't like her answer, it was more than I'd had before. "Thank you."

Carefully standing on trembling legs, I dried myself and made my way to the table where the food was laid out. The urge to topple into bed was hard to deny, but I'd feel better for eating. Damn it, Andas could have poisoned it…I didn't think that was something he would do though—at least not to me. But did Unbalance have any boundaries, or was I being naive and stupidly hopeful to imagine he did?

I bit into cold cut meat and had barely chewed before I shoved flaking pastry into my mouth to chase it down. This food was nowhere near as good as Cinth's cooking, but it would help restore me. I needed to be strong to face what I was going to have to do.

Gaia had referred to Cormac's sword. Did she mean

power was locked away inside of the weapon much as Sigella had been locked away in the harp? Or had Gaia been suggesting that I should use Cormac's sword on Andas. Run him through? That was what you did with swords, after all.

I grimaced and lowered the chunk of fruit I'd been gnawing at.

Suddenly I wasn't hungry.

The door flung open, and I turned to see Andas standing in the doorway.

I stood naked as I faced him. "What? I thought my execution wasn't until the morning."

"You were speaking with someone." He growled but didn't stalk closer. His eyes roved over my body, and I watched as his breath hitched and the colors in his eyes swirled faster. A storm brewed within them. I wanted to be caught in that storm. My own breath fell short from the heat of his gaze. His focus slid over me the way I wished his hands would.

"I miss my friends," I said simply. "I miss Kik, most of all. I keep imagining what he might say to me if he were here." That was easy. Kik would give me a hoof to the face if he'd been here.

I shrugged and forced myself to turn from him, and immediately felt the heat of his gaze lower to my ass.

I picked up a piece of food and put it in my mouth, pretending I wasn't keenly aware of Andas on every level. In truth, I wasn't sure what to do to seduce him in this moment.

I licked a trickle of fruit juice off my fingers and swept my silver hair aside, so it didn't get sticky.

Behind me, Andas choked.

"You truly...miss that foul-mouthed creature?" he said after a moment.

I glanced back and lifted a shoulder. "He was the closest thing to a brother that I've ever had. I miss him with all my heart." For a second time, I put my food down. I should stop thinking about murder and death while I ate.

There was a moment of silence, followed by the scrape of the door closing.

But had he shut the door and stayed, or left? My heart raced as I checked, fully expecting to find him there.

He was gone, and the sharp pangs of disappointment were deep and...unsettling.

Because Gaia had been clear that I had to use the sword. The sword was the key to undoing all this.

That would probably mean ending his life. While I trusted the reverence I felt in Gaia's presence, I wasn't sure I could do that. I'd *never* been sure I could do that. In the same way I now saw the scale of problems differently than the average two-legged fae, did Gaia perceive the scale of this situation differently than I did? Did she think nothing of Andas dying? Or perhaps it suited her agenda for him to die, and she considered my grief as natural and acceptable collateral damage?

I wanted to ask her more questions. I wanted guidance in all this because while some balance existed in the path I followed, there was still so much I didn't understand.

"Though I'm getting used to that," I said begrudgingly. If I lived long enough, maybe I'd desensitize to the sense of the unknown, just as I was desensitizing to suffering. I mean, look at me, trapped in a castle of the being who'd trapped my soulmates in his body, and I am still trying to seduce him while also gearing up to run him through with a sword. Suffering had less and less influence on my actions.

I flopped into the bed and rolled myself under the thick, velvety covers. I sighed and closed my eyes, sleep crashing over me.

No peace came. I slept for hours, only to be startled awake by my thundering heart. My throat was raw and my mouth dry. The room was dark, but I wasn't alone.

I could feel him there, in the shadows.

"That's a concerning quality." I didn't know whether I should pull the blankets higher or throw them off, and I could guess which option had appealed to me more in sleep by the heat coursing through my body.

"You were screaming in your sleep." The reverberation of his voice sounded more like Aaden than ever before.

Clearly I hadn't had the dream I'd assumed.

And then his words sunk into me, and I touched my throat, understanding dawning. "Oh."

He was suddenly by the bed, the shape of his body

was slightly darker than the windowless room. "Why don't you want to kill me?"

I swallowed. "I don't know what you're talking about—"

"You were screaming that you didn't want to kill me. Why not? We're enemies, you and I. That will never change."

Of all the things to scream. I bit back a groan. Had I said anything about the sword?

His hand found the side of my face, and he brushed his fingers along my jaw with an exquisite gentleness that I remembered from Aaden.

I let myself lean into his hand, let my lips brush against his palm.

He hissed and pulled back as if burned. "Enough screaming."

And then he was gone a second time. Or were we up to three?

I lay in the dark, still feeling his touch. Still tight with the need for more. I threw my arm over my head.

I didn't want to kill him, no.

Like Andas, I knew that another Unbalance would come into creation if he were to die—because one of us couldn't exist without the other.

So now I found myself considering Andas's confession.

If I had a choice, what would I choose? The predator I knew, the predator who carried two of the most important souls within him? Or a predator who'd try to kill me instead of only threatening to do so and kissing me instead?

I groaned and rolled onto my stomach, wishing I had a release for this frustration. My power was still dim inside, distant like a vision in the desert. But that didn't matter, at least not right then.

Nothing mattered except for the tightness of my body.

I was out of the bed and grabbing for my still filthy clothes. But that wasn't quite right, as it turned out. Someone had cleaned my clothes while I slept. The leathers and tunic were spotless, and the scent from a purple flower filled the room. Beautiful.

Swallowing hard, I dressed, then stuffed leftover food into my mouth. Exhaling first, I scooped up Cormac's sword and then glanced at my boots. I left them behind. Ungrounded as I felt, I wanted stone under my feet.

I strode to the door, fully expecting it to be locked, so when the door opened easily, my instincts took note.

A trap?

I didn't think so. At least not one that was going to hurt me. Maybe this was bait to draw me out. Maybe not. I just didn't know with Andas.

"You keep things interesting at least," I muttered under my breath, unable to keep the smile ghosting over my lips.

I made my way through the small castle and down

to the main courtyard. There was no one around—not that I'd expected anyone to be in a castle created by Unbalance in the middle of some isolated mountaintop.

Breathing slowly, I focused on the weight of the pommel in my palm. I allowed my body to absorb it so it could learn to counterbalance the weapon's weight. My body craved some activity after the long sleep, so I let myself work through fighting patterns I'd been taught long ago. I felt confidence return. I knew how to look after myself. I knew how to make hard decisions and take risks.

Like challenging the Old Man.

Or dodging the Naga.

Racing against the tarbeasts.

Sweat dripped down my body, and as the sun rose, my frustration and discomfort slid away from me. This was my path, for better or worse.

I was doing the right thing by listening to Gaia.

The earth and rock underfoot warmed and softened, and I found the tranquility of balance that I'd missed for the last day. I continued to flow with the power that circled around me, not realizing my eyes were closed until a flutter of dark energy disturbed the warmth I'd created.

Gray, death, and the smell of rot.

I spun and opened my eyes.

A gray fae lurched forward, his hands outstretched. No, not one gray fae...

A thousand.

More. They filled the courtyard and beyond. The entire plateau was covered in them. Everywhere I looked, gray fae filled the space.

They surged at me in a wave, their mouths open, their hands clutching for my body.

I could have killed them all at once if my power had been at its peak. But it wouldn't have been right—they'd been fae once, and it wasn't their fault that they'd been pulled into Unbalance's clutches. Clutches they'd never escape.

Worse? I saw creatures of Underhill among their ranks.

"You left us," they hissed.

"You promised you'd save us."

A hollow shout. "We rot because of you."

There were too many, and their words hammered into me, along with their sheer numbers.

They'd suffered so much, and I had no choice but to fight them. The sword was light in my hands as I drove it through fae after fae, removing heads and piercing hearts. I felt each blow ripping me apart, too, just as I'd felt the loss of the creatures I'd left behind in Underhill.

"Andas." I screamed his name. Was this my execution then? He couldn't do it himself, so he'd set his creatures on me while I was still weak.

"I'm coming, kiddo!"

My world crashed to a stop as a land kelpie burst

into view, his long, icicle-crusted mane tinkling like tiny bells.

This wasn't happening. This was a dream, or a cruel nightmare. It had to be.

But I felt the warmth of the rock under my feet and the thunderous rumble as his hooves lanced the ground.

Kik spun into view, booting the gray fae away from me. "Kid, don't freeze up on me, come on! Let's go!"

A hand clawed at my arm from behind, and even though Kik was here—impossibly here—I said, "I can't leave him."

I spun and struck the gray fae holding me.

The feeling of how the sword entered the fae struck me first. The gray fae tended to be crumbly and easily tear. That wasn't what I felt as my sword slid into this fae. The grunt registered next, not hollow or hissed or eerie, but the grunt of a man.

Andas stood, still gripping my arms with his hands. He didn't wear a shirt, and was barefoot like I was, dressed only in a pair of pants. His eyes swirled with greens and golds and blacks.

"I suppose you win," he said.

Only then did my horrified gaze fall to the blade I'd buried deep into Andas through his middle.

I caught Andas as he fell to the ground. The gray fae slid away as if they'd never been, and even my thoughts of Kik disappeared as the realms narrowed to the force of darkness cradled in my arms. "No, no! I didn't know it was you."

"It's better this way. Living that way would have ruined us both."

My hands shook, and his words didn't penetrate my panic. "I don't…I don't want you to die. You can't die!"

His eyes fluttered. "Why not? Now you will be free of fear for a time."

Was that what he'd wanted for me? "Just don't die, I command you not to die!" Fear lashed at me. This was Cormac and Aaden all over again. "I won't do this without you!"

A small crease appeared between his brows. His eyes were unfocused. "Without me? We were destined to exist on opposite sides." A sigh. "Fate was cruel to us, Silver."

I swallowed hard. Fate was cruel indeed, and she wasn't fucking winning this time. "Kik, pull the sword on three."

"You got it, kiddo." He clamped his teeth around the pommel.

"One," I shouted.

"Why would you save me?" Andas lifted his hand and touched my face. "Let me go. This feels right. I have no wish to fight or kill you. This is best."

So he'd said. "Two."

"Leave before I am reborn. I hope you win. Be… happy." His hand slipped and I caught it.

"Three!" I screamed.

Kik yanked the sword out, and I dropped my mouth to Andas's lips and pulled on what little power I had, pushing the silver essence into him to heal the sword wound and knit him back together. Fire, sweetness, dark, light, black, gold—the kiss was everything in this world and something that had not yet existed. Something real but impossible.

Set against the stark fear of losing him forever, my other worries seemed small. Insignificant. Worth it.

Andas.

Cormac.

Aaden.

Silver.

Four souls seeking a path through the darkness.

I wouldn't lose them this time. I refused to walk through immortality alone. Whether Andas liked it or not, he wasn't dying today.

CHAPTER 10

I sat with my legs hugged to my chest, my sight fixed on Andas's immobile form. I hadn't sat this way since childhood, but the seismic feeling of rightness and wrongness within me had insisted on this position.

Andas was alive.

And he...might have something to say about what I'd done.

"Excuse the strong language, but are you fudgin' crackers? Why did you do that?" Kik exploded for the umpteenth time.

I did shift my sights from Andas then. If only to absorb another dose of the strangeness that was my best friend returned from death. "Fudgin' crackers," I repeated.

Kik shrugged a shoulder, eliciting a ring of icicles. Where once he'd been a glory of shining, pure whites and blues, now he was mottled with blacks and grays. His icicle mane had changed from a crystal-like appearance to one of dripping ink, though it still rang the same way. His hooves were cracked and veined with black.

And yet there was no trace of darkness in him that I could detect.

It was as though his outside finally reflected his insides.

Except...

"Kiddo, one day you'll meet Gaia, and you'll find the inner strength to get rid of all the bravado and curse language and shirk everyone's expectations to find who you really are. And who I am is a love-spreading, kind-talking individual who supports those he cares about."

Kik had found Gaia.

At first I'd thought he'd lost his mind, but the use of 'fudgin' crackers' had me convinced that Kik was telling the truth. "Right."

Kik hoofed the ground. "Hey, thanks for murdering all those gray fae so I could get through the last bit."

I blinked. When I'd seen Kik in the stars after the kraken attack, apparently I'd tried to drag him back to the world of the living. He'd been in some kind of limbo for a time, but the death of however many hundreds of gray fae I'd slaughtered had paid the price for his life. "Andas sent them to me."

My focus returned to Andas. Had he known such a sacrifice would complete Kik's journey back? And how had he even known Kik was in limbo? I blinked as the answer came to me. *The scale realm.* Andas had been able to access that realm for a while after Kik's 'death'.

He'd known Kik could come back under the right circumstances.

Why did Andas do that for me?

I whispered to Kik. "Losing you was like losing part of myself, and it doesn't feel real that you're back. I'm scared to believe you're really here."

He butted me with his nose. "You think a little thing like death could separate us?"

I swallowed and lifted a hand to scratch his head. "My mistake."

"I love you, kiddo. I'm sorry I called you fudgin' crackers. I didn't mean it."

"I think I can handle it," I muttered back. "You need to see Peggy."

He tossed his inky mane. "You think she'll dig the new look?"

I was Balance, and even I could only see so much of the future. Still, I knew what he needed to hear. "Yes."

Kik jerked his head at Andas. "You'll be okay with this?"

"Well, he'd hardly kill himself, would he?"

"Suppose you're right. He'll be pissed, though. He wanted to go."

I grimaced. *Yep.* Andas might have something to say about me binding myself to him. "If you see Sigella and Orlaith, let them know what's happening."

"I'll be busy, kid. I haven't been reborn that much." He opened a portal, and I heard Peggy's gasp before Kik stepped through the opening and promptly closed it.

My lips twitched, but my smile was quick to fade.

Then there was me and Andas.

He rolled onto his side, and my heart leaped into my throat. He hadn't moved in two days. I'd had all that time to explore the new power I'd gained from the bond.

Enough power to make one thousand castles.

I'd had two days to foster an impossible thought that no one would ever understand, maybe not even Andas.

All I knew was that when I'd pushed my essence into Andas, I'd felt how Cormac and Aaden were balanced within him. I'd felt how they couldn't merge because Andas's essence unbalanced the entire equation. The greater forces had given him so many different powers to merge in order to become Unbalance, but then they'd left him incomplete.

They'd left room for a fourth to enter the equation.

And so I'd entered myself into the equation, and then each soul within him had balanced perfectly. Rather than widen the rift, I'd eliminated it. Cormac and Aaden truly were him now. Their essences had faded into the black, although in the right light, I could still see glimpses of green and amber in his eyes still, just like I could see different parts of them in his physique and mannerisms.

And yet the heavy weight in my chest wasn't quite grief.

By healing the rift, I'd said goodbye to them—and also welcomed a permanent connection to them that I'd long felt was our fate. But if I could bear that, if I could find more inner strength and endurance for suffering than I'd ever thought possible for one being, then maybe there was a messed-up, never-before-anticipated future for us.

A future for Unbalance and Balance.

My mind trembled at the very unhinged thought. Had desperation pushed the confines of my mind too far at long last?

I had a failsafe, I reminded myself. My life was tied to Andas's, and his to mine. If I'd doomed us all, then at least there was a straightforward way to end this.

"What have you done?" His terrible voice filled the courtyard. Taking him inside hadn't felt right. I'd kept him warm with my magic instead.

My pulse tripled, and I waited for it to calm before answering, "Bedding you wasn't the answer, after all. Though I would've liked to try."

He asked again, and *his* calm didn't fool me. "*What have you done?*"

"I bound myself to you."

"To gain power," he hissed. "You have reset the scale between us."

He was right, though that was never my intention. Historically, Balance and Unbalance had always been at war for dominance over the realms. Whoever had more power tipped the realms into darkness or away from it. I'd always seen the powers of balance and unbalance as two separate entities, but now I could see those powers fought for the greater share of a single power, constantly tugging opposite ends of a rope. I could also see that while I'd reset the scale and Andas and I were bizarrely and impossibly equal and opposite in our powers right now, this reset wouldn't last. One of us would tip the scale soon enough and the eternal war for power would start all over again. "I did. To save you."

"I didn't wish to be saved. I didn't wish to be chained to you." He blurred to his feet and roared, "What have you done?"

I stood, too, and closed the distance between us. "There's a chance we can figure this out."

"You!" His eyes bugged. "You think there's a happy ending to this. Are you—"

"Fudgin' crackers? Yes. There's no happy ending, but there could be an existence together."

Andas ran his hands through his black hair, and his eyes glinted with amber and green. "You had it in your grasp. I was dying. Balance was yours for the taking."

"Just as Unbalance was yours for the taking when the kraken killed me. Why didn't you take it?"

"Because I feel what they felt for you," he growled in my face before whirling away.

Yes, he did. And he'd been able to cast that aside in part when there was a rift in him.

Now he couldn't. Just as I never could.

Cormac and Aaden were *in* him forevermore.

"You have doomed us both," Unbalance said. "You have ensured doom for all."

"There is a chance," I replied. "I would gamble on that chance. I would ask you to gamble on that chance too."

And there it was. I'd never had the chance to ask Cormac if he'd be mine. Aaden had known what he meant to me, but Andas had already started to claim him by the time we'd reached Unimak. I'd never had this conversation with either of them.

Andas was silent. "You have made a fool's gamble. There is no future where you and I can be. You know this. I will not torture myself in that way, and I will not torture *you* in that way. You made the choice to bind us, and I will hate you for it, Silver."

"Hate is the easy choice," I whispered.

"Hate is what we have left," he answered.

Sulphur. I could've stopped him from passing through the portal or followed him with ease. But that wouldn't help matters.

I absorbed the devastation he'd just caused. I swallowed it like a bitter-tasting herbal tincture that would help me grow stronger.

Andas intended to continue spreading darkness as usual. We were anything but usual now, but I couldn't force him to see my way. I could only hope that he would come to it on his own.

For now, I had a tribe of people who'd be worried over my whereabouts.

I cast out my awareness to Sigella and Orlaith. They were both in the Irish court. Kik and Peggy were...

I pulled back from *that* immediately.

I opened a portal to Sigella and strode through.

She wasn't here alone.

I inhaled the strong, spicy scent of incense, a cloying aroma that dulled my ability to smell anything else. Exactly the scent I'd expect the sense-dulled ruler of the Irish court to burn.

"U-Underhill," I heard him stutter from behind me. "Mistress of Underhill. You weren't expected."

Had anyone ever expected my mother while she lived? Did Underhill usually send a letter of warning?

I glanced back.

The Ríchashaoir didn't bow, but he did dip his head. "Welcome to my court. Let me apologize one thousand times for the nature of our first meeting. I was operating off the Oracle's information at the time, and I hope you won't hold your kidnapping against me."

I didn't, truthfully. It was a tiny thing in the scheme of things. A little kidnapping. I studied the Ríchashaoir's future pathways and no matter what I said or did here, he'd have the same bland existence—eat, cheat, repeat.

I didn't answer him, instead staring past him at Sigella and Orlaith who sat on a small couch beside the fireplace.

Keefe sat between them.

"How did you get on?" Sigella inquired, taking a sip from a dainty teacup.

Keefe hiccupped, and Orlaith glared at him.

Trouble in paradise?

"I bound myself to Unbalance and healed the rift in him. Cormac and Aaden are now part of him in truth—they are all of one essence. I feel there is a way forward through this, however Andas doesn't agree, and in the end, I might need to kill myself to take him with me."

Silence met my words, and Sigella's sip was painfully loud.

"I might have to side with Andas on this one," she answered.

The Ríchashaoir gasped. "You *bound* yourself to Unbalance? We're all doomed!"

Shit, I'd forgotten he was there. And why did everyone keep saying that word?

Orlaith had immediately locked gazes with Keefe, but she turned to me and said, "You listened to me and screwed his brains out, didn't you?"

I shook my head. "No, but I bound our essences together. Permanently."

Sigella set down the teacup that was shaking in her hand after my news. "Is that all?"

All I was willing to divulge for the time being. "Mostly."

Keefe sprawled back on the small couch, a bottle of absinthe dangling from his fingertips. There was a sharpness in his gaze as he studied me. "You've leveled the playing field."

Sigella focused on me. "You stole his power?"

"Just a consequence of the bond," I answered.

Keefe thumped his head on the back of the couch. "This changes everything."

Tell me about it.

"Yes, it does," Orlaith said in a sharper tone.

Sigella narrowed her gaze on them as the Ríchashaoir blurted, "What does it change?"

Before I'd fully turned to look at him, my mind registered a sudden change in the Ríchashaoir's future paths. A new one had formed out of nowhere. No, not nowhere. *Keefe* had formed this future for the Ríchashaoir, and it led to a dead end. A dead end that was already upon us.

Keefe sure moved fast for a drunk.

I turned to find the shards of the absinthe bottle shoved under the Ríchashaoir's ribs. Blood and alcohol dripped from the tips of the glass, and the magic Keefe had daggered into the court ruler in tandem with the bottle attack had already ensured his fate.

Orlaith screamed, "Father! That wasn't the deal. He was mine to play with."

Keefe regarded her with a serious expression. "Peace, daughter. My role has changed."

Father. Daughter.

I let the shock pass over me. Keefe swept a flourishing bow, and when he peeked up at me, there was a shimmer. He became a hunched old man, the same version of him I'd first met when he'd gifted me Orlaith on my mother's orders. "You."

He straightened. "A pleasure to meet you again, Underhill."

"You're in Andas's power." And he was Orlaith's father. That explained a lot.

"His power? Not as such. I *was* his last henchman, the Trickster. And I find I am trickster still, but am I still in his power? That remains to be seen. These are unprecedented times indeed."

Orlaith threw herself in front of him as I lifted a hand. "No, Silver, please! He's my father."

Sigella's voice was ice cold as she rose to her full height beside me. "And what plan did you have for Silver at the Lake of Jealousy? You didn't overhear anything in the Alaskan court, did you? You were told to lead her there. By *him*."

"I did overhear it!" Orlaith retorted, but she paled, and my heart plummeted at the sight.

I thought she'd set me up while an unwilling and unaware slave to Andas's darkness. But she'd done so at the mere bidding of her father, who had been a henchman of Andas at the time.

Orlaith rushed to say, "I was unsettled. I had my body back, and then my father showed up. I thought he was on our side, and when I realized he might not be, I tried to stop you from going to the lake."

She'd sent me to the kraken.

"Lies," I boomed, my fury bursting outward. "You knew what he was asking. You urged me to go to the lake, and only later did you try to reverse what you'd done with further subterfuge. You could have confessed the truth many times, but instead you decided to keep your betrayal a secret. You nearly killed me." My voice had come out in a whisper. "I nearly *died*, Orlaith."

"I wanted to tell you the truth," she said, wringing her hands. "I didn't know how, and then I...I didn't know if I should."

I felt myself harden. There were few people I trusted and let in. Keefe hadn't ever made it to my inner circle, and Sigella was still on her way there. But Orlaith...I'd trusted her. I'd let her all the way in.

"You didn't know if you should try to keep me alive," I said hollowly. "How didn't you know the answer to that?"

Her voice cracked. "I don't know, Silver. I didn't know what to listen to. I could only see some of the picture."

Keefe had already opened a portal, but I didn't

budge my gaze from Orlaith's shimmering eyes to look at where he was going.

Her voice trembled, "I don't know what I am anymore, Silver, but my choices aren't as clear as before. I don't want to hurt you, but there are other considerations for me too. I can't tell those things not like I could before."

Before, when she was a bat and imprisoned away from darkness by my mother. Orlaith's sentence had ended too soon, and the consequences of that were becoming clearer by the second.

"I don't know who you are either," I replied coldly.

Keefe held out a hand to his daughter. "But I do. Daughter, your place is still with me."

Orlaith didn't immediately take his hand, but after another look at my cold face, she did. The sight made my stomach drop.

Her action felt permanent.

The trickster stepped through the portal first, and even the sight of the scale realm on the other side couldn't penetrate my hurt and shock. Then again, Keefe had closed the scale realm in the first place 'with Sigella's help'—and the prison realm inside of it too. By doing so, he'd freed Orlaith from her bat form. And apparently he could still access the realms, unlike me.

True to his name, he'd tricked me and Sigella well and good.

"I do love you, Silver," Orlaith warbled and broke our stare to turn away.

Then the trickster's daughter, a trickster and a traitor herself, moved through the portal after him.

CHAPTER 11

"Will you go after them now?" Sigella stared at the place where Keefe and Orlaith had portaled away. Traitor and Trickster, that's what I'd call them. The daughter-father duo.

The hurt of Orlaith's betrayal had cut far deeper than I wanted to admit.

I shook my head. "I can't access the scale realm, and I have bigger things to deal with."

If Orlaith wanted to be with her father instead of me, then good riddance.

Sigella spun her hand, and a second teacup and saucer appeared. She swirled her tea and gazed into it. "This one is yours."

She handed it to me, and then picked up her teacup again. I held mine and peered into the amber brown liquid. I found myself hesitating to drink. If Orlaith could betray me, then what of Sigella?

As if she could hear my thoughts and uncertainty, she laughed. "You're getting smarter, Silver. Trust isn't something you should give to anyone."

I studied her over the rim of the cup. "Not even you?"

Her smile was sad. "I wish I could say with certainty that I'll always be trustworthy, but time and challenges have a way of changing people. Perhaps one day you won't be able to trust me. But today…today is not that day." She raised her cup and sipped. "And today we needed something stiffer than a cup of tea."

I sniffed the liquid and sipped it too. The sharp snap of alcohol rolled through my mouth and down my throat. The burn was pleasant and left a tingle in its wake, warmth in my belly.

Perhaps if anyone had looked in on us, they might have fainted from the sight. The Ríchashaoir's body lay a few feet away, blood pooling around him, while we drank tea with our backs turned to him.

But he was gone, and of no consequence now, and I didn't feel one way or another about his departure. He'd played his part in this story, causing as much grief and heartache with his position as anything good.

"Do you have a plan?"

I paused with my teacup partway to my mouth. "Why are you being nice? Why aren't you calling me a fool for trusting her? I thought you'd have plenty to say about what an idiot I've been."

Sigella sighed and rolled her hands, her cup and

saucer disappearing. "Because I was a fool too. I...I believed Keefe to be what he said he was. So we're both idiots, and it would be ridiculous for me to call the kettle black at my age."

I tipped my head. "What kettle is black?"

She reached for my cup and saucer, and they disappeared as she grasped them. "What it means is that I can't chastise you for making the same mistake I did, Silver. I lowered my guard when I shouldn't have. It won't happen again." Her voice hardened, and in her eyes, I saw a hot anger from a lifetime of romantic disappointment. Keefe had given her hope for something more, then snatched it away.

I closed my eyes, the few sips of alcohol and tea I'd taken soothing the rough edges around my heart. But balance was tugging at my feet, urging me away from the scene. I'd felt my magic urge me to the lake's edge, but I'd never felt it this directly. Then again, I'd received a massive boost of power.

"We have to go," I said, then started following the sensation through the Ríchashaoir's castle, my eyes half-closed. Perhaps I should tell someone the Irish ruler was dead. Another would take his place, a better fae, but it wasn't a *small* deal.

And yet I didn't, because the tugging at my feet was very insistent.

Sigella had quickly fallen into step beside me. "Where to now? You have an unbreakable connection to Unbalance. Can you reach him to take his power? If we can keep his power, then it will render his darkness useless. What's the next step in this battle?"

I grimaced because neither of those ideas were good—at least not yet. "I could do both, but he's angry with me right now. Taking his power is not my goal. I wish to find a way through this, with him."

The words were out, and I didn't even wish to take them back.

Sigella refrained from scoffing, though she did clear her throat several times as if she were choking.

I glanced at her. "Was your tea full of lumps?"

She'd gone pale, but her lips twitched. "Yes. I think it must have been." She opened and closed her mouth, but my 'plan' seemed to have rendered her mute. I couldn't complain. She'd taken it pretty well, all things consider.

I strode on, obeying the tugging on my feet.

When we reached the outer doors of the castle, the alcohol-induced relaxation had burned off enough for me to realize how utterly silent the halls were—we hadn't passed a single fae, human or creature from Underhill on our walk.

I stopped in my tracks. "Where is everyone?"

"Out here," Kik's voice echoed in from one of the windows open to the courtyard.

Sigella jerked. "Who's that?"

"Kik came back from the dead. Forgot to say."

She muttered under her breath, "Is anything impossible anymore?"

"Probably not." I picked up my pace, jogging forward.

"You gotta see this, Kiddo! It's...well I don't know what in the ding-donging heckles this is," Kik brayed.

Sigella was behind me as I ran out of the castle gates. I rubbed my arms, looking for Kik and Peggy in the sky. "The sun is above us. Why is it so cold?"

There wasn't any wind to chill the air today, yet the temperature suggested we were nearly nightfall, not the crest of day.

There was something else too. Something...about the air.

A dryness that reminded me of the Desert of Loss in Underhill, a freezing place without water for a hundred miles in every direction. I'd crossed it once and would've died but for finding a bulbous hohu.

I licked my lips, wondering that they felt so dry when the day was chillier than usual. "This is not natural."

"No," Peggy said darkly from beside Kik as they landed.

"You should see it from up in the air, Kiddo. The water is gone. Everywhere." Kik moaned, "What will I do without a drink? I'm a thirsty boy. If I faint soon, it's dehydration. I'll need CPR, Peggy. We should get a jump on that."

Peggy tossed her head. "You've defied death once, my love. You'll be fine."

He stopped stumbling and whipped around to look at her. "Say that first part again. The 'my love' part."

"That fucker," Sigella hissed, catching up to me. She slapped her hand against her thigh. "*He* did this."

I dragged my focus from Peggy and Kik. "Andas?"

This didn't reek of Andas to me. I mean, *why* would he do this?

She growled. "No, this feels like Keefe. He said something about the most precious thing in our world being water. How terrible it would be if it were taken."

He'd said that, and she hadn't thought anything of it? Then again, we'd just sipped alcohol from teacups next to a dead body. It wasn't exactly a normal day.

I noticed the hundreds of fae gathered in the courtyard for the first time. They lurked uncertainly thirty feet away, their faces fearful at the changes which they could sense weren't normal. Drought wasn't unknown in Underhill or Earth, but this was something more. Too immediate and intense, and I could scent a sinister essence on the breeze.

"The waterways are empty?" I asked Kik and Peggy. Each part of nature possessed a unique essence, like fae creatures, and I couldn't sense any water essence around at all.

"River, creek, lake, and ocean that we could see," Peggy said in undertones.

If this was Keefe working from the scale realm, then

we should all be very fucking worried. He and Orlaith had been gone for less than an hour.

I ignored the court fae, who were likely waiting for their Ríchashaoir to appear and explain everything. "Kik, Peggy, we need to see if this is isolated to Ireland. We need to check the Alaskan court."

Kik flicked his inky tail. "You got it!" He stomped a hoof and a portal opened. He and Peggy slipped through it, their bodies pressed flush against each other as they disappeared to the other side of Earth, to a part of the world where the ocean *should* flow heavily into rivers and inlets.

I paused, glancing back at the Irish court. Earth-dwelling fae needed everything spelled out for them. Amplifying my voice, I called out to them, "Remain inside, and do nothing you don't have to until the water returns. Though the air is cold, you must conserve your energy."

Terror-filled eyes turned my way.

"What's happening, Underhill?" one fae shouted.

Not Mistress of Underhill, just Underhill. I blew out a breath. Yeah, even I'd realized the title change might be permanent by now.

"There is great evil that would destroy us," I answered. "I go to stop it."

The words felt so formal, and not quite my own—more like something my mother might say—but that didn't make them any less true, and part of me knew these fae needed to believe I was different and powerful.

I strode through the portal to the Alaskan court, and Sigella stepped through behind me. Kik had delivered us to the main courtyard of the palace, and there was no one to be seen.

A more intense cold slammed into me like a sharp slap to my face, stealing my breath. *Too cold.*

Keefe's attack wasn't isolated to Ireland.

"Silver!" Cinth waved at me from the second-floor balcony. Kallik, in her hooded Oracle robe, stood beside her. "Everyone's inside in the warmth."

"Go to them," Sigella said, then grabbed my arm. "Silver, I can feel the scale realm. I don't believe Keefe has locked me out of it."

There was more she wasn't saying. "You want to go there."

"I might be able to find him and stop this."

"And if I need you here? And shouldn't we put more thought into your plan to attack Keefe?"

Her smile was a flash of teeth, there and gone. "Call for me, Underhill, and I will come. As for the rest...I don't know that planning ever got you very far. I wasn't aware you knew the word."

That was the truth. "Learn what you can. Don't endanger yourself."

Sigella stepped back and fell through an opening that led into the scale realm. I tried to follow her, but my foot froze to the ground. How was Keefe managing that? And against *me*.

"Be careful." I whispered to Sigella.

The portal closed, and the cold in the Alaskan court crept up my body.

I strode into the palace, grateful for the immediate warmth beyond the entranceway. Kallik met me in the hall. "This is bad, sister."

"I know, do you see a future through this? Around? Something?" While I could sense how to navigate interactions and situations to ensure the best balance, my sister's vision of pathways was unique to her power. She didn't see the future or past or present in terms of balance like me. She simply saw what could be and what had been. I understood now that her power was limited by her inability to sense balance, and anything she told me should be properly weighed with those limitations in mind. The path to balance often involved tragedy and pain and suffering which the Oracle may believe were futures to avoid.

Her lilac eyes locked on mine. "What I see is that the pathways have stopped. I can't see anything or anyone. I can't see the fate of the birds outside, let alone the fate of realms and powers like yourself."

The oracle couldn't see. Yes, if Keefe was behind this, we should be very worried indeed. "What does that mean? Has that ever happened to you before?"

I could already sense the answer was no.

She lowered her voice, checking to see whether the

hall was clear. "It's as if the fates of everyone and everything in the world are about to end."

The pressure, tug and pull of balance around my legs made me stumble. "That…that's impossible." Hadn't I just had a conversation about that word with Sigella though?

Kallik pulled me into a side room and removed her hood.

Cinth, Ronan and Faolan were waiting inside beside the fireplace.

"Water's the most important thing to this world," she said. "Few creatures, and no human or fae can go more than a few days without drinking it, but there are deeper consequences. We rely on water currents to move heat from the center of Earth to us at the poles. Any countries close to the poles will be plunged into freezing temperatures, while any countries near the equator will face scathing heat. Here, we might be able to melt any ice or snow we can find, but if there's no water, then there are no marine creatures, and we'll be without our usual winter food source."

"And those at the equator won't have any water at all." I added.

Keefe was a genius. I'd kill him, but he was a genius. By putting him in the prison realm, my mother had accidentally taught him a powerful lesson. There was only one watering hole in the prison realm, after all, only one source of life. He was simply scaling that up and applying the same idea to Earth.

But how was he powerful enough to play on this level?

Gaia's voice whispered in my mind. *You should understand the need for balance best of all.*

Balance. *I* was balance. *Are you saying that Keefe is a force of balance too?*

You are balance. You are Underhill. This one exists to balance that which might be. The direction of his force must be determined.

Oh, good. I was worried she'd give me too many clear answers.

I tensed in case Gaia received that thought, but she didn't offer any more cryptic explanations. From what she'd given me, I could assume that she—and the other greater forces—were behind Keefe's sudden rise to power...and maybe the sudden changes in Orlaith too.

"The humans are blowing up my phones," Cinth said. "Every reserve, every river, even the bottled water is gone. As if it were just sucked dry in a matter of moments."

"The humans are blaming us, of course," Faolan said, his face tight and lined with worry. "What will they do when half the world is plunged into a modern ice age and the rest becomes a furnace?"

I pursed my lips. "It is our fault. Or at least, it is the fault of one fae. Their error is in condemning an entire race for the actions of one person. *Two* people. Orlaith is involved too."

Kallik gripped my shoulder. "I'd hope she'd turn from that path. I'm sorry."

"You couldn't have told me?" I asked her.

"I could have, yes, but there was a chance it would have gone a different way, and now her path is as invisible to me as everyone else's. Her father included."

Cinth lifted her hands. "Wait, wait, wait. So Orlaith is controlling the water alongside her father? Who the hell is her father? And how could Orlaith do that to you? She was Team Silver all the way."

So I'd thought.

I forced myself to straighten my spine. "Keefe is Orlaith's father from the prison realm. Orlaith led me into a trap on his orders. He's a trickster, and he was the third henchmen of Unbalance, but apparently he's not tied to Unbalance anymore."

Faolan whistled low. "He fooled us all."

"Can you stop them?" Cinth asked. "No creature can go long without water. The marine life will be dying in droves. Humans won't be far behind, and neither will we."

"I don't know." I looked at her, seeing fear, panic, and worry. I wished that I had a better answer.

"Our children will die. We will all die, Silver," Ronan said quietly. "Tell us what we need to do, and we will help you. But we need to act quickly."

Each of them was hoping for an answer that I didn't have. I had to find a way to stop the Trickster directly, but he was safely hidden in the scale realm—inaccessible to me—and killing him would ensure the end of things between Orlaith and me. Apparently, part of me still held out hope for reconciliation.

There was a soft tug at my feet, and I focused on the force of balance there, feeling out what it wanted me to do. Or more specifically, *who* it wanted me to find.

I lifted my head.

"She's got an idea," said my sister.

Andas would be allowed into the scale realm, and lack of water would kill his creatures too. If I could convince him to stop Keefe, then we could figure this out. He might be furious with me, but I could try to convince him that the battle should be between us and only us. Whether that would work was anyone's guess. I could only see our meeting and everything beyond was smoky and obscured—as unclear as the situation and as uncertain as the decision of all the players involved.

I'd always thought my mother was all-seeing—that she could stare into the endless future. Perhaps she really had possessed that foresight, but I sure as hell didn't. There was no clear path through the stars because that required all the creatures sharing the path to feel clear about their decisions. As it stood, only Keefe seemed certain on what he wanted to do, and the rest of us were still figuring out our response. Until we got there, there was only the next choice, then the next.

I said, "Sigella is tracking Keefe already, but I can't

reach her in the other realm to help her. Only Unbalance can restore our water source. I need to find him."

Kallik moved first, drawing me into a hug. Her arms were tight around me as she whispered in my ear, "We rely on *your* sight now, sister. Balance, follow its lead for us all."

I pulled back. "You trust me?"

Why did everyone trust me? I was just surviving from one moment to the next, and my life had been this way for long enough that I felt certain it would be this way to the end.

She smiled, though it was sad. "I've always trusted you, Silver."

Kallik kissed me on the forehead, leaving me with more strength than before.

Cinth grasped me in a hug that squashed me into her bosom. "May the goddess speed your journey, Silver. If there's anything we can do…"

"There is one thing," I told her. According to my sister, the realms could end at any moment. It was possible I might never see my sister or Cinth or *anyone* in this room again. I'd learned to never show fear, and I wasn't about to start now.

The unwilling queen of all fae held me at arm's length. "Anything, Underhill."

"Save me some beetroot tickles."

Her smile wobbled, and tears gathered in her eyes. "You think I'll be here to bake for you?"

I shrugged. "I don't know, but if we survive this, then I want one of those pastries."

Her face fell. "You don't know we'll survive."

I turned from her, and the voice that came from me wasn't really my own. "The path is chosen. Now I must walk it alone."

Alone.

Without Kik, without Peggy or Sigella. Without my sister. If Andas was to give up the help of his henchman, then perhaps I would have to do without the aid of my helpmates.

I closed my eyes and felt for my connection to Andas. Finding it was as easy as breathing.

I opened a portal and stepped through.

Dark.

I held up a hand and tightened my power into a tiny flame. "Andas, I need to speak with you."

I could sense him here, even if I was unsure where here was—a cave, but not the cave where the naga had made their Earth nest. This one was damp, and the moisture was greedily drawn into my skin after the dryness of the air at the courts.

Unbalance didn't answer.

I moved slowly into the dark. As if there were a compass built inside my chest, I walked straight to where he was perched in the dark.

"What are you doing here?" he snarled. "Should you not be out there, saving the fae?"

I frowned and set my tiny flame into a niche on the

wall. "I would, but I can't reach the scale realm. Your trickster has closed it. But he'd let you in. You've probably been able to get in this entire time."

Andas didn't answer.

"That's why I am here." I continued. "I...will you stop your henchman? He's unleashed chaos on Earth, and he's surely doing the same to Underhill. Millions will die without water, not only fae, but humans too. Your people and mine."

The shadows cast on Andas's face made his expression difficult to read. "And what would you give me to stop him?"

He hadn't responded with a no. That was better than nothing. "What do you want?"

"My power back." He cupped my face with one hand. "Give my power back to me, Balance."

I'd felt how bonding to him had equalized our power. It made sense that we were destined to war over a finite amount of magic. When he had more, he ruled the realms. When I had more, I ruled the realms. It was simple, at least to me. And this time, a power trade was reasonable. "If you stop Keefe and promise the water will never again be used like this in our battle, then I will give all power I gained at our binding back to you."

His hand pulled my face toward him. "Swear it."

Our lips were so close that just by speaking they brushed one another. "I swear it."

He exhaled, and the warmth of his breath pulled a

groan from me. "On something of value. Someone you love? Perhaps your sister?"

His words settled on me, cooling my growing desire. I didn't gamble with the people I loved. "No. Take my words or leave them. I swear that if you stop Keefe and save the realms from this drought, I will return the power you held before our binding. Or you may take it back, I don't know how that works."

I'd known that one of us would tip the scales to become more powerful soon enough.

Andas yanked me forward so our lips were pressed tightly together, his tongue snaking into my mouth as if tasting me. I returned the favor. Smoke and ice, he tasted different now than before our binding.

As quickly as the kiss started, he broke it off and stood. "You'll regret giving up my power, Underhill."

He sounded irritated with me, and I stared at him from where I sat crouched on the ground. "I regret nothing, Andas. Not even you. If I don't make this deal, then no one will be alive to feel anything, including regret. You can congratulate your henchman on a job well done."

His eyes had widened, but he smoothed his expression. Had he thought about what I'd said earlier? I was willing to take a gamble that we could share a future together. An unprecedented, maybe impossible future together. Had he considered taking that gamble with me?

We held each other's gaze for a leaden beat.

"Will you go to the scale realm then?" I asked.

He shook his head. "I haven't been able to access it for a while now."

I frowned. "Keefe locked you out too?"

"First as a ruse so you'd believe he was on your side. Though I do wonder if it was ever a ruse, really."

"What—"

Andas strode through a portal and was gone.

"—do you mean?" I trailed off and waved away the sulphur from his portal.

Still crouching, I let my hands drift down to press against the rock, wet with moisture while the rest of the world was dying of drought. Of course Keefe wouldn't leave Unbalance without water, even if something was going on between them.

I sighed, wondering if I'd just traded one misery for another. Andas would stop Keefe and then…then I'd be back to where I'd started—so much weaker than Andas. But at least those I loved would be safe and alive while I figured this all out.

How long would it take for Andas to find Keefe and stop him? He'd said he couldn't go to the scale realm any more than I could, but I assumed that he could summon his remaining henchman to him the same way I could call Sigella, Kik, and Peggy to me.

Warmth flowed through me from the wet rock—a comfort, perhaps from Gaia herself. There was no tug on me in any direction, no indication that balance wished for me to move, which kept me still. That was a rarity, and it reassured me that this had been the only choice.

Whatever darkness that resulted would need to be born.

I opened a small portal to check on those I'd left behind, kind of like those annoying looking orbs that Cinth kept floating around the palace. Maybe the drought had already been reversed. Kik and Peggy were inside the Alaskan palace now, with Kallik and Faolan. They were all wrapped in blankets by a roaring fire.

The temperatures in the poles were plummeting fast.

"She'll kick his behind good and hard. Very hard." Kik bobbed his head, shivering.

"Hopefully soon," Faolan said, drawing Kallik closer.

Peggy lay on the floor covered in a blanket, her wings tucked and her nose resting. She was breathing hard, which suggested the lack of water was affecting her even worse than Kik despite his dramatic stumbling. "Underhill will save us."

I closed the small portal and tried to open one to the scale realm to see Sigella. When that didn't work, I opened another to check on my people. The naga appeared least affected by the drought, although they kept very still in their underground nest. Old Man was curled up tight—against the unnatural cold. The Irish and Alaskan courts…

Everyone was miserable. Some were already sick from dehydration.

My chest tightened at the sight of children lying still and lethargic. Andas would stop Keefe. He had to. If for nothing else than to get his power back.

Only, when I checked the rivers, they weren't refilling.

What about my home realm?

I opened a portal and stepped through to Underhill, not far from the Old Man's cave. Unlike near the poles of Earth, heat slammed into me here, as if I'd walked into the flames of the dragon's mouth itself.

I stumbled away, eyes squinting against the blazing suns. Next, I portaled to the purple sea, only...there was nothing there. No water. Heart sinking, I stood on the bottom of what had been a vast, dangerous ocean. I could only be happy that most of the creatures who'd lived here had made it through to Earth, or their decaying bodies would surround me now.

Except...

I could feel them dying on Earth. Their pain and suffering clawed at me, and I cut it off quickly, so I wasn't dragged into panic and insanity. I covered my mouth with a shaking hand. The rawmouths, the kraken, Earth's water creatures. *Millions* of creatures would die in this way. I'd feel the loss of them. After, there would be a void in me, and I couldn't bring myself to portal and see such a horrific sight as well as feel it. What would this mean for the future when the realms were deprived of their crucial roles in the life cycle?

And why would Andas allow Keefe to destroy Underhill like this? I didn't understand, but I had to save those that I could.

I turned on the spot, shading my eyes. Without much hope of finding anything better, I portaled to different parts of Underhill. The Cloud Forest. The Hopeless River. The deep jungle. Every place was dry as if deprived of water for years, though some locations were cold and some were scorching hot.

A hand clamped onto my arm and yanked me through a portal and back to the dark cave. The repeated location of our meeting surprised me because Andas constantly leaped around. I'd felt it through our bond as well as experienced it firsthand. He didn't usually go to the same place twice.

"Did you stop him?" I faced Andas in the dark, his hands sliding to my waist as he held me steady.

Despite everything, my entire being yearned for his touch and love. "Why isn't the water back?"

Andas tightened his hold. "I cannot reach him. He's no longer tied to me, Silver. I'd felt it happen, but I'd hoped I could still draw him back under my power."

No. Keefe's musing words before he'd left for the scale realm gained clarity, and I grabbed hold of Andas's arms. "How is that possible? How can he have so much power?"

"Just like your Orlaith betrayed you, so has the

Trickster betrayed me. Your decision to bind us has come with consequences." Andas didn't let me go despite the accusation in his words. Maybe in the dark, when he couldn't see me, then submitting to his desire to hold me was easier.

I pressed my forehead to his chest and considered the theory. "The trickster and traitor were pushed into this role when I healed the rift in you." My heart sank as I said the words because they were correct. This was what Gaia was talking about.

"And so you were wrong about what we might become, as I expected," Andas answered. "There is no way for us to co-exist. The greater forces will not allow our alliance. See the message they have sent us?"

He was right in part. In comparison to the actions of Keefe and Orlaith, Unbalance suddenly seemed the lesser of two evils. I'd tried to draw Andas and me together, and now everyone was in mortal danger from a trickster who'd been given the power to stop us, and by goddesses and gods, no less. "Then we have one choice. We must find a way to stop Keefe together. As for the bond...I'm not willing to give up on that yet."

"Not even to save everyone you love when Keefe makes his next move?" Andas's tone was mocking.

But I didn't know if I could give up our tie, not even for everyone else. And what did that say about *me*?

His mouth dropped to the edge of my ear, and he grazed it with his lips. "You will give me my power back if I help you stop the trickster and the traitor. The deal hasn't changed."

"Depends. Is that all what you want from me?" Lugh's left nut, had I really just asked him that? Had I lost all dignity? If Andas was correct, pursuing this bound I'd forged between us could kill billions. How far was I willing to take this?

I couldn't say.

All I can say is that his next reply hurt far more than it should have, even if the words were a lie.

"That is all I want from you," Unbalance stated, cold and unmoving.

CHAPTER 12

"Keep telling yourself that," I whispered. "That's what you'd like to think, but you want far more. You need far more."

Just like I did.

Unbalance was like a statue. He still gripped my waist, and I clutched his shirt in my hands.

"No one gets to tell us what we can and can't have." A ballsy statement when Gaia might use her magic to kick my ass at any time, but the words were out, and I had no urge to take them back.

Andas's fingers twitched, and I could feel through our bond how much he wished to touch me and believe me. I could also feel his steely resolve, which was a credit to both men who'd formed him.

"You will force me to make the decision, won't you?" he said roughly. Andas grabbed my wrists and drew my hands off his shirt and body. He held them by my sides. "You'll force me to kill you."

"You won't kill me," I said calmly.

"I won't have a choice," he roared. "There won't be anything left if I don't. We are as much pawns as everyone else in the realms, Silver. You must accept our fate as I have."

But I could see through him now. I had access to his essence. "You *haven't* accepted our fate. You hope as I do."

"The hope of a fool."

"Then fools we'll be until we're forced to be otherwise." I twisted a hand free and lifted it to his face. Balance didn't tug at me, and I could feel a calm in Andas too. "There is no path to be walked in this moment but ours. You must feel it too. Will you walk it with me?"

Whatever had to be done about Keefe wouldn't happen in this instant, and where I would've needed to explain that to anyone else, Unbalance accepted my words without a blink. His power was opposite, but in many ways it was the same.

His jaw clenched under my hand. "If I walk this path, I will never find the strength not to walk it."

"You would waste this gift?" I replied. We were being given a lull, and I wished to take advantage of it.

"Why do they give us this time now, when the realms are withering to nothing?" he snarled.

I studied his lips. "Because the demands on us will

never stop. There will always be creatures dying or wars erupting. If we won't take the stolen moments that belong to us, then we don't deserve a chance. This is our test. Will you fail it for both of us?"

I kissed his jawline, and he stiffened. I kissed closer to his mouth, and he groaned. "Walk the path with me, Andas. Why not see where it leads? How can you fear the possible demise of the world more than the demise of us?"

He gripped my hair and pulled me away. I had a bare second to feel crushed by the finality of his rejection before he said, "I don't fear anything more than the demise of us. I fear giving it power. I fear hastening our demise. I fear that hoping now and taking all you offer may deprive me of years of your company, even if I can only see you from afar."

I smirked. "You'd rather be miserable for a long time than happy for a second."

Andas's throat worked. "There's a long list of things I'd rather. On the top of that list is that we were two average fae—or even idiot humans—with none of these burdens."

His grip in my hair loosened, and both of us were breathing hard.

"And if we were two average fae, together in a cave, with no demands on our time?" I said with difficulty. "What would you do then?"

Andas smiled slowly. "We're not two average fae, my Balance." His dark essence seeped into the cave, and my silver essence poured out to match it. Andas glanced at our magics, then back at me.

"If you plan to turn from this, Andas, then do it. Please don't toy with me." I gritted my teeth and made to pull away.

He gripped *my* tunic and dragged me right back. "But that's exactly what I plan to do to you, Silver. And you'll be very happy we're not two average fae by the end."

I wasn't sure who moved first.

I gasped as our mouths met, teeth, tongue, lips, and all. We'd never done this. We'd never chosen to damn the consequences and cast aside our responsibilities and just *kiss*. My body had been denied for too long. Far too long.

I ripped at his shirt and my tunic at the same time.

"Slow down," he growled.

Unbalance was telling *me* to slow down. I panted, "I can't."

I was desperate and didn't care who knew it at this point. I looked up into his eyes…and realized that he was barely hanging on too.

"When we're driven apart at last," he hissed. "What we share here is the dream I'll torture myself with until my bitter end. This will be perfect."

I pressed my thighs together. "How long does perfect take?"

Andas grinned. "Longer than you'd like. But I can't

have you combusting." He held my hair and craned my neck. "Don't look away. I want to see it."

I looked into his dark green and amber gaze and didn't budge as he dragged a finger down my vest, slicing it neatly with his magic. My trousers came next.

Unbalance tugged the two sides of my vest apart with his free hand, and then he did budge his gaze from mine. He'd never looked more serious as he took in my bare chest, and my nipples tightened further under the intensity of his stare.

Dark eyes slammed back to mine as he palmed one of my breasts.

An exhale fell from my lips, and he smirked, drawing up his essence to circle and squeeze my nipples. I jerked, eyes widening.

"Yes," he breathed. "You see all that will be done to you."

"And all I'll do to you," I replied. Observing and learning was my strength, was it not?

His magic toying with my breasts had lit a fire in me, but Andas maintained his hold on my hair and stared into my eyes again as he pushed apart the two sides of my leathers. The material fell from my hips and ass, still clinging to my legs, and that somehow made me feel more brazen than if I'd been naked before him.

I expected his hand to lower between my legs, or his fingers to pulse inside me, but Andas pressed me against the wet rock and inserted his knee between my thighs. The friction was immediate, and I stopped breathing.

"I want to see Underhill grind against me," he whispered, lapping up my startled reaction. "Show me what an animal you really are."

There was no hiding the reactions of my body from him. "This is your idea of perfect?"

He nodded. "I am still Unbalance, after all. Do you still desire me?"

If Andas wished to scare me off, then he shouldn't have called me an animal. Because really, I was far more like an animal than one of those court fae.

I moved my hips, rewarded by the flare of his eyes.

Mother be. The sensation was immediate. I could sense the precise movement that would feel best. I circled this time, and my instinct was rewarded with a hotter flush of pleasure. "I've given up on anything but instinct, *my* Unbalance."

"Tell me," he said, his voice low, fervent even as I moved against his thigh. "What do your instincts say?"

My words twisted in my moan. "That there are many rewards to be had if one can just suffer a little."

Andas clenched my ass with his other hand and helped me circle against him. "Is this suffering?"

I shook my head.

"Open your eyes. Look at me."

I listened, and the greens and ambers of his eyes didn't mean Cormac and Aaden any longer. They were one person now. They were Andas, and I wanted *him*.

The force of his stare was uncomfortable. My rocking grew jerky.

"Scared, little Underhill?" he growled.

The mocking edge to his words wasn't convincing, but the challenge was there all the same. I was too far fucking gone to care. Andas was right—this might be the one and only time we'd be allowed this intimacy. I'd torture myself with the perfect dream until *my* end as well.

I wasn't holding anything back.

Gripping his shoulders, I moved against him and then gripped his hair with my other hand. I dragged us nose to nose, our gazes locking and holding.

The cold and wet of the rock under me was forgotten as pleasure tightened my body and mind. *At last.*

"At last," he echoed, voice hitching. "Fall into me, Silver. I've got you."

And I knew it. Part of me had always known it. That might not make a difference to anyone else, but it mattered to me. To him. We might be drawn apart again by what we were, but it would never be by choice.

Try as I might, I couldn't focus on Andas's eyes as pleasure dragged me under the surface. Languidness spread through me, even as he arched me over the rock and released my hair, even as he slipped his fingers between my legs and crooked them within me. Whatever he rubbed only amplified the waves of fire hitting me in that submerged place. I heard wordless encouragement. I heard my scream when one climax battered against a fresh surge. I made it to the surface and took a frantic breath, only to be shoved back under, choking on my own breath in the doing.

"I want it all," Andas growled.

And then his mouth joined his hand. Except his fingers hadn't stopped, and neither did his magic. His tongue. His mouth.

There was no whispered encouragement this time. My body was rigid with lightning, and still I wanted everything he offered. He'd asked for the animal. Here she fucking was. This time I screamed my way through the collision of one pleasure's demise and the other's rise.

I screamed until he'd wrung the last of whatever the fuck had just happened from me with his slow licks and the pulses of his clever fingers. Tears trickled over my temples from the sheer magnitude of what we'd created and shared.

And I wanted more. Always more of him.

He rose from between my legs and pulled me upright to perch on the rock, bringing us flush. He'd taken the time to slice my clothing from me. I banished his, then took a moment to absorb his beauty before gripping his length and guiding it to where we both wanted it.

"Silver," he said as he paused at my entrance, his

guttural tone jolted through me. "There's no going back."

I felt it too. I felt that we'd sealed our fate. I'd either regret or rejoice this memory for the rest of my existence.

My body felt heavy with calm. My mind too. There was a tranquility in me that I'd never experienced before. Never. There was nothing in me except what I felt for this being I'd been designed to destroy or to be destroyed by. I was meant to love this fae.

He was meant to love me.

Each bliss bestowed upon us would be gratefully received for its rarity and for the suffering we endured between times.

I used his shoulders to lift slightly and sink down on his length. *His* eyes widened at my soft sigh. *His* breath halted as I worked my hips to accommodate him.

"You've made your choice then," he choked.

I nodded once, then paused when his cock pressed against a barrier deep within me. The same fire erupt in *him* then.

"And you've made yours," I taunted.

Unbalance growled, gripping my thighs as he pumped into me. Once. *Hard.*

I gasped through the slight pain, gripping his arms tight.

He hissed, "I have, and we both know this ends in

doom and despair. You should've left me to die, Silver." He bowed his head against my chest. "Why didn't you leave me to die?"

CHAPTER 13

I could not think as Andas moved against me, *in me*. Whatever other things I might have said, were gone, disappearing under the onslaught of sensation.

This was more than pleasure, this was connection and history and pain, and I felt the bond between us tighten as I breathed him in, tasted his skin, feasted on his mouth as if I were starving and he was my last meal.

No hesitation. No regret. This was where I was meant to be—with Andas, skin to skin, our hearts beating frantically as if they, too, would touch as our bodies did. Wild, we were wild and in this together. We were free in this moment as we might never be free again.

Andas thrust into me over and over, harder each time. There was nothing gentle about this, nothing soft and slow. We were chasing a peak that neither of us could see or define. And I loved every fucking second of it. This was my path—Andas was the fate I'd been walking toward every step of the way. The rightness of our bodies together was so strange considering who we were, yet I didn't question that we were fated to be together. Not anymore. I'd made my choice, and so had he, for good or for ill. We were in this shit together.

The swirling of a coming climax coaxed me to try and match his thrusts, but all it gained me was a growl and a slap on the ass that made my whole body clench. A moan slipped from my lips. I tipped my head back, leaning it against the cold damp rock.

"Sweet goddess," the words slipped from him as his rhythm faltered. He gasped as my body milked his, tightening in waves from that one smack.

"Yes?" I purred the word.

His laugh caught me off guard and then he picked up speed again, and we were climbing once more. The third climax was stronger than the first two—or was it three? His magic made demands on my body on all fronts, along with his hands, mouth, and cock. I was drowning in the sensations, lost to anything else. Waves of bliss rolled through me, touching every part of my body, and his body melded to mine as he roared, coming hard, as undone as I was.

I matched him, screaming his name as the dam burst inside of me, as if I were coming apart at the seams and only the barest of threads held me together—all of which were tied to him. Shudders wracked my body as I tried to catch my breath, falling slowly from the high, sweat drenched and struggling to make sense of our tangled bodies.

Our foreheads touched, my arms were limp over his shoulders, legs wrapped over his hips. His hands trembled where he rested them on the swell of my hips, the skin under them tender from where he'd held me tight.

The light in the cave was dim, but I could see enough; the trail of sweat on his cheeks, the bruises already rising on my arms. I licked my lips, tasting blood.

What came after this part? Our relationship had no template, so there were no directions as to how to move forward. I doubted that he'd follow me around like Kik did with Peggy. I doubted that he'd allow me to take the lead, as Faolan did with Kallik. We'd shared something irrefutable. But how the hell did we navigate the rest? Of all the impossible things I'd made possible, this truly seemed impossible.

And yet, I'd never shied away from hard work. "Andas?"

He swallowed audibly. "What?"

"What do we do now?"

He huffed a laugh. "Fucked if I know."

Well, that was…unexpected.

He stepped back, his cock sliding from me, and I

almost grabbed at him to draw him back to me. But our moment of grace had ended, and I could feel that as surely as I'd felt this time was meant to be ours.

I set my feet on the floor and pushed off the rock. My back had been pin-pricked by the rocks, but I didn't mind. I'd endured far worse injuries.

He turned, giving me a view of his bare back. I couldn't help the gasp that escaped me. Andas froze as I moved, drawn toward him. My fingers tracing the designs that had been etched into his skin.

Not a wolf.

Not a sword.

A new symbol that was purely his covered his back and slid down his arms, as if a painter had been busy with him while he'd moved inside of me. They were feathers, as if he had wings. I brushed my fingers over the design, fully expecting them to feel real. The skin on his back flexed and danced as I traced each one.

He looked over his shoulder at me. "What is it?"

"Feathers. Crow feathers. They look real."

The bird that existed on Earth and in Underhill and signified magic and warfare for the fae. Fitting, for what he was now.

Andas took my hand, spinning me so that my back was to him. His fingers traced over my shoulder blades and spine, following a design that I could feel. I knew what it would be before he said it. Another creature that existed in both realms.

"Raven feathers, but white and silver, not black," I said.

I didn't have to see the painted wings to know what it looked like. I knew it down to my soul. Andas spun me to face him. "A bird seen as a protector. Fitting. You are a mother."

Gaia's voice rippled through the cave. *You've both been marked, bound together. Now you must seek what comes next.*

Andas cocked a brow. "Was that a fucking goddess?"

"Gaia," I replied.

He stared. "Does she visit you often?"

I smirked. "Can't tell you all of my secrets."

And that was the crux of it. We were still on opposite sides—and would be, for the rest of time. The intimacy we'd shared still hovered between us, but there wasn't time to dwell on it, no space to savor it, because we had to find a way to stop Keefe.

The world was dying all around us.

I tried to feel guilty for taking the time with Andas, but it had been the right step, not just for my journey, but for his too. At some point I had to be *me*.

Andas huffed and snapped his fingers in my direction. Cloth swirled around me, wrapping me in white and silver material that hugged my legs and torso, leaving my feet bare.

The pants were snug but comfortable, with plenty of movement to them. The vest that covered my chest bore a pattern of raven's wings.

"I'll get this filthy in minutes, you know that?"

His smile was brief, and it made my heart flutter. "I wove it to repel dirt and stench."

My mouth twitched upward. "That's the most thoughtful gift anyone's ever got me. It will be a challenge, then, to make it stink. I like a good challenge."

Drawing on my power, I flicked my fingers at Andas, and dressed him in the perfect opposite. Black material from pants to vest, and heavy boots. I wiggled my toes against the ground, not feeling the sharp rocks or cold. He hadn't given me shoes, and that felt right. He saw me as I was—a woman who'd rather roam through savage places alongside her wonderful creatures than the halls of any palace.

"Gaia has blessed you," Andas said. "But this won't stop everyone from dying if we do nothing."

I nodded, sobering with his words. He was right, and Gaia had said as much. "Do you have a plan?" I asked. "You know Keefe best."

"I will deal with him. He is my issue. You should stay here."

My snort was barely out of me before Andas fell through a portal in a swirl of darkness and was gone, leaving me alone in the damp cave.

"He really did that," I said to the dark. Maybe he didn't know me for shit.

"Idiot." I muttered under my breath. Sigella was in the scale realm with Keefe and Orlaith, and even if I was locked out of the scale realm, I was far from helpless. Standing idly by wasn't in my nature.

I'd already tried to open a portal to Sigella, but perhaps I could check up on her essence. I could see her future right alongside mine still, and that had to mean something.

Carefully, as if I were creeping up on a herd of alicorns, I stretched out my magic in my mind to touch her path. *Weary. Furious. Hurt.*

I could still access her essence. Maybe I could open a portal *through* her. I drew on my power and pushed a tiny amount—no more than she could bear to hold—into Sigella's body. Her wounds closed over and new energy filled her, but her body wouldn't hold my power for long.

I opened her eyes, then pushed my magic through her essence to open a small portal to me.

For an instant I was looking at Sigella and looking at myself too. I quickly closed Sigella's eyes and retreated somewhat until I was left only with the single view of Sigella in the scale realm.

I could tell this portal was different, and sure enough, when I touched my fingertips to the portal, my hand didn't go through. I couldn't physically reach her.

Her arms were bound above her head with iron chains, and she'd been stripped to nothing but a ragged blue shift. Although I was relieved that she hadn't been beaten black and blue, anger snapped through me.

"You fucker, Keefe," I growled.

Sigella shook violently from holding my power, but she answered in a voice hoarsened by thirst, "He holds all the water in the worlds in a single bottle, Silver. You must find it and release it, or all the water creatures will die. In time humans will die without them. Already, those who survive this drought will suffer great famine."

Fierce hope rose within me. "Where, Sigella? Where do I look?"

"Not with him." Sigella's eyes fluttered shut. "Somewhere else. Maybe Earth."

Maybe? That was a big fucking search area. "Not Underhill?"

She didn't respond. I had to get her out of there. There had to be a way to get through this portal to grab her. She wasn't in bad shape, but who knew what Keefe's plans were.

The viewing portal went black, and I was shoved from Sigella's essence as if Keefe had stuck his hand through and jabbed me in the chest. Only it wasn't Keefe. I caught a glimpse of red hair and fierce eyes before I was pushed all the way out.

Kik might not swear anymore, but he'd taught me every horrific word possible, and I hurled them all at the cave walls until my rage subsided somewhat. I wished I could say Orlaith had at least apologized or explained her betrayal. As things stood, it appeared she'd made her choice for good.

I rubbed my hands over my face. "A single bottle. That's what I have to go on? *Maybe* on Earth."

A single feather from one of the rainbow flock, dropped deep in the jungle would have been easier to find. But I knew who could help me.

Opening a portal, I stepped through it into the Alaskan court. Night had fallen—the summers were short here—and the dark had brought a freeze with it. Hurrying up the first set of stairs, I made my way to the room where I'd left my friends. My family.

They weren't there.

I circled on the spot and tried to lock onto their magics, but it was as if they were gone…

"No." I breathed the word, horror making my heart race. They couldn't have died. Not in the few short hours I'd been away. I cast out my magic to my sister, then whirled when it located her behind me.

"They're hiding below," Kallik said, entering the room. "We've done all we can to shield them from this slow death, and our spells will make it hard to find them."

I turned to face her. "They're alive?"

"For now. We've put as many people into a magical sleep as possible to help reserve their energy. We've had the Irish and Louisiana courts do the same. Only a few of us have remained awake. For the worst, should it come."

Kallik was pale, and her lilac eyes seemed larger than ever. "The humans are preparing to initiate attacks on all three courts, Silver. To destroy us with their weapons and bombs. We have forty-eight hours before they give the order."

I reached for her hands. "I know what I must find, I know how to return the water to the world." Well, maybe not exactly, I was hoping Sigella was right, that I would just need to find the bottle and release the contents. "I just don't know where it is. You still can't see the paths?"

Kallik closed her eyes. "Only one. Your path is intertwined even more with Andas's. Why isn't he with you?"

"He thinks he can stop Keefe by himself." I paused and frowned. "Keefe. Can you see his path? Or Orlaith's? They're the ones I need to understand in this."

If either the trickster or the traitor had a path visible to Kallik, that might help me find the one bottle.

"There's nothing more," she answered.

My heart sank.

"But I can tell you something about him that didn't seem relevant to me before? It's all I have."

"I'll take all the help I can get."

"Keefe is not his true name, and Trickster is merely the name he's given himself. His real name is tied to your first meeting. The subterfuge seemed small at the time, and it wasn't connected to any dire future. I myself go by Oracle instead of my birth name..."

"You did what you believed was right," I told her. "Thank you for that. There could be something there."

Where did I first meet Keefe? I cast my mind back. I'd first met him as an old man when he gave me Orlaith, but when did I meet the *real* Keefe for the first time? "I first met him in the cave where the tree of life was sprouting. I…" I thought back to that time, trying to replay it in my head. "He'd been drinking and…" There had been bottles behind him, bottles he'd drained.

Could it be that easy?

Could the bottle be stashed in a place we'd visited twice over, a place that we wouldn't think to check again? It would be like burying a treasure in a place you knew the hunters had already looked. Indeed, it was exactly the kind of strategy I would use.

There was only one way to find out.

"I think…I think I've figured it out." I grabbed my sister in a quick hug, surprising us both.

I portaled away from Alaska to Ireland. It was morning here and there was ice on the ground and hanging off the trees.

There was no time to waste.

I drew my power to me and raced into the cave holding the tree of life. Kallik's words hummed under my skin—Keefe's name wasn't his name, and that felt important in discovering how to unravel his power.

I slid to a stop outside the cave and immediately felt a change in the place. The naga were underground, hunkered down deep under the cave. For now, they were safe, although none of us would be safe for long.

I ran into the cave, using my power to pull a small fire into my hand and light my way. I should have hesitated, though.

The tree of life had grown since I'd last visited. Now, it was waist high, thick with dark veins and a few silver ones too. The tree rustled and breathed as though a wind blew through the cavern, the silvered leaves glinting as they picked up scant bits of light. The naga were quiet below my feet, but I could sense them there, aware of my presence.

Propped against the far wall was a single bottle, clear, with water swirling in it as if currents were trapped inside.

My instincts flared.

This was too easy. I moved toward the bottle and was hit with an invisible force that threw me back across the cave. I smashed into the stone, hearing and feeling the crack of my ribs. Stars rippled through my vision as I pushed to my feet.

"So much smarter than I gave you credit for." Keefe said, his voice bouncing around me. "I said to myself, 'Keefe, should you bury it too', and then I answered myself, 'No, she's an idiot.' But the joke's on me." He chuckled to himself.

I reached for my weapons—none of which I had on me. I'd left them all behind. Like a fucking fool. I'd *never* done that in my life.

Keefe stepped from the shadows, smiling. "You think you can save this world from me? Already the marine life is dying in the millions. Millions of humans will follow when they die from dehydration, or hypothermia, or heat stroke. Soon enough, the very air they breathe will change. These things are already happening. You have already failed."

"You were created to play a part, Keefe," I said. "I believe your part is to die. This is a challenge to prove my worth and nothing more. A blip in the history of my life. Humans will live on. Marine creatures will recover and grow stronger again."

He laughed, his grin wide, though his eyes had narrowed. "Such optimism. And what of your precious Sigella? Shall I kill her as *my* challenge? What of my daughter?"

"The Traitor?" I asked. "Orlaith made her choice. And Sigella has survived worse than you."

"The Traitor," he mused. "The Trickster and The Traitor. Sounds like a good time to me. But surely you have not discarded my daughter so easily."

I circled the tree, moving closer to the bottle. "I can't say what will happen to her now, her path and the part she plays are her own."

Keefe waggled his brows "We shall see. But enough of paths and serious things. I am a Trickster at heart, you know this. What challenge shall we have, then, to see if I hand the bottle over to you?"

I tried not to stare at him with my mouth hanging

open. "You think I would believe that you could honor such a challenge?"

He pressed his fingers to his chest. "I may not be Underhill's chosen, Silver, but I am special in my own right. If I give you my word, I will hold to it."

Keefe held his hand out, palm facing the dirt, and flexed his fingers.

A length of wood rose from the ground, planked flat like a table. A chair sprouted in front of it, and bottles appeared against the wall behind it.

Hundreds and hundreds of bottles, all with the same swirling water inside of them. The same current.

"A game of wisdom." Keefe walked from behind the bar of bottles and whipped a white towel from the empty air, flipping it over his shoulder as he leaned forward. "You faced two henchmen before me, Underhill. Beasts. Monsters. But I am not a monster. I am more like you than perhaps you have realized."

I didn't doubt him. Gaia had told me that Keefe was pushed into power to balance 'that which might be.' At the time, I hadn't connected that she meant a relationship between myself and Andas, but Gaia had been telling me that there would consequences to our love. Keefe had been granted the power to balance the alliance between me and Andas.

He pulled a glass from the air and placed it on the long bar with a slight thunk. He cracked a bottle open.

"What do you mean, you're like me?" I moved toward the table.

"I can't just give you the answers," He laughed, smiling as if we were old friends. "But you weren't exactly educated either. Not like other fae at least." He hummed.

I spread my hands and executed a mocking bow. "So educate me, wise Trickster."

His grin widened. "You're much more fun than Andas. He tried to chop me into little pieces. Good thing I didn't let him do that."

Hot, icy fear sliced through me.

Keefe wouldn't have been able to kill Andas, right? I stretched for the connection between myself and Unbalance, only to find it wavering and dull, as if he were injured or worse…dying.

"Ah, I see you have an idea of what's going on?" Keefe sighed. "I do so like a good game, particularly one where the stakes are high and time is limited. Now. Here is my game. I will let you choose the bottle. If you are correct, you shall release water back into the worlds."

"And if I choose wrong?"

"Death and suffering, my dear. Yours. Andas's. Eternal servitude for everyone you care about. They'll learn to love me when they learn I control all water. If they don't learn to love me, then they'll learn to fake it. Either way is fine by me."

"All the water you stole will return to the same places it came from. Every drop," I replied. "You will never take it again. That is a fair deal considering what you seek to take if I lose."

He held out his hand again, palm down. He flexed his fingers, and I felt the air snap. "You have a deal."

What I wanted was to run toward Andas laying injured. Dying. But *everyone* was dying.

And Keefe wanted me here, *entertaining* him, which made me furious and also more determined.

He motioned to one of the chairs. "Have a seat, young Underhill. It's time to choose your drink. I suggest you choose wisely."

CHAPTER 14

I considered the rows upon rows of bottles behind the wooden bar from my seat at the makeshift table. Some bottles were huge, and others tiny—only the size of my thumbnail. Some gleamed, and a thick dust layer coated others. Some had cracks and rusty caps, others were made of crystal or amber. All held the same swirling water.

And only one bottle would save the world, Andas, and me.

The bottle I'd first seen upon entering the cave sat front and center, and I gazed at it for a time, wondering if the Trickster was brazen enough to display the very bottle I wanted. Or had he placed it front and center to trick me?

That choice felt too risky.

"What's your selection?" he asked.

I slanted him a look. "Five seconds have passed, Keefe. You didn't set a time limit."

He pouted. "But I have many things to do."

"You can wait."

Real fury lit in his gaze then, and I wondered at it. But he'd tucked his anger away the next instant. I'd seen it, though, and I thought I knew what it meant—Keefe didn't like being told what to do. Someone had controlled him before, and he hadn't liked it.

I returned my focus to the bottles. "My mother held your reins for a long time."

He snorted. "She never held my reins. But she thought she did."

"You spent how long in the prison realm? You were under her power there."

"There is a difference, young Underhill, when a prisoner knows he will not always be imprisoned. When his sentence is finite. And now make your choice and stop attempting to figure me out. Many have tried. Many have failed. I'm tricky like that."

He laughed at his joke, and I hovered my magic over the bottles.

"The first bottle you touch, magic or otherwise, is the bottle you choose," he said in glee.

"You didn't state that in our deal," I said.

"And neither did you," he snapped. The cave trembled with his change in emotion.

I wondered anew at his sheer power. Such power could only be ancient, which seemed to confirm that binding myself to Andas had triggered the change in Keefe.

I hovered my magic over the bottles. They all felt the same, and I'd need to use my power to cut through the disguising magic cast over them.

This was never going to be that straightforward.

The tree of life rustled around me, and the slight shine of the fluttering leaves caught my peripheral vision.

I tilted my head, my mind humming as I shifted my focus from choosing the correct bottle to learning, as I did when confronted with any new predator.

One bottle contained the life of entire realms…

The tree of life sat mere feet away. Could like call to like?

I pulsed a surge of my magic into the tree trunk behind me. I'd already learned that attempts to purge Andas's essence from the tree wouldn't work—that purging darkness from anything or anyone never worked. So instead, I again layered my magic onto the tree. Before, I'd merely blanketed the leaves, branches and trunk with my power to save the tree, but now I layered my power until an equal amount of my magic glowed in the trunk as darkness blackened it.

Last time, the tree had tripled in size, but I felt something shift within the tree as its balance was restored. I could feel the tree looking to me for guidance. I had a claim on it now, and the tree understood that it had two masters, and that I was one of them.

This tree had made me hope, hate, regret, fear, and rage. A *tree* had made me feel all of this.

I had great respect for what this tree could do, and so I whispered my request to the tree of life, and it shuddered.

"You can't use the tree," Keefe spat out.

"This isn't a game where you will make up the rules as we go," I informed him coolly. "You have said that I cannot use my magic directly. Fine. I say that I will be allowed to use anything else at my disposal so long as my magic and body do not touch any bottle that is not my final and only choice."

The Trickster crossed his arms, then glanced over my head at the tree of life. The corner of his mouth tugged up. "Oh, why not. Go on then."

His easy acceptance of my demand didn't fill me with confidence.

I whispered to the tree again, and with a second shudder, it parted with a third of its leaves. I encouraged the leaves to fall on the bottles. One each.

I watched to see if any of the bottles reacted to the life touching it. None of them glowed or pulsed or shattered.

Nothing happened at all.

"Ha!" Keefe burst out. "Anti-climactic. Still, you are merely a fae, and a fae mind can only fathom so much."

My brows drew together. He spoke as if he *weren't* fae. Keefe had a tendency to reveal information when he felt he had the upper hand. He'd be the kind of hunter to crow over his fallen prey, only to have the prey kill him with its dying breaths. Me? I didn't waste time.

I'd kill Keefe one day, and if Andas—whom I could feel growing weaker with each passing minute—died after whatever Keefe had done, then I would also torture Keefe to his dying fucking day.

I blinked at a plucking sensation deep in my chest. I followed the sensation to the underground naga nest. The pull tugged at me still, encouraging me to try something I'd never attempted before but had witnessed my mother do.

I dove, in all but body, into one of the queens and opened her eyes. "Yesss?"

"Nessst mate," said the young king. "You make a great choicccce for usss."

I nodded my serpent head.

"We made nessst here," he said. "Rootsss grow ssstrong around us, into our nessst, and we let them. We are togethherr with tree of life. We seee what it sssees. Water hasss alwaysss called to us."

"What do you ssseee?" I asked through the queen's mouth. Naga indeed had a gift for seeking water. It was a large factor in where they chose to build their nests.

The eldest queen answered, "We sssaw nothing, but her leavesss burned through the magic desssigned to masssk and trick. Leavesss on each bottle are a window to contentsss."

My heart skipped a beat—well, the queen's heart

that I'd borrowed. The leaves had created a hole in Keefe's magic, and the naga could see into the bottles through their new connection to the tree of life. "You know whiccch bottle is the righht one?

The naga nodded, from toddler to the eldest queen.

The young king dipped his head. "Underhill was wissse in placing usss here for thissss moment."

Underhill hadn't known any of this shit would happen. But their good opinion meant something to me, so they could go on believing in me. "How can I payyy the debt for thissss information?"

"You havvee sssspent a time in one of our owwn." She gestured to the queen I occupied. "Sssshe is ssssilver-toucched, and a great treasssure."

"Ssshow me." I left the queen and returned to my body in the cave with Keefe.

He was talking. Had he been talking this entire time?

I kicked back my chair and touched my magic to the naga king's essence. I'd entered Sigella's body recently, but now I drew the naga king into mine while holding my magic away from his essence. If it touched him, he'd die. I could feel the naga king's awe as he tip-toed inside the mother of all creatures. I could sense his fear and wonder and confusion at all he would never fathom of my power.

You may move my hand, I told him in my mind.

He replied in a whisper, *Great Underhill, you honor me beyond measssure.*

Walking behind the bar, I let his essence guide my hand.

Down the row I went, two-thirds of the way and past the bottle I'd first noticed.

The naga king's magic pulsed through me, stopping me in front of a non-descript amber bottle covered in a thin layer of dust. Some rust on the cap. Not stately or eye-catching.

Average in every way.

The water issss here, Great Underhill, said the naga king.

I believed him. *Thank you,* I silently replied, then waited until the king's essence had retreated to his own body once more.

I picked up the bottle.

"I'll give you one chance to reconsider, young Underhill," said Keefe.

His words were too careful. Too mocking.

"This is my choice."

If our roles had been reversed, I supposed Keefe would have made a speech about his cleverness here.

I popped open the lid and the contents wisped into the air. Only a ding-dong would mistake the tiny droplets for what they appeared to be. The power stored in each of the droplets made my head swim. I was doubly stunned by the incredible power Keefe would have required to collect the water in the first place.

"Cheat!" Keefe bellowed. "That should have been impossible."

I laughed then. Why did people keep using that word? It was particularly ironic that *he* was using it, given he'd just collected the water of the realms in a bottle. "It was impossible. And then it wasn't."

"Cheat," he said again.

This was the real Keefe. He didn't cope well with his plans changing. Or with being tricked. I'd learn to be more adaptable. If I had a tantrum every time things didn't work out...

Well, there wouldn't be any time left in the day.

I nodded at him, imagining how nicely his skin would part over the fine edge of my dagger, and then I portaled away.

I'd let my gut decide on my destination, not even registering where it was taking me until I arrived in the middle of a sparse forest to find Andas buried to his neck and shoulders in the cold ground.

The enormity of my decision to portal to him above anyone else shook me to the core.

I'd gone to him, not Kik and Peggy. Not my sister and Cinth.

Andas was alive.

Conscious, but barely.

I crouched by his head. "Why aren't you better? I returned the water to the realms."

His breath was labored. "You did?"

I opened a portal to the rawmouths' lake on

Unimak. Of course, it wasn't theirs any longer. I'd felt them die within me early on, as I'd felt most of the water fae die before cutting myself off from their pain. Some of those who possessed the ability to also live on land had survived. When this all ended—if it ever ended—then I'd mourn everyone lost. I'd get used to the void in me where they used to be.

The lake looked just as it had at the naga king's coronation. "The water is back."

Andas sighed and closed his eyes. "Keefe got me good."

My heart hammered, but I said calmly, "Where are you injured? What do you need?"

"Help is on the way. I couldn't portal them here."

He didn't have any henchmen left, but I heard a familiar scuffle and then the drag of hundreds of feet. "Your gray fae."

"Stand back, Silver. They get ahead of themselves sometimes."

That was a fucking understatement.

I bounded to crouch on a boulder fifty feet away as gray fae converged on Andas like addicts. And that was exactly what they'd become—addicted to his darkness. He was their fix.

I watched as they dug at the ground and tugged on him.

I heard his furious roars as they failed to extract him.

After a few minutes, I dropped down into their midst and walked back to him.

Andas coughed pitifully, and I jerked to a halt.

No, they *hadn't* failed to extract him. His head and shoulders just ended where they should continue. He was like one of those stupid head and chest statues in the Alaskan court. "Keefe…chopped you up. How are you alive?"

Chopping wasn't an accurate description. I couldn't see any wounds. There was no blood.

"He didn't *chop me up*," Andas said, glaring at a gray fae creeping up on me. "Stay back, all of you. She is mine."

My stomach flipped. "Andas, you're dying. You need to tell me how to help you."

"Keefe has locked me in the four realms. I am whole, but my head and chest are here, one arm and leg are in Underhill, the other arm is in the prison realm, and my second leg is in the scale realm."

"Why can't you portal yourself out?"

"Because he locked me here," Andas ground out.

Something wasn't adding up. "Why would that kill you?" He had to have another injury.

"It's not killing me," he said on an exhale, looking about seven-eighths dead.

I jerked his head back via a ruthless hold on his black hair, then shouted in his face. "I will be *very* fucking angry if you give up everything we've worked toward so far because you want to keep secrets."

Andas met my furious gaze with one of his own. I saw the stream of thoughts behind his eyes. I saw him come to the realization that he had no other option.

"I can't stay in one place for long," he said in a low voice. "Keefe was aware of that."

Andas couldn't—

"What?" My jaw dropped. "Why can't you stay in one place?"

Then I thought about the way I could always feel him leaping around. He'd portaled us somewhere after the kraken attack, only to leave me for a time so he could continue portaling around without me connecting the truth. "Why?"

"It doesn't matter why."

I tilted my head in confusion. Had Unbalance always done this?

If Keefe had locked Andas in place, then I'd expect the reason Andas had to constantly move about was crucial.

I schooled my features, then wrapped my silver essence around his head and neck and the tops of his shoulders. I opened portals around him next. The portal to Underhill was easy. I ripped out the barbs of Keefe's magic in Andas that were pinning him in place. Ignoring Andas's screams, I pulled his arm into Earth to join his head and chest. I'd need to keep the portal open until I freed the rest of his body though. I couldn't pull his leg through without ripping it off the rest of his body.

I had a feeling he wouldn't thank me for that.

I took a breath. Getting the pieces of him hidden in Underhill had been easy, but it would be the only easy break we were given.

To my surprise, however, I *could* sense and access the prison realm. "This will hurt."

"The last one fucking hurt," Andas retorted.

"This will hurt more." I held my magic at the ready, and when I'd opened the tiniest possible portal to Keefe's realm and territory, I ripped out the barbs and yanked Andas's other arm to Earth. The upper half of his body was all in one place.

"I can't access the scale realm," I said after trying. I'd opened portals through other beings before, but I wouldn't be able to force my way into Andas.

He stopped cursing and groaned. "Go through our bond."

Really? That was useful information. I should catch him on the verge of death more often. I dove into our bond without any resistance, and I had a feeling he couldn't have closed our bond even if he'd wished it. Which could just as easily go the other way, so I shouldn't celebrate too much.

I easily pushed my magic toward his leg, and when the sensation changed to that of wading through mud, I gathered that I'd entered the scale realm. If that hadn't alerted me, then the savage barbs of magic stabbing through Andas's leg and pinning him in place would've done it.

I couldn't sense anything outside of Andas's body, but now wasn't the time to look around the scale realm.

I said silently, *I can push out Keefe's magic. Can you do the rest?*

I felt his nod, then he replied, *On three.*

I didn't do countdowns. Diving into Andas again, I sent out a wave of silver and disintegrated the barbs filled with Keefe's swirling magic.

Andas roared, and I retreated from his body, then lunged to grip his arm and help drag him out.

A portal opened, and Sigella stumbled out.

I released Andas and caught her by reflex alone.

Andas finished yanking his leg into Earth and blurred to his feet, weapons drawn and pointed at Orlaith, who stood on the other side of the portal in the scale realm, black ribbons snapping behind her.

The red-haired beauty stood defiant and surer than I'd ever seen her. There were no pleas to braid my hair. No nervous bat babbling. Her silver dress was streaked with black. Whatever internal dilemmas she'd experienced when first returning to her body, she'd obviously figured them out. And by figuring them out, I meant that she'd embraced whatever darkness remained in her. If I couldn't see the bands of darkness in her, then the state of her dress would've been enough to tell. I'd learned by now that my creatures were silver. What surprised me is that Orlaith still had any silver at all on her dress.

"Don't get caught again. I can only intervene so much," said Orlaith to Sigella. She cast a quick look at me, and I saw her anger toward me. And her pain.

I wasn't sure how to take her comment though. Did she mean that Keefe was in control, but she could still go against him if she wished? Or just when she chose?

And what would make her choose us consistently? I couldn't rely on Orlaith to do the right thing anymore. She was unpredictable.

Sigella lifted her head from my shoulder. "Thank you, Orlaith."

"Not all of us have forgotten that we were once friends," said the fae, slamming the portal closed.

Considering she'd sent me to a kraken to kill me because her father said so, I found that hypocritical. But again, consider me surprised that darkness hadn't completely claimed her and that she'd saved Sigella. I wanted to feel hope that Orlaith could still be saved—that we could return to being what we once were.

I also knew that could never be.

I exchanged a long look with Andas.

"You good?"

His body was in one realm and all attached. Things could be worse.

Andas nodded, then glanced at Sigella. "Yes, but…I need to go."

I knew what that meant: he had to move.

I released a heavy exhale. "Go. Be safe."

"I'll find you soon." Andas trailed his fingers over

the raven feathers on my back, and they tingled at his touch.

Then he was gone.

"How are you faring?" I asked the ancient fae still in my arms.

Sigella grunted. "Like I'm going to liquify Keefe, put him in my favorite teapot, and drink his insides along with a beetroot tickle."

"Let's get you cleaned up and fed." I also had to check on the others now that the water had been restored.

I looped an arm around Sigella's back and we walked through my portal into...

Chaos.

Screaming.

Fae staggering and blurring. Children limp in their mothers' arms.

A human fell to her knees before me. Her face was turning blue. She couldn't breathe. *Water* spilled from her lips.

"She's drowning," Sigella said in horror.

Drowning from the inside out. Whipping my magic forth, I pulled the water from her lungs. And didn't stop there, because I noticed the cells of her body were at the bursting point. It was as if someone had injected too much water into every single part of her body.

The woman toppled to the ground, dragging in great gulps of air.

"He put the water back. I asked him to put all the

water back where it came from," I whispered, and then shouted at the closest fae, who was frozen in horror but not drowning. "When did this start?"

He turned an unblinking gaze my way. "J-just a minute ago, Underhill."

"Why now?" Sigella asked.

"Because Orlaith returned you, and he got angry," I said grimly. "He decided to interpret my request another way."

I strode toward the nearest drowning human, already knowing I couldn't possibly save them all.

More death. More suffering.

Looked like the Trickster was having the last laugh.

CHAPTER 15

They were all drowning right in front of me.

"Motherfucker," I growled as I continued pulling water from the lungs of the humans around me. "How are the fae, Sigella?"

"They're mostly taking care of each other. Few will be lost," she said as she mirrored what I was doing, pulling water from the humans in the Alaskan court.

When the last of them were done, I sprinted for the palace.

We had to move fast if we were to save any more humans than those directly in our path. Given the water in their lungs, we had minutes at best. *Minutes.*

And an entire world of humans to somehow save. Impossible. Once more, that word was there, as if waiting for me to deny it.

"Silver!" Cinth cried out from across the courtyard

as she raced over to us. She clutched a viewing orb in both hands.

"The humans inside, are they okay?"

"We've helped all we could."

I took the ball from her and studied the humans within. They were bathing in the river and drinking their fill. I sagged in relief. "It was just an attack on the courts."

"Yes, the Irish Court too. I'm waiting for an update from them."

"I'd feared we had an entire world to try and save."

Cinth leaned closer and began to whisper at the orb. It showed different places—humans in tall buildings and in fields—many of them had congregated at waterholes.

"Stop," I said sharply. "Go back to the last one."

Cinth whispered a command and the boat filled with humans appeared again. They were falling to the ground.

"They're drowning too," Cinth said. She changed the location. "But other humans are okay."

"He's toying with us," I said, then swore. "Portal fae to these humans now. They're under orders to pull water from lungs and put it into the earth. Sigella, ask Kik to help with the portals. Cinth, send word out to leaders without delay. We need to be alerted as soon as an area is targeted and humans start to drown. Tell them we'll send help, but we need to know *immediately*.

I want every orb in this palace and the other courts in the hands of a fae so they can scan the realm for signs too. We'll only have minutes to respond. Go now!"

"Understood," Sigella said.

Cinth was hurrying back into the palace.

I opened a portal to the humans I'd seen in the orb. "Every fae who isn't helping a human right now must go through this portal. Empty the humans' lungs into the earth! Work fast. They need our help."

Bewildered fae ran through the portal at my command and I held it open.

This wasn't war; this was triage. And we could expect that Keefe would continue this attack until the very last drop was returned.

Peggy galloped up to me, Kik following with Sigella.

A fae raced up to Kik, an orb in hand. Kik wasted no time opening a portal for more fae to race through and face the fresh threat.

We couldn't possibly keep up with these threats, as Keefe would well know. Which was the reason he was releasing water this way instead of in one large load. He wanted to torture us for as long as he could.

There had to be something else I could do.

"Fly with me, Silver," Peggy said. "Try drawing the water to you. That is the only possibility I can see working." She bent her head, and I leapt onto her back without a pause.

Hope. I had to hope.

"Hurry the fricky deedle dum up, ladies," Kik yelled his strange new brand of encouragement at us as Peggy powered us above the Alaskan court, high into the cloudless sky.

I recalled Andas's words as we rose higher. *Gaia has blessed you.*

I sure as hell hoped he was right.

I held my hands out wide and reached for the strands of power that tied me to Earth and Underhill and the water within them.

Whatever I was going to attempt, it was now or never. Death crowded me, and for a split second, I thought I heard Keefe laughing from realms away— howling that he'd finally won. A being with his character would like to watch the fallout to his subterfuge.

To be entertained by our despair.

Peggy slowed her wings, and we coasted on a current.

"You can do this, Underhill. Each of the five elements should speak to you, just as Earth and Underhill can speak to you. Call the water back home. Once it's away from Keefe, then he can't release it into the humans."

Her lilting voice was a song, and the warmth and reassurance and surety in her tone resonated in my bones like the vibration of a tuning fork.

"Earth below me, water within me," I whispered.

I imagined the realms' waters. I imagined billions of

dusty, amber bottles—a replica of the bottle I'd selected to 'save' them. I imagined those billions of bottles were killing them now, bucketing too much water into their cells.

I held my hands wide to connect to the sheer size of what I was attempting, and then I called the water to me.

The amber bottles I'd imagined shook and rattled around—many of them inside their hosts. The bottles fought my call to return the water to its proper place. Keefe had guarded his despicable act with magic to prevent anyone from tampering with his efforts.

But the water would come if Keefe's magic could be disrupted.

That was the only way.

"Andas!" I screamed his name, hoping that he would hear me. I opened a portal swiftly to him, blindly following the connection between us. He was still on earth.

Peggy flew through it, trusting in me.

Andas stood at the edge of a city. Cars had pulled over in a mess of bonnet and boot. Sirens screamed and whined over the chorus of wailing, gurgling people. At least Cinth had managed to reach leaders to raise the alert.

Unbalance said, "They're dying. This doesn't benefit me any more than it does you."

"His magic is guarding the water." My voice was

calm, too, and strange to hear as panic crashed against my ribs. "I can call the water back, but not with his magic in the way. He's blocking me, and he's fucking strong."

Andas frowned. "Perhaps…perhaps I understand him better now. Count to sixty. Then try again." He portaled away from me.

"Do you trust him?" Peggy asked. She landed where he'd stood, on top of a rolled truck.

"Yes. Count for me. Tell me when time's up."

All around me I could feel the humans dying. I could *hear* them drowning from the inside, as if they were my creatures too…but that didn't make sense. They weren't of Underhill. I'd never felt them like this before.

Though if they were somehow connected to a realm, then…then shouldn't they fall under my protection too?

I slipped off Peggy and pressed a hand to the ground, but Gaia answered my question before I even asked it.

She said gently, *They have never been tied to the powers of balance. Like reluctant toddlers, they believe they can do it all on their own. But if you save them now, they will become yours to protect. You will forge a tie between them and balance. They will not want your help, so your guidance of them must be careful.*

I closed my eyes and leaned into the sensation of the humans' essences. There were so many of them.

Like specks of snow in a blizzard, or insects in an Alaskan summer. Their lives were so very fragile...

Yet for all our magic, we fae had still been forced out of Underhill. My people may not be drowning today, but we could drown tomorrow through a different attack.

"I can't even look after my fae, let alone these stupid fucks," I muttered. And yet, how could I let them die? Mere minutes ago, they'd had smiles on their faces. Hopes and aspirations. Children.

"Ten seconds," Peggy said.

Their hearts, an entire city's worth of them, began to falter. One at a time. Some slipped away faster than others. I'd lose some—the newfound connection was tenuous—but I'd save more than we lost.

Peggy tapped a front hoof in time with her words. "Ready yourself. Three. Two. One."

I yanked at the water in the humans, those closest to me first. I dragged the water out of their lungs as quickly as I could. Brutally.

I opened myself to the world of the humans then, and I tied them to the cluster fuck that was me and Unbalance and whispering goddesses.

As I connected to the humans, their sensations, languages, and fears crashed into me. They'd nearly burst from too much water, and I was about to burst from fusing to them. I felt the seams of my body and mind explode outward.

I went to my knees and buried my hands into the

earth below, digging my toes in for traction as I submitted to what could be my death. I clung to the only thing I could. The efforts of my magic to drag water from the humans. Fast. Faster. Over and over, water out, water out, quicker than I could think.

The tearing strain was like nothing I'd ever experienced before.

A scream built in my throat as my magic grew hot like an overworked weapon, but I couldn't stop. It had locked on its course, and I was no longer in control of the result, or of stopping.

I felt it was going to kill me. I couldn't fathom how my body was still intact and not sprayed across the earth.

There wasn't room for fear or rage.

I was one with this, and at the mercy of this.

With the Earth.

With its water and life.

With its occupants.

The brutal forging between me and an entire realm calmed suddenly, like a door shut against a storm. My body started to tremble and shake from the shock of what I'd experienced. My mind buzzed. I knew what had happened, but also couldn't have conveyed it to myself or anyone else.

"Those who could be saved have been saved," Peggy said. "The water is returned to its proper place."

"I need. A moment." I slumped forward, my face hitting the ground, dirt shoving its way into my nose. I breathed through my mouth for seconds or minutes or an entire hour as my mind stopped trembling and my new connection to the humans settled into my essence.

I groaned. The sensation was akin to one of having eaten far too much. I was holding too much inside of me.

"Fuck you, Keefe." I muttered.

The full feeling got worse. And worse.

I gasped. "It's not over."

"No." Peggy agreed.

How the fuck wasn't this over? My last thought was that this reminded me of the bow I used to have. The one that never missed its mark but would drive me to my knees with the power it demanded in payment. With great power, came greater consequences, and this one was a fucking doozy.

"I didn't die the first time," I wheezed.

The world swirled around me, wind and earth, and tangled my silver hair in my face. I struggled to make heads or tails of where I was. I mean, I could literally see a tail—I was staring at Peggy's rear end.

Were we flying?

I vomited off her side. Then again for good measure. Fuck, I was dying.

"Silver, do not die," she commanded.

Shit, I hadn't actually believed I was dying until she'd said that. I focused on the surging, catastrophic waves of emotion and awareness crashing through me. Losing some of Underhill's creatures had nearly undone me, and now the humans were overwhelming me with their grief and fear. They'd lost many, and their collective hearts were broken. They were screaming inside. And I felt every bit of that.

I struggled to make their pain smaller within me. The scale was hundreds of thousands of times larger than what had happened when Underhill's creatures had been lost to Andas's darkness. And I couldn't cut the humans off. I'd only just tied them to me.

"We need a portal," Peggy was saying over and over.

"Portal," I slurred.

"To the court," she said.

A portal to the court.

I waved a hand and created a sluggish portal, not even sure I'd fully achieved the task. I really was dying. *Shit.* After all that.

"Here," Cinth yelled from somewhere below.

Were we back at the palace?

Peggy did a nosedive, and only the jutting cartilage of her wings and her skill were keeping me on her back. My face was by her ass. Which I'd vomited all over.

"Mother never would have arrived like this," I groaned.

The Pegasus landed lightly, and I toppled off her side to the cobbled ground.

Cinth ran forward and heaved me upright. "You did it, Underhill. You did it. The fae we portaled helped as they could, but it never would have been enough. The humans have stopped dying."

"She needs help, not an update," Peggy snapped.

Cinth tightened her hold on me. "What's wrong with her?"

But the full feeling was dissipating. I belched. "Think I'm okay now. It was just the last... bit." I fucking hoped.

The queen waved a hand in front of my face. "Are you sure? You look unwell."

Peggy walked around me, helping to prop me up with one of her wings. "She had to connect to all the humans in the world. It nearly overloaded her capacity."

There was no nearly about it. I could attest to the fact that my capacity had certainly been overloaded.

Strength flowed into me, however, and the bloating feeling settled. I felt fuller in general, but my magic was working to give my connection to the humans its place within me. I'd grow used to the feeling soon enough. "I couldn't save all of them. Many died."

"But *most* were saved." Her face was pink. "That disaster could have eradicated them to near extinction."

I nodded. "No animals were affected?"

Ronan, never far from his queen, joined us. "No. The returning water only seemed to affect the fae and humans. Nothing else suffered."

"The ones worth controlling were the ones he attacked."

Cinth fell into step beside me as I marched toward the war room. I could feel Kallik there.

"We need to be prepared," I said to the queen as we strode through the palace to the war room

"For what?" Cinth puffed.

"I'll tell you when we get to the room. No one else should hear this."

She paled, which made the burn marks on her face stand out. "Of course."

"Queen Hyacinth," said a fae, racing up to us. "European leaders have united in support of us in light of the aid we granted."

A woman tapped at an orb, falling into stride behind us. "Leaders in most other continents are calling for a summit to decide our fate."

Another sprinted to catch up. "Five countries are threatening immediate repercussion and eradication of fae on Earth."

Hyacinth's breathing was shallow. Rapid.

I didn't stop. "Do nothing. The queen will give orders presently, once she has time to assess our position and needs."

The fae erupted with questions, and I stopped in my tracks, facing them.

"Do I need to repeat myself?" I asked.

"That's not really a question," Ronan said. "Just stop before you piss Underhill off even more."

The woman squeaked and dropped her orb and it floated away. The picture within was a room full of shouting humans dressed in the rigid clothing important ones seemed to favor.

I resumed walking and shoved into the war room a beat later.

"You okay?" Ronan asked Cinth behind me.

"I'll be okay when I'm not queen," she said, tears in her voice. "What if our babies were human, Ronan? What if next time, whatever despicable act Keefe or Unbalance take, hurts fae?"

"Our children are safe," he soothed us. "We won't let anything happen to them."

"Yet I should be by their sides now, not here," she said sadly. "They'll be afraid. They'll feel what happened, even if they were lucky enough not to witness anyone dying today."

There was a heavy silence, then the queen took a steadying breath, asking, "What do we need to prepare for?"

I waited for Ronan to shut the door behind us, nodding at Kallik, who already sat at the other end of the room with Faolan.

"He'll attack again," I said. "Keefe won't go down quietly. We beat him this time, but the guy has an issue with being controlled. His vanity must've taken a hit, which means he'll have something worse waiting for us next time."

"Perhaps he'll be content with the chaos for a time," Kallik said.

Faolan sighed. "He's created it in droves. That's for

sure."

Chaos had been embodied in a few of the ancient darker gods long since departed from this world. Then again, Gaia liked to chat to me, so presumably those powers weren't as long gone as fae had always supposed.

"You still can't see his path?" I asked, already knowing the answer.

"When the paths ended, I thought we were all meant to die. But they haven't returned. They're shadowed, kind of like when I look at your path or Andas's. Nothing is showing until the last possible second." Kallik's lilac eyes were piercing. "Do you know why that is? Why am I losing my sight?"

I had my suspicions, and I also suspected Andas might have something to say about that. "Keefe is fighting both Andas and me. He tried to kill Unbalance. He keeps switching sides, which would make his path volatile. Perhaps that's why the paths are shadowed."

She said quietly, "And what of the billions of other paths I should be seeing?"

Ronan, in the act of sitting at the table and encouraging Cinth to do the same, didn't hear Kallik's comment. "Is it not a good thing if Keefe is switching sides?" he asked.

I shook my head. "He's not assisting either of us. He's just switching who he attacks. We cannot live in a world without Unbalance, any more than we can live in a world without Balance."

Sigella slipped into the room. "There's always more to a war than what's obvious."

As if on cue, the orbs hovering around the perimeter of the room lit up and turned to face Cinth. They were filled with humans in rigid clothing.

Ronan cursed under his breath and stood abruptly to leave. Who the fuck had okayed this call?

Hyacinth, queen of the fae, did not look particularly confident as she stared back at them. She clutched her hands on the table, and when she asked, "What do I tell them?" I garnered they couldn't yet hear us. From their glares, I was assuming they could definitely *see* the queen.

I put my hand on her shoulder. "I will help you."

She looked at me and a sigh gusted out of her. "You'll help me. How?"

"They need to understand this fight is not against them, but *for* them. That we are on their side," I said.

"I tell them that all the time. They won't believe me. Not after what Keefe has done."

I could've dived into her body to speak through her, the way I had done with the Naga queen. But this wasn't a time for tricks or subterfuge. Not with humans I was bound to protect.

"Then let me speak to them."

"Please do," she said, her relief very apparent. I saw guilt flash over Kallik's face. She'd put Cinth in this position, after all. She hadn't had a choice at the time, but it couldn't be easy for her to see her best friend living a life she hated.

Cinth slid out of the chair, and I moved into her spot. My legs were tired, my body exhausted, my mind spinning. But I wouldn't sit. I stood, straight backed, and probed within for my bond to Andas.

Not for power.

For confidence and reassurance.

I felt him there with me. And Gaia propped me up too. My connection to my helpers strengthened me also. The words would come, they had to. I couldn't be foul-mouthed Silver. I had to be Underhill of the silver tongue.

I blew out a breath and nodded. "I will speak to them now."

The orbs lit with a soft, pale green light.

I dipped my head toward the humans, grounding myself, and then let the words flow. "Leaders of the human realm, I am Underhill. Protector of all realms, mother to all lives."

"Doing a damn poor job of it," snapped a man in a suit, his tie loose.

Anger, loss, grief, revenge. "We moved as quickly as we could against an enemy who sought to destroy human and fae alike. Saving as many of you as I did nearly killed me. And I am one of the most powerful beings in all realms."

A murmur rippled through the orbs.

"You saved us by yourself?" asked another human.

They understood my power now. They understood that they should listen or at least think before speaking. "We portaled fae to as many cities as possible. They saved several of you with their magic, and I worked alongside them to help the rest who were still capable of being saved."

A woman dressed all in purple, a crown on her head, stared at us. "And the fae? What losses did you have from this enemy?"

I could have lied, but I needed to forge a bridge of trust and truth. "We lost many to the water being removed, just as your peoples did. Fewer of our people died when the water was returned, as we have innate magic. In this we can be glad, as if we'd both been incapacitated, we would have shared extinction.

Not that Keefe would've killed all of us. Where would the fun in that be? I had no doubt he would have left a hundred million or so alive to toy with later on.

Another round of murmuring erupted.

The same man who'd first spoken did so again. "Why shouldn't we just bomb you? Why shouldn't we eliminate a threat that has been on our doorstep for years? I said so after that giant declared war on us, and fae have proven time and again that they can't be trusted." He banged his fist on his table. "When do we say enough?"

There were many who agreed with them. What animal wouldn't want to better its survival prospects?

I turned to him. "The threat is not fae. The threat to

human life is from the monsters that would remain even if we were gone. If every fae from every court was destroyed, no one would remain to stop evil from growing. We are what keeps this world in check. We are what *ensures* your survival. Destroy us, and your last line of defense disappears *if* you manage to succeed. Then you will have to face the next monster on your own."

"We could face monsters. We have all the weapons—"

"Hush your fool mouth!" A woman in a deep blue sari held up her hand and glared in the man's direction. "You think monsters respect bullets? Have you not seen what this single monster can do? Stealing every last drop of water from the entire world…This is the time to learn more about fae. We need them more than they need us. *They* weren't the ones drowning. We can fear them, or work with them. And it seems an obvious choice to me."

Her words caused a flurry of people shouting over one another. My connection to them flared, and I used it to silence them.

Some blinked, and the eyes of others bulged. They recognized their silence had been an unnatural one. They felt their smallness.

I said, "I have chosen to protect you all and claim you as creatures of balance. As such, we will continue to fight the monsters and do all we can to keep them from your doorsteps."

The leaders stared at me, and some of their mouths hung open. Perhaps stealing their voices hadn't been the smartest move, and yet I needed them to hear me and hear me well. "The human and fae share this. We exist together or we die together." I leaned forward. "I would prefer that we do not die."

I released my hold on them but no one spoke.

My words had hit the mark.

I snapped my fingers, and the orbs went red.

"Holy shit, that was..." Cinth swallowed hard. "Do you think that was wise?"

Kallik nodded, a soft smile on her face. "They're afraid, Cinth. They were listening. Not all, but enough. Each of them had a brush with death, and that should humble them instead of driving them to unite against us."

"I'd stopped hoping that they'd see sense," Cinth whispered, but hope was plain on her face.

A freezing breeze announced Andas's arrival as he portaled to my side.

Cinth gasped, and Ronan burst back into the room, his hand on his sword pommel.

Andas ignored them—and Kallik, who hadn't reacted in the slightest to his arrival.

"You heard?" I asked him.

A grunt. "That was necessary. They needed an ass kicking. I don't know if humans are capable of holding themselves together, but they'll need to while we deal with...*Keefe.*" He spat out the Trickster's name as if it tasted foul. There was something in the way he said it that tugged at my instincts.

"I take it you feel the humans too?" I asked him.

He threw me a look. "Yeah, thanks for that. I thought I was going to die. Twice."

"Did you vomit everywhere?"

Andas grimaced. "Tied to fucking humans. I was happier without them, even the really fucked-up ones."

Cinth's eyes were as big as saucers as she glanced between us. The stiffness in Kallik's body informed me that she was also struggling. Then again, she'd battled the last Unbalance while tumbling through a never-ending chasm in the Earth. That would naturally leave an impression.

Unbalance and Balance shouldn't be able to exist in the same room. We shouldn't be able to chat. We were oil and water.

Except, because of me and because I'd bound myself to him, we weren't.

And because I'd bound to him, Keefe had received the power to kill millions of creatures. Yet I could stand beside Andas and not be driven to kill him, or to be killed *by* him. I could be Underhill *and* share love with another.

How many would I sacrifice for that? Unease stirred in my gut, probably because the answer to that question was decidedly blurry.

Unbalance held out a hand to me. "Silver, are you ready?"

I said to the others, "Send word to me via Kik if Keefe makes a move. We'll try to form a plan to remove him for good."

Cinth darted a look between me and Andas.

I took his hand, feeling the bite of Unbalance against my skin, no worse than a thorn. Which is how this had all started anyway. "I'm ready."

CHAPTER 16

*Andas took us to a wide yet shallow braided river.

"How long have we got here?" I asked.

He shot me a look, then muttered, "About twenty minutes."

"You can stay longer than that."

"It becomes very uncomfortable."

I thought back. "We were together for longer than twenty minutes in the cave. You were uncomfortable then?"

Andas frowned. "No, I wasn't."

I did a sweep of our surroundings, then perched on a flatish rock. "Tell me. I'll figure it out anyway."

"You know what I know," he muttered. "I can't stand in the same place for long."

But why?

"There must be something more to it." I narrowed my gaze on him. "There must be."

His jaw clenched. "I've wondered if…the fae I'm made from."

"Aaden and Cormac," I supplied. "Those were their names."

"I realize that," he said tightly.

I lifted a shoulder. "Why does it bother you?"

Andas rounded on me. "Because you loved them, and I don't want to know that you've loved any other. I want to possess every part of you, even your past."

I nodded. "I feel the same way."

I'd surprised him, and he lost some of his fury.

He rubbed a hand through his black hair. "Both felt adrift in their own way. Cormac because his family's morals clashed with his own. And Aaden because he never felt like he belonged. I wonder if my inability to stay still derives from that."

Could be. "Do all Unbalances struggle with it?'

"I cannot access the memories of past Unbalances. Just as you cannot access the memories of your mother."

That made sense. "Then we should explore why you can stay in one place longer when with me."

He flashed me a grin. "I had excellent incentive."

My blood warmed at the reminder. Would that mean we had more time to explore each other again. "Or did Gaia put a hiatus on that aspect of your nature as part of her gift?"

"Ask her when she next calls, would you? The uncertainty is fucking annoying."

I bet it was. "How did you get to Keefe?"

"Attacked his daughter."

My stomach lurched. "Is she okay?"

"Alive. Saving her will take it out of him and buy us some time."

Orlaith had chosen her path in this, but I couldn't imagine life without her in it. I still held out hope this was all a giant misunderstanding. "Everyone needs balance. Orlaith is Keefe's weakness."

"And counterpart, I think," Andas said. "I'm unsure how much she's involved in his plans, but she does have a say, or at least is privy to the details." At my look, he added, "I've been watching them."

When I opened my mouth, he said, "No, you can't know how. What did you say about keeping your secrets?"

I bit back a smile, then sobered. "You know more about Keefe than you're letting on. Keep your secrets about your spies, but tell me more about him."

Andas jerked his head. "Let's move first."

We walked through the portal, and I barely took in the vast desert.

I rested back on the cooling sand, and Andas lay next to me.

"His name is Sucellus. Or was. Long, long ago."

"A god?" I whispered. "They still exist among us

then." I'd always assumed that Gaia and her like existed in another realm completely.

"He *was* a god," Andas said, shaking his head. "When his barbs paralyzed me, I was able to glean some information about his past. Once, he was great. Friend to Gaia and the common folk. Farmers and hunters paid homage to him, welcoming his abundance and power of fertility for their crops. But as the millennia passed, their adoration lost its warmth. He turned to his lesser affinity, that of wine. He began to enjoy the power of intoxication, and more of his power was poured into this aspect of himself—stolen away from the powers which created abundance and harvest for all creatures. He strayed too far from his purpose, and an effort to oust Gaia from the almighty throne saw him thwarted and cast out of the ranks of the ancient powers."

"His power was taken." If not, my mother never could have placed him in the prison realm.

Andas nodded. "His magic was reduced to a trickle, and he was left at the mercy of your mother, who had no knowledge of what he'd been."

No, or she never would have sent him to deliver Orry to me. "He knew that the power would come back to him."

Andas glanced at me.

I nodded. "He said as much. He always planned to return."

He hummed. "Perhaps. I can't say. But I saw the moment he regained power."

"Then he *was* given his power to counter us once I bound us together?"

Andas sighed. "Yes. It took two powerful fae males, a tree of life, and a bond to Underhill to create a strong enough vessel for me, but an empty god provided the perfect vessel for other gods and goddesses to fill with the power to balance us."

I exhaled. "Shit. I can't believe he was a fucking god once. What does that make Orlaith? Did you see anything about her?"

"Nearly time to move,' he said. "Orlaith and Keefe aren't blood related. I believe her lifestyle, which embraced many kinds of intoxication, originally called to his nature and lost power. For a short time, they shared a bed, but that side of their relationship changed when she was imprisoned in bat form, and neither of them view the other in a romantic way any longer from what I could see."

My brows shot up. "I hope not. She calls him father."

"That was his alias in the prison realm, but that is how they've come to view each other since imprisonment—as father and daughter. He is as ancient as time itself, remember, and gods and goddesses don't see things the way we might. That aside, the urge to protect and mentor Orlaith has led to respect and love. I'm unsure at what point Keefe decided to plant some of his essence in her and to take some of hers into him, but this has created a bond of sorts between them—a familial one."

I pulled a face. "He put a leech in her?"

Andas cut off. "How did you guess?"

"Your sluagh tried to kill me with leeches." When he blinked, I said, "Sigella mushed them up and made them into tea, don't worry."

He blinked again. "There's no one like you in the world." He looked almost sad as the words left him. "Who would I become without you? I live in fear of losing you."

And I lived in hope of sharing a life together. But then my nature was to hope and believe in light places, and his was to seek out caves and dark corners.

Keefe's nature tended to bring about some messed-up shit, and I'd heard Kik tell mares to call him Neigh Daddy too many times for me to forget. Believe me, I'd tried.

"So he was her customer for a while, then grew to love her and implanted his magic in her. Now he sees her as more of a daughter figure." I sucked in a breath. "If we can burn his magic out of Orlaith, then she might stop being a moron."

Andas didn't say anything, and I could feel through his essence that he, like me, had no idea if that would work. He stared off over the dunes, and I pursed my lips as an idea came to me. Bound as we were, our essences always touched now, but it was just a soft feeling. A constant reminder of where he was and how he fared.

I poured into our connection now. I rested my essence alongside his as if we rested in bed together as an old mated couple might.

He didn't budge his stare from the dunes. "What are you doing now?"

There was a resigned weariness to his voice that startled me to laughter. "I'm glad you've given up on guessing."

His lips quirked. "Your unpredictability will make life interesting."

My heart skipped a beat. He spoke as if we might have a future. I couldn't think past each day, sometimes not past each hour or minute.

Andas stood. "I need to move."

There was no 'we' about it. "Try to stay."

He rolled his shoulders. "It itches, and then it gets worse. Believe me. I don't want to leave."

"So why don't you stay?"

"Because it's not just discomfort. The magic gathers to shun my darkness."

I shifted my focus to the magic under his feet and swore. "Whoa."

He was right. The *realm* was rejecting him. "It's like this in all realms?"

"Yes." His hissed reply spoke of his increasing discomfort. If I hadn't been able to feel the change in the magic, then I would have been able to glean the effect from the quivering of his essence. "Anchor through me. The magic doesn't reject my presence."

Andas blew out a breath, but I felt the press of his essence against mine. I wrapped my magic around his, and his essence stopped shaking.

He tilted his head. "The discomfort is less. Still there, but less."

"Told you there was an answer."

"And will you always stay by my side and wrap your magic around me?" he mocked.

I brushed the sand off my leathers, then rested a hand on his chest and pushed up to kiss his mouth. "Just give me a chance," I whispered to him.

His burning gaze told me everything he felt and all the hope he didn't have. Fine. I could hope hard enough for both of us. He could fear enough for both of us.

"But," I said, lowering, "I see what you mean. We'll figure out a better solution."

Andas battled a smile but lost the war not to chuckle.

"What is it?" I asked.

He shook his head. "Just wondering how I'll survive the force of you."

I had that thought about him daily. "You won't. The humans have changed their tune. An alliance between them and fae is imminent." I smirked. "Sorry about that."

Andas's chuckle turned sinister. He cupped my

cheek and kissed my temple. "I'd expect no less considering you're currently the greater power between us. However, as things stand..."

The exodus of power from my body drew a scream, which arched toward him. My body sagged in the aftermath, and Andas lowered me to the sand, kissing down my neck before tracing his nose up to my jaw. My head lolled and he gripped my chin, drawing my face back to press his mouth against mine. His tongue tasted me.

I glared, and it was Andas's turn to smirk.

"We had a deal," he reminded me.

Strength was returning to me. Strength, not power. I could feel that Andas had turned the tables again. If I'd needed to save a world of humans from drowning now, I wouldn't have had the ability. "*I* bested Keefe."

"Then how was I able to take your power back?" Andas challenged. Something on his face changed, and he focused intently, as if listening to something from very far away. A slow grin spread across his face.

"Do I want to know?" I asked between gritted teeth.

"Probably not. You'll find out soon enough."

Then I wouldn't chase it. "I'll get that power back someday."

Andas lost his grin, and when he extended a hand down to me, I took it. He steadied me while gripping my arms. "I don't doubt it. There is an ebb and flow to such things, but the ebb and flow is usually not so swift, nor...painless."

I heard his unspoken question—

Can you bear that?

I couldn't answer him, and Andas didn't truly expect an answer because how could we know if this would all end in fifty years? How could we say that we wouldn't be trying to kill each other again in a month?

If Keefe hadn't removed us entirely by then.

"Day by day. Suffering by suffering," I told him.

Andas slid his hand down and squeezed my ass.

I slapped his hand away. "I'm still pissed at you. I had plans for that power."

"As do I." Andas kissed the side of my mouth. "The time of darkness is here, my love."

He flung off my magic and was gone in the next breath.

As for me? I'd been immobilized.

My love.

I felt Kik's essence slacken as he moved toward me.

"Ah knuckles," he howled, closing the portal behind him.

The land kelpie had sunk up to his knee joints in sand.

"You look stumped," I told him.

He scowled. "Watch it. I can still hoof you into next week."

"Did you discover something about Keefe?"

"No, you took too long, and I got it in my head that you should be chaperoned around the master of darkness."

I quirked a brow. "You want to chaperone me?"

"And why not?" He tried to draw himself taller, but only sunk further into the sand.

I could think of about one hundred reasons why not. "What advice do you have for me then?"

"Don't give it away. He'll leave you as soon as you do. Trust me."

"Too late. And he didn't."

"He—you did what?" He struggled in earnest, and I watched as he sank lower and lower until sand filled his mouth.

Kik extended his neck and spat the sand out, the rest of his body no longer visible. "I'll shove my hoof so far down his throat that he'll be coughing ponies!"

He continued ranting for a few minutes, but then stopped shit-talking and rolled an eye in my direction. "You just gonna let me keep spitting creative and violent intentions like that? What's got you? Constipated again?

I bit my lip against a smile. Andas had just ripped away the lion's share of our power, and I imagined he was on the way to start wars and spread darkness through the realms. I'd do everything I could to stop that. But…he *loved* me.

I beamed at my friend. "Constipated, yes."

"Then let's get you some prunes. I got your back, kiddo. Climb on because I am literally stuck. I'm gonna need to open a portal underneath us."

A frantic tugging in my chest stole my breath.

"Not to the court," I told him. "The naga are calling."

"On it, kiddo. Are they under attack?"

I couldn't tell. But they weren't the only important thing in that cave. Not by a long shot.

CHAPTER 17

I leaped on Kik's back, and he opened a portal directly beneath us. We fell through and the world turned upside down, twisting and turning as Kik fought to right himself.

"Blinking finking and nod, I can't get feet under me!" he bellowed as we toppled from the height of the treetops.

"You don't have feet," I reminded him.

His answer was lost in the anarchy of our plummeting fall.

I tugged on the surrounding magic, softening the ground beneath us. Kik landed on his side, and expelled a great gust of air, forming one word. "Fudge."

There wasn't time to ask what fudge had to do with anything, but if he hadn't cursed after that landing, I had to wonder if he really had been reborn.

The thought had no sooner flitted through my head than I was off his back and bolting to the naga cave.

The nagas' voices reached me first, hissing and screeching. *Fighting.* They were fighting.

I couldn't get to the interior of the cave fast enough, and when I arrived, the scene before me left me breathless.

The naga surrounded the tree of life, and Keefe stood in the center with the sapling. He looked up at me and smiled. "You're surprised? This tree is as crucial to life as water. I will rule now, Underhill. Good luck with the fall out."

His hand was wrapped around an upper branch of the tree. His knuckles turned white, and I expected him to yank the entire tree out by the roots. Instead, he raised a sword and swung for the 'v' formed by the nexus of the branch and the trunk.

He cut it clean off.

A wail rose from the naga, and several lashed forward at Keefe, their fangs exposed, only for their attacks to slide off him.

He disappeared.

There will be a consequence to his action, Gaia whispered. *Protect your people.*

Fuck me. I'd expect no less at this point.

The tree of life bled where he'd cut it, and the steam curling from the wound warned me all wasn't well. Earth shuddered, but I was already surging forward.

A backlash was coming.

I pulled magic from the earth and rock around us and threw a blanket of woven power over the tree. "Hide, all of you!" I yelled to the naga.

They slithered into the soft sand, all except for the king and the queen that I'd spoken through recently.

"We ssstay." They locked hands and swayed, singing softly. Their words whispered across my skin as the pressure under the blanket of power increased. Smoke poured from the wound in the tree.

I had to stanch it, or we'd all die.

I eased through my own magic to access the space closest to the tree. The heat rolling off the steaming wound blinded me. Lifting my hands, I stretched my fingertips toward the tree and traced around the trunk until I found the cut.

Hot. Angry.

Afraid.

Strange to think of a tree of having emotions, and yet this was the tree of life, so why wouldn't it feel every aspect of life as we did? I thought of Andas, of Kik and Peggy, and of Kallik and Cinth. All those who'd come into my life during these last few months. How much love and understanding had grown between us.

How much strength existed within my family, both chosen and blood.

That was the balance to the anger and fear.

Love. Trust. Understanding.

I lay my hand over the red-hot wound. Pain

slammed through me, ribboning up my arm to my torso. The tree's blood poured over my fingers and set my bones to rattling.

"I will fight for you too," I said through gritted teeth. "You brought them back. You gave me a chance to love, and that's everything in this world."

I clung to the images of those I loved, and how they made me feel. Even Orlaith, when she'd been Orry. I held on to the love I felt for all of them, and then released it through my burning palm.

I didn't know how long I knelt in the sand. My blood mingled with that of the tree, but the pain slowly receded, and my hand cooled but still tingled from tiny bolts of electricity that danced across my palm.

I dared to open my eyes.

The tree had grown, its leaves a simple silver now, rather than a combination of black and silver. I stared, feeling the rightness of what had happened.

Well done, young Underhill. Sacrifice and love are the path to balance against darkness. Love is what you needed to learn. Love for those you protect, and the willingness to make sacrifices to see them safe.

"I thought...I thought I'd been doing that." I whispered, not quite sure how to take my hand off the wound.

Gaia didn't answer, but I took her words to heart and committed them to memory. The tree's longer limbs wrapped around me, gently stroking my arms and face as if acquainting themselves with me. Just as gently, the tree pulled my palm from the wound.

I'd expected pain and a violent burn. The image of the tree of life was etched into my palm, charred black like a new tattoo.

"Thank you," I said in a hushed voice.

"Underhill."

I turned to the naga king. He walked forward, and I lowered my web of magic around the tree so he could draw closer.

He took my hand without a word and brushed his fingers over the black charring. The burn fell away to reveal healed skin. The image of the tree remained, although now it was silver. Unless someone stared at my hand, they wouldn't see it, but I could feel the tree in me, and I would forevermore.

"Bounnnnd to the tree of life," he said. "We will protect it with our livesssss, mother of all."

I wrapped my fingers around his. "You already did."

His forked tongue flicked out once. "Clossse the cave, Mistress of Underhill. Clossse it to all."

Understanding hit me. "You'll be trapped forever."

He swayed. "Ssssafe…we will tunnel below ground, make more cavessssss. Underground riverssss for water and food. Protect the tree."

"The king issss right," the queen whispered from behind him. "We will be ssssafer. The tree will be ssss-safer. It issss an honor to sssserve this tree that isss yoursss."

She bowed her head, her skin glinting like a new coin.

They were right, and yet…I hesitated before speaking. "I honor you above all others. King of the Naga and Gold Queen. I will visit you often, and I thank you."

They bowed their heads and sunk down through the sand to join their tribe.

Alone, feeling bereft at the sacrifice they'd made—and wishing I saw my path as clearly as they saw theirs—I portaled from the cave.

Kik did a double take when I appeared outside. "I thought you couldn't do that from the cave."

"Now I can. The cave and the tree are mine."

I'd claimed the humans, and now the tree of life. The Earth realm was mine. Yes, I could feel balance shift toward me again. More power flowed in my veins. Which meant less would flow through Andas's veins…

I touched the rocks around the cave and felt out every tunnel leading into the place. I closed them off, filling tunnels with solid stone until no ready pathway in existed.

No sunlight for my naga family. My heart ached, but they'd made their choice and sacrifice, as had I, and I felt the rightness of it.

Except…

Trees needed light to thrive.

Keeping my hand on the rock, I used magic to form holes the size of my fist through the rock, creating openings that led all the way to the inner cave. But that wouldn't be enough light for the tree to thrive.

I lined the holes with silver, drawing ore from the earth to coat the sunlit holes, reflecting light to the tree and visiting naga.

That would be enough light and air, and the tree's roots would need to handle the water.

"Now where?" Kik butted me with his head. "I saw that knucklehead Keefe run out of here. The second his foot was outside the cave, he portaled way."

"Any idea where he went? Did you see anything on the other side of his portal?" I already had an idea, but I needed it confirmed.

My connection to the tree of life hummed within me, a power that rivalled the strength I'd had after bonding to Andas and claiming a half-share of his power for a time.

"The scale realm." Kik grimaced. "But you're locked out of there, kiddo. I know it. *You* know it."

I smirked. "I don't think I am."

Kik's eyes went wide. "What?"

I rolled my hand, my magic curling around me more strongly than ever before. Balance tugged at my feet, and my path was suddenly as clear as the naga's had been.

"Take me to Peggy. I need to speak to her and Sigella. They're together." I could have portaled us both there, but something warned to conserve my power.

Kik dropped lowered to one knee, allowing me to

climb on his back. "You got it. Off to see the most beautiful mare in all the realms."

I smiled, even as fresh fear battered at the hope building inside of me. What if I was wrong? What if I fucked everything up? Andas and I were extraordinarily strong, but we were both magical creatures. Keefe and Gaia…they were magic *itself*.

"Breathe, kid," Kik said. "I can feel the tension in your butt cheeks. You're grabbing at my back hairs."

I laughed and wrapped my fingers in his mane as he portaled us from the resting place of the tree of life to the Alaskan court.

He trotted through the courtyard, and a pent-up breath left me when we didn't arrive to find dying fae or drowning humans. My last visits hadn't been the most relaxing.

The sound of wings thumped through the air, and Peggy landed behind us soon afterward. Sigella on her back.

My brows rose. That was an unexpected sight. Had Sigella bested her somehow? Peggy didn't allow just anyone to ride her, and while the two were mostly civil enough with each other, I'd never perceived any friendliness between them.

"That was an excellent idea." Peggy tipped her head at the ancient fae.

"Couldn't have done it without your help," Sigella gave Peggy a deep curtsy.

My brows rose further.

They were mocking each other. I squinted at them. No, they were *serious.*

I forced my eyebrows down from their shocked heights in my hairline. "Are they drunk?" I muttered to Kik under my breath.

But he looked as confused as me.

"What are you two up to?" Kik grumbled. "Having all these smart, beautiful females around makes me nervous."

Peggy snorted. "Your flattery improves every day, my love. You need only mention that I am the most beautiful and smart of all to perfect the art."

I slid from Kik's back. "Sigella, I need your thoughts on a matter. And Peggy, don't go far, I believe I'll need your help next."

Peggy winked at me. "At your service, Underhill."

I strode across the courtyard a way, and Sigella fell into step beside me.

"What is it?" she asked.

"How do I kill Keefe?"

Her silence didn't scream encouragement. "I don't believe you can. The greater forces made him who he is for a reason. Without eliminating the reason—which I gather you wouldn't be willing to do—then Keefe must remain. In some capacity."

In some capacity. I hadn't considered that.

"Gaia tends to these realms, but what of the other gods?" I asked, then dared to add, "Like Lugh?"

She snorted. "How lovely if he was living one thousand tortures for locking me in a fucking harp. Gods don't die, though, they sleep. Or they choose to let their lives fade to almost nothing. That's as close to death as they can get. Keefe has chosen violence instead, though that is not what he was created for."

"Power," I mused as Peggy and Kik joined us. "He wants power and control." That was very clear by now. "So if he can't be killed, he could be imprisoned again. Or put to sleep."

Sigella rolled her wrist to draw a teacup from the once-empty air. She lifted it to her lips. "The old gods need to choose to fade. He won't make that decision willingly this time. I suspect he did agree to his last imprisonment willingly."

I sucked in a breath. "Because of Orlaith."

"Likely." She sipped at her tea, and I stared at the cup.

I swallowed, recalling the leech tea she'd once forced me to drink. "Would one of your teas incapacitate him?"

Her gaze sharpened. "My teas can do anything. But, again, he would need to drink of his own free will."

My plans shifted and adjusted with her words like currents in the ocean. "Then I would have you make that tea, Sigella. If I can't kill him, he must be subdued."

"Silver." The queen's voice rang out from across the courtyard.

Cinth ran toward me, her hair a mess and her skirts covered in flour and sauces.

"What is it?" I asked, and the question felt repetitive. If my life was always to move from one crisis to the next, perhaps I could do away with that question altogether.

A sheen of sweat coated her pale face. "The humans... While some are grateful for our help, others are coming to attack us. Now. They said a fae with dark hair informed them that we are planning to weaken the humans and take control of this realm for good."

I knew it was him before she said "Andas."

"I'll go to him now."

"Why are you so calm?" she demanded. "Don't you care?"

I considered that. "Yes, of course I care. But the realms are in a state of Unbalance, therefore darkness creeps in more readily than the opposite."

I could tell Queen Hyacinth did not understand that one bit.

"The damage is done," she said, bursting into tears. "I've been baking all morning, trying to find a solution. There isn't one."

I didn't understand why baking would help her find a solution. It certainly wouldn't protect her people from weapons, but I sensed it would be an unwelcome question. "What was your last communication from the humans?"

"They're calling for me to step down. Demanding a new queen take my place. The fae are too loyal to say so, but I can tell they're losing faith in me. They just love my cooking too much to anger me." She bowed her head, and I placed a hand on her shoulder.

Knowledge buzzed to life within me.

The leadership would change. And it would be an opportunity for balance.

I said, "You've been an amazing queen, Hyacinth. You were foisted into this position by powers beyond anyone's control. I trust you. I know you've only ever wanted to do your best in a situation you hated from outset to close."

Her sob echoed through the courtyard, and the few lurking fae turned to look. I pushed my power in their directions until the courtyard was clear.

"But I don't trust myself," Cinth said. "I'm a queen for fair times and simple challenges. This is so far beyond me, Silver. I'm done. I can't do it any longer."

I looked past her to find Kallik watching us, cloaked as the Oracle.

"What does the Oracle see?"

My sister left the shadows of the small doorway into the palace that the human servants tended to use. "The pathways are closing to me, Underhill. I had expected to remain Oracle for the rest of my existence, but the power is fading.

The paths hadn't closed off for me...

"The world is changing because of the new bond between myself and Andas," I said. "Perhaps your sight will come back in time, daughter of a king. Or perhaps the power of the Oracle has faded so that you might claim the title you were born to have."

Kallik's breath caught. "You can't be serious. The title was meant for *you*."

"I am Underhill. I cannot be the Queen of the Fae. If you are not an Oracle, then you must take up this mantle. Hyacinth has bridged the gap beautifully. Now it's her turn to live as she would choose."

Kallik didn't answer. She'd never wanted to be Oracle. She'd never expected to be queen. Just as she and Faolan had found their footing in the realms, she was about to make a second sacrifice for the good of all fae.

And she'd do it. Because she *was* the daughter of a king—and queen—and she'd been chosen by my mother to rule. I was choosing the same.

Cinth started to cry. "Thank you, Underhill."

Her words were barely intelligible. She *was* a queen for fairer times of beauty and light, of beetroot tickles and bruadar. Not a queen made for warfare and battles. Not a queen created in the fires of sacrifice and death so that others might live.

Kallik was that queen. I tipped my head toward my sister. "I will not force you. But you have seen much that no other queen has seen in your time as Oracle. There was a reason for that. There was a reason you fought Unbalance. Your time to hide has come to an end, my sister. I hope you feel ready now, as you never did upon accepting the mantle of Oracle."

I *felt* my sister's sorrow as she fell to one knee. "I will do as you bid and trust in your judgement. There is none other for this task, I know. Though I will lose some freedoms, I'll gain others. The freedom to speak without fear of altering the future. There's joy to be had in that."

She lifted her lilac gaze to mine as she slid her hood back to reveal her long, dark hair.

I struggled to swallow the lump in my throat. "We will work together, as Underhill and the Queen of the Fae always should have."

The Oracle had served her purpose.

I touched the hundreds of magics in the palace and commanded all creatures into the courtyard. Fae started to exit the palace. They slowed and started whispering at the sight of Kallik kneeling before me, and of Hyacinth behind me, joy and relief etched onto her face.

The whisper was taken up, swelling with shock.

Kallik. Daughter of King Aleksander. Kallik. Returned. Alive.

Cinth started to leave.

I glanced back. "She will need you still, Hyacinth. You know that?"

Her eyes overflowed with tears. "I will always be there for my friend. She is the sister of my heart, and I don't blame her at all for the life I chose to lead until this moment. It could not have been any other way."

Their friendship was unlike any other I'd witnessed.

I turned to the gathered fae.

"Kallik sacrificed much to serve my mother as Oracle." My voice boomed, silencing all. "Now, she returns in this time of need to the position for which she was born. She is Queen Kallik of All Fae, and she has the blessing and respect of Underhill."

That was the best I could do for her. As terrible as it was that the humans were at our doorstep, the bigger threat was still Keefe and the piece of the tree of life he had stolen.

The fae crowded toward Kallik, and I moved back, heading out of the palace gates. Kallik would navigate this, of that I had no doubt.

"That worked out well. I was sick of the cook's blubbering."

I slid a glance at the ancient fae beside me. "Sigella, will you brew the tea for Keefe?"

"It will take me a few hours, but yes. I'll prepare it gladly."

"I'll return to the palace for the tea then." I found Peggy amidst the crowd and sought out and held her gaze.

She nodded, indicating she would be waiting for me too.

I closed my eyes and followed my connection to Andas, feeling him far across the world, creating rampant chaos and darkness in the humans. They were easy marks, especially now.

I sighed. Then, creating a portal, I stepped through it and into absolute tumult of a camp of human men.

Soldiers.

More than a few lifted their puny weapons to me. I could have used my power to blast their weapons into the dirt or shatter the humans like glass, but I waited until the fear left their postures and spoke one word.

"Andas."

My heart fluttered as Unbalance walked between the men, dressed in a uniform that matched theirs. He flicked his hands in their direction. "Come to see my handiwork?"

I lifted my chin. "I'd have thought you'd outgrown the need to dress up and play with dolls."

"Your sarcasm falls short, my Underhill. I see the quickness of your breaths and the pressing of your thighs. Perhaps I should wear this uniform more often."

He wasn't wrong. I pursed my lips. "Perhaps you should. I have a way to stop Keefe."

"Do you?" His mocking tone made the other men laugh, as if they knew what was going on. As if their minds were his.

I pulled a face. "Do you need to control them like that? They're filled with darkness. They'd follow you anyway."

Andas lifted a shoulder, and the soldiers did the same. "You have the luxury of obeying your power with abandon. Mine is a beast that must be controlled.

If I do not siphon it in small ways, then it will control me in large ways."

Before I could open my mouth to ask if he enjoyed it, Andas cut me off. "Be sure you want an answer to that question. I am what I am, and that cannot change."

My heart mourned the loss of the soldiers, but I let their suffering flow over me because there was no other option in this moment, and—in truth—I'd seen the reality of what my life with Andas would be. Only time would convince me that I could bear it.

I did my best to ignore them, asking, "What if there was a way to allow you to stay in one place?"

His laugh slid from his face. "You…it's impossible. You can't always stay with me. I can't keep anchoring through your essence."

My turn to laugh. "People keep saying that word to me, and yet here we are. Me, doing the fucking impossible yet again. The answer was simple, really."

I waited.

Yes, I was going to make him grovel.

"And what's the answer?" he said from between clenched teeth.

My lips curved. "What will you give me if I tell you?"

He considered that. "Much."

If we were speaking as Balance and Unbalance, I might have given him a harder negotiation, but I'd come here as Silver. I lost my smirk and said softly, "This one is for free. Because I want you to be happy and able to rest. The reason you can stay in one place when anchored to my essence is because I have always been anchored to my home. Recently, though, my anchor shifted from Underhill to Earth, as did my power. I feel the need to reside here now, and it occurred to me in that shift that you don't have a home. Unbalance has never had a home, if I'm guessing right. I have a way to ground you to a realm. Underhill will become your own, and in this way, your essence might rest and settle."

The human soldiers reflected Andas's slack-faced shock.

"You…" His voice hitched and he tried again. "You would give me a realm? You'd give me *Underhill*. Why would you do that?"

While I'd feared that my power—and that of all fae—was tied to Underhill, and that we would all slowly weaken, I now knew that wasn't the case. Claiming the humans was the final part of the shift in me, and Earth was my new anchor and home. My creatures wouldn't be harmed by any changes to Underhill, or the changes to Earth that would inevitably happen over decades in response to my power.

In fact, I had a feeling that in a few hundred years, Earth would appear a great deal like Underhill used to. Maybe I wouldn't tell the human leaders that.

In short, I had no need of the old Underhill, and no fear about releasing it to Andas.

Along with all that, there was another reason as large as the rest. "Because I love you too."

CHAPTER 18

"Keefe doesn't do anything without reason," I said to Andas. "He's a trickster, not a fool."

Andas had set the human soldiers loose in every direction, and I tried not to consider what they'd been ordered do. Balance tugged gently at my feet, urging me to go rather than stay. Stopping Keefe would affect the balance more than intervening here.

Andas was watching me when I managed to tear my focus from the soldiers of darkness.

"You won't act?" he asked.

"Not in this."

"You said Keefe doesn't do anything without reason…He took a cutting from the tree of life."

I nodded. "And why would he do that? The tree of life is what anchored me to Earth. Keefe has already claimed the prison realm, but the scale realm eludes him."

"You believe he'll use the cutting to attempt to anchor a second realm to him." Andas's gaze met mine. "You'd have me use that cutting to anchor to Underhill."

"Yes, but you'll need to change the name. I'm Underhill, and I'm going to call Earth that in time."

The corner of his mouth quirked. "Deal. Plan to get the cutting?" He barely got the question out before he started laughing.

I narrowed my eyes. "What?"

"I just realized that I asked *you* what the plan was."

Scowling, I said, "I can plan."

He tilted my chin. "You could. But the plan wouldn't work, and you'd end up doing something else. So you've learned not to waste time on planning at all."

Couldn't argue with that.

I stole a kiss from him. While it wasn't nearly enough, it was far better than the alternative of nothing. "Let's go."

"Where?"

"To grab a cup of tea." I walked a short distance before turning. "Put on a disguise, please. The court fae will explode and get glitter everywhere."

Andas cocked a brow, then I watched as his features morphed into Aaden's face.

"You have a messed-up sense of humor," I informed him. "Someone else. *Not* Cormac."

He grinned, then his black hair burned to orange, powerful muscle turned lean, and he grew taller.

"That will suffice." I dragged us through a portal to Sigella's side. She was in the palace gardens where we'd first said goodbye after I'd finally freed her. She'd planned to explore and enjoy her freedom.

She hadn't gotten far with that.

"Not done yet," she snapped.

I grimaced and retreated a distance with Andas, who watched her stirring and mashing intensely. Sigella was flashing between her prim form and her more savage form. A chunk of flesh shot out from under her mortar and splatted on the manicured tree beside her. Something wiggled under her palm before she shoved it in her mouth, then spat the chewed remains onto the grass, only to scoop the pulp up again, dirt and all, then add it into the teapot.

"To be clear, *Keefe* will drink this tea, correct?" Andas muttered.

"I'm almost certain."

I felt his gaze on me, but I couldn't give him more reassurance than that.

His focus shifted upward, and a second later, a rumbling shook the very air. A long and thin object fell from the bottom of a human plane. It shot against the palace barriers, and I gasped at the ball of fire and smoke. A series of the same weapons exploded against the barrier, and there was a shattering like glass as the barriers gave way.

How strong were these weapons? They were already through.

I drew up my magic to create new barriers.

"Stop," savage Sigella snapped in my face as she gripped my throat. "Not your place now. Look inside."

Andas drew his magic hard and fast, but I lifted a hand to stop his attack on my helpmate.

Deciphering the carnage of tendrils surrounding the palace took a moment, but I could see that while hundreds of essences were tangled in the fate of the Alaskan Court, I wasn't. I couldn't be.

The humans were attacking my fae creatures.

And yet...

Humans were also my creatures now.

As a mother, how did I decide which of my children should be favored? The answer was that I could favor neither. I could simply direct them away from darkness where possible and hope better times waited ahead. Sigella was right to intervene.

"You're right," I told her.

She snapped her teeth in my face, then retreated to her tea making.

Andas released his power. "You allow your henchmen too much leeway. I would not tolerate that."

Maybe that was why he only had two baby henchmen on his side, but I didn't tell him that as another plane moved in overhead.

"No," I whispered. "Get a new barrier up."

There were at least thirty planes in the sky.

Beside me, Andas breathed in the heady rush of power he'd be receiving from the dark acts of the humans, but I was focused on the lines of uniformed fae appearing from within the palace. And at the head of their ranks—my sister and Faolan.

They held hands, combining their magic into a bomb of their own. I jerked forward a step with Andas as they released it.

The plane exploded.

I sucked in a breath, and the ebb and flow of power between me and Andas was almost as startling as the confirmation that the humans had made their decision to go to war against fae. With each attack from the humans' planes, I grew weaker as darkness rooted in them. But with every plane that exploded, strength returned to me as dark acts were prevented and their vessels destroyed. Had my mother known that such a give and take of power existed between her and the previous Unbalance?

"They can't have truly known," Andas said, answering my thoughts. "Balance and Unbalance have never been bound as we are."

Perhaps so, but my mind was occupied with how constantly the state of power would change between us, and how we would ever manage to navigate that and not hate each other in time.

More planes.

More fae.

More planes exploding. More bombs hitting the palace.

Kallik would win this round for me, and Andas clearly knew it as well as I did. Balance would emerge the victor today.

"Nearly there?" I asked Sigella.

When I looked at her, she was sitting at a small breakfast table that hadn't been there before, sipping tea and watching the battle between fae and humans.

"Yes, it's ready." She hesitated, then pushed a teapot forward.

I walked over but didn't pick up the pot. "Is it Keefe or the act that makes you hesitate?"

"The act." She took a breath. "I have felt how it is to be trapped in a place by men. Several times now. To do that to another…" She took another, larger breath. "Feels incredible. I wish I could pour the tea down his throat myself."

Right. No remorse or guilt then.

I picked up the pot. "You can spend a few hours by his side gloating once the deed is done."

"I anticipate it." Sigella flashed briefly to her more savage persona. "I will eat his soul for supper." She flashed back to her normal form and didn't add anything more.

I cleared my throat. "Great. See you later."

I'd connected that when Sigella felt particularly bloodthirsty, her savage nature was more likely to appear. That version of her was someone to avoid.

Beyond that, I still knew little about Sigella's powers or where they came from. I also expected that centuries would go by and I'd still know little. Sigella was too smart to make her power easy to figure out.

Once we'd left the garden and Sigella's earshot, Andas said, "A little unpredictable, but I'd love to get hold of that one."

"She's mine. You got the one with a skull horse and lethal corset."

"Looked the part, but she was limited. The hunger distracted her."

Peggy stood with Kik under the tree where they'd rested together when I saw Kik's death. His first death.

"It's time?" she asked.

I frowned at her essence as she moved forward to meet me, and then my heart leaped into my throat.

She was with foal.

I glanced at Kik. My best friend would be a father. Peggy, a mother.

And their foal...

Andas's shallow breaths confirmed he'd spotted the same path for him—darkness and a long, long life.

But Andas wouldn't ride the foal, and the identity of its rider remained shrouded.

"Underhill?" Peggy said, and I gathered it wasn't the first time she'd called to me.

I forced a smile. "It's time. You mentioned once that Pegasai limit their riders because their riders become family. You can sense my distress. Does that include future stress?"

"I can sense what will aid in your overall sense of wellness."

"Now or in the moment?"

"At each turn," she answered.

I nodded. "I thought so. What I must navigate next is complex. I'll need your aid."

Peggy drew her wings tighter. "Wellness for you might not mean wellness for others. In some situations, you might choose personal suffering to accommodate the wellbeing of those you love. This is why I rarely tell you what I sense."

"Send a pulse through our connection whenever you sense happiness for me," I told her. "I will decide the rest, and I understand what you say of suffering."

Andas stiffened beside me but didn't venture a comment.

I took his hand. "Let's go. Once you have the cutting, the wound will require your essence. And we must plant it in your realm without delay."

"His realm?" Kik asked.

"Earth is mine now," I told him. "What was Underhill will become the home of darkness."

"Now that's a renovation," he replied.

Peggy snorted, then lowered so I could climb onto her back. She didn't stay lowered for Andas, and he didn't seem to have expected it.

I nestled between her wings, gripping the teapot that I hoped would make a god sleep.

"You're sure about this?" Andas said, his dark eyes wary and...scared.

For me.

For us.

We both knew this was liable to explode in our faces.

I opened to an essence in the prison realm. Orlaith had helped Sigella while also making it clear her loyalty was to Keefe...though the proof that her essence was still open to me seemed to contradict her declaration.

I touched her essence to Peggy's. Andas was already attached to me.

Peggy sent a pang of her power into me. "I see a future with Orlaith that benefits both of you but the purity of your friendship will never return."

Vague...Hopeful. Hurtful.

"Hold on," I said to Peggy and Andas. "This could hurt. I've never done it before."

"Fuck," Andas mumbled.

I'd entered Sigella's essence to take over her body and open a portal, and I'd invited the naga king into my body also, but I'd never created a portal inside of someone's essence to physically move through a person. What could go wrong?

I seized Orlaith's essence and pushed myself, Andas, *and* Peggy inside of it. I'd only have seconds. One being was not meant to hold so many, especially not Balance,

Unbalance, and a Pegasus. Plus a half-kelpie and half-pegasus foal.

I opened a portal in her essence to the scale realm, then forced our bodies through the other side.

Toward a dangerous being more powerful than myself.

I stumbled into the scale realm and managed to steady myself against Peggy.

Andas glanced at me and exhaled in a way that suggested he'd doubted my ability and was quite shaken.

Chuckling sounded, and I blinked through the spinning in my head to focus on Keefe sitting on a jutting rock, swinging his legs. Orlaith rested unconscious in his arms, overwhelmed by having Balance, Unbalance, and a Pegasus forced through a portal within her. Her essence was all over the place, obliterated. I'd taken too long to move us through, but she was salvageable yet.

Andas circled away from me and Peggy.

Keefe kept us both in his gleeful sights, amusement putting a wry twist on his lips. "I wondered when you would team up. How convenient for me."

I hadn't been sure how I'd convince Keefe to drink Sigella's tea. But from the way he cradled Orlaith in his arms…even though he was chuckling and smiling…

What had worked for Gaia could surely work again. His glee could just be a show, but Orlaith's obliterated essence might work in our favor.

I tightened my hold on the connection that still

existed between me and Orlaith. I drew all one million specks of her essence into my grip.

Then, ignoring the pleading of my heart, I began to strangle her essence.

Orlaith thrashed in Keefe's arms, foam appearing at her mouth.

Keefe stopped chuckling.

"I hold her existence in my hands," I told him, though he already knew.

Andas stopped opposite me and crossed his arms. "I suggest you listen to her. She'll hound you until you do."

Yes, I fucking would.

I held up the teapot. "Let's have a drink."

"Wine," Keefe said on a breathless exhale. "Sigella's wine."

Huh. I'd missed that.

Then again, I supposed tea wouldn't have appealed to the god of intoxication.

CHAPTER 19

*K*eefe's focus shifted from me to Andas and back again, then to the tea pot I held, and finally to Orlaith in his arms.

The dark power that was Andas rippled around Keefe before he could move and wrapped both Trickster and Traitor inside, binding them tight. But that wasn't enough to keep Keefe in place while we convinced him to drink Sigella's wine.

I opened myself to Andas, and he drew on my power—silver to offset his darkness. He wove my power around them both, too, and the flex of his hands as he tossed it like a thick rope had my heart fluttering.

Shaking myself, I adjusted my firm hold on Orlaith's essence. Seeing her as she had the potential to be without darkness—smart, feisty, and determined. Loyal, yes. But only when her humanity had been stripped away did her steely core of loyalty shine. I studied how her essence sparkled and glittered against my skin. She'd clung to me in part because I had power, or at least she'd believed I had power. Maybe she'd known all along that I'd become Underhill.

That thought hurt more than I wanted to admit.

But I did understand that as a bat, Orlaith had been different. She hadn't been able to hold the darkness that had earned her a spot in the prison realm, in a similar way to how Aaden and Cormac couldn't have held the power of Unbalance alone. So maybe everything I'd shared with Orlaith had been true. Perhaps I could mourn the loss of my bat friend while knowing that Orlaith had never wanted to become this version of herself again either.

I pinned Orlaith's essence to the scale realm and to me, so she couldn't float away and escape.

Keefe flexed against the magical rope that Andas had tossed over him. I expected him to fight, or to truly lose his mind and batter abuse at us. There was no escaping our combined power, and we could all see that. Now he'd be forced to listen.

All he did was let out a low groan, without so much as *trying* to break a sweat. "Damn...you guys got me good. In all my years, and there have been a great many of those, I've never seen Unbalance and Balance work together. You could take on Gaia herself."

I rolled my eyes. "We have no issue with Gaia. She's not the pain in our asses."

Keefe laughed, but the sound was hollow. "I

thought…No, it does not matter what I thought. I see that I cannot loop my way out of this path. I thought this day would end differently."

I'd noticed how he circled his pathways into a maze before. If he couldn't do that now, then Keefe must really be trapped. I was just surprised he'd accepted it so easily. Which made me feel this was yet another trap.

"And that is?" Andas growled. "Dead, I hope?"

"I would be as good as dead if I were stupid enough to drink *that* down," Keefe stroked Orlaith's face gently. "Sigella's wine…I would never wake from its power. She made it strong enough for Lugh himself to sleep."

I narrowed my gaze. "So you're just…giving up."

Keefe looked at me, and behind his drunken facade, I saw the god Sucellus peering back at me. Calculating. Careful.

"Give up?" he mused, still stroking Orlaith's head. If that wasn't a sign of balance working its magic, then I didn't know what was. As invincible as Keefe had seemed, he'd had a weakness. We all did.

"Depends," Keefe said after a moment. "Can you stand here forever? I can simply outwait you."

Andas flexed, and the magic we'd combined bore down on Keefe, who just smiled.

"You can hold me here; but you can't kill me," he said. "We've already learned that, haven't we? And Silver will never kill her friend, her one true friend whom she's already saved so many times, will she?

Because what if Orlaith realizes the error of her ways? What if the darkness in her recedes?" Keefe rolled his head from side to side, the rest of his body trapped, then laughed. "So. Now what?"

Two images came into view, next to Orlaith's limp body. One of the bat Orry floating in the air, and one of Orlaith the woman. No one else seemed to notice the images but me.

Her voice whispered through her essence and into me. *It wasn't like that, Silver. I love you still, as a friend and as my family. You see both sides of me, as no one else ever has, not even my father. But I am, and will always be, bound to traverse between light and dark. That was who I was before, under your mother's rule. It is who I am now, under your rule. It's Gaia's bidding. The bat...those were the best parts of me, and I am glad you saw those pieces first. Maybe you, unlike your mother, will choose to see something different in those creatures who walk between Balance and Unbalance. I have a purpose. I know it.*

I frowned, wishing I could read her better. Like any creature, she'd do anything to save herself—I'd seen that as fucking clear as day. The rest though...the part about walking between Balance and Unbalance and having a purpose...

She hadn't intended the meaning to be literal. She was saying that good people could still do dark things and hold onto the good in them. She was saying that life wasn't as clear as light and dark.

But I found my mind dwelling on what she'd *literally* said.

Keefe sighed again, drawing my attention from Orlaith. "A moment is all I ask, then. Bring her back so I can say my goodbye."

"You think we're fools. That we'd believe you'd do as we command for a simple goodbye?" Andas snorted. His power wove tighter with mine, holding Keefe in place, though the old god hadn't so much as flexed his neck muscles. "There will be no last-minute escapes this time, Sucellus."

Something tugged at me.

I'd said goodbye to my heart not once, but three times. Once for Cormac. Once for Aaden, and again when I'd realized they'd become Andas forevermore. While I'd gained from those goodbyes, I'd still lost hope that I'd ever have my men back as they were. What would I have given to have been able to say a final farewell, or to have touched them one last time?

Anything.

Everything.

My heart constricted, and I struggled to breathe around the emotions swelling inside me. Sadness, pain, and grief were chief amongst them. I might not fully understand, Keefe and Orlaith's bond, but they were tied together. By choice, and by bonds they'd woven themselves. There was great power in choice and intention when it came to love.

"You can say goodbye," I said.

Andas whipped to look at me. "You can't be serious. They'll try to escape. Right now he isn't fighting, and do you know why? Because our power is unstoppable when combined, Silver. Even for a god."

I stared hard at him, needing Andas to understand there was more to what I was doing. We needed to sort out some kind of hand signal system. "I know what it's like to wish for one last touch from the one you love, and then to have that taken from you."

Andas's eyes locked on mine, and I saw a softening at the edges. Would anyone else have spotted the way his face smoothed? I didn't think so. I loved him, for all that he was, but I'd been through a fuck ton of dragon shit to get to this point.

He nodded.

He trusted me, and that felt monumental. Because *it was*. Unbalance trusted Balance, and she trusted him right back. Maybe that wouldn't prove enough to keep us at peace with each other, but I'd remember his nod for the rest of my days.

Keefe sighed, and I turned as he spoke, a careful smile on his face. "As always, your kindness and compassion—"

My voice was cold. "I'm no fool. Though I know you think I am."

Keefe believed he knew what I was capable of, and what I would and wouldn't do. Which was foolish because even I didn't know my limits any longer.

But I couldn't see pain—even in Keefe and Orlaith

—and not try to restore harmony. That was the curse of my power, and the curse of being Underhill.

Even so. It didn't mean I'd be easily walked over.

I kept staring at Orlaith's limp body and the vision of the woman and bat hovering over her. The vision was her very life waiting on my next choice. Her essence clung to my skin, as if she intended to soothe me regardless of what choice I made.

Or soothe me into lowering my guard and letting her trick me once more. Her body twitched,

and I saw her eyelids lift as she peeked at me from Keefe's arms.

Everything I'd pushed down since Orlaith betrayed me burst to the fore.

So much for letting compassion lead the way. Snarling, I tightened my hand on her essence, bearing down on it without mercy to take her to the brink of extinction. Her body bucked, and her eyes fluttered. For *real* this time.

"You…can never be trusted again, Orlaith," I hissed. "It's best for you to be gone. Better to keep the memories of you than to make new memories of your treachery and deceit. I will say the last goodbye, to a friend who never was."

I drew myself together and kept my eyes on Orlaith as I plucked away one droplet of her essence at a time. I let all my hurt and fury and shock guide my hands.

Her body began to fade in Keefe's arms.

Tears streamed over my cheeks as I let my heart

break at last. Let it be the last time I'd ever see the friend whom I'd thought would be with me through so many of life's adventures.

"Goodbye, Orlaith," I said, and lifted my hands to disperse the last of her into the world. "May you be reborn into a gentler path."

I paused, however, at a soft nudge in my back. *Peggy*, I realized, and the thought was enough to interrupt my rage.

She was letting me know this might not be in my best interest. My hurt heart definitely thought Peggy was wrong, but my heart was just one part of me.

"Don't!" Keefe shouted. "Don't! Please, she is all I have left."

But could I leave her alive, knowing she had such power over me, knowing that my heart would always want to protect her, even when I shouldn't? The answer was no. Her image slid away as I drove the pieces of her further apart, plucking them from her physical body. "I am the Underhill that my mother was," I growled. "I *will* make the hard choices—the ones that cause suffering, if it is the right thing to do."

I was as strong as my mother had been.

Keefe tightened his hold on Orlaith's limp body. "I…I can see that, Underhill. I deeply regret that I didn't see that quality in you before now."

I raised an eyebrow, holding the last of Orlaith's intact essence in my hands. "Then you have a choice to make."

"I will drink." The words slid out of him on a great exhale. "I will drink the wine. That's what you want, yes? To put me from your minds for the rest of forever? To bind me to the uselessness and permanence of sleep."

Well, if he was going to offer.

I was shocked that he'd sacrifice himself for Orlaith. Shocked, but gratified, because this was the reaction I'd needed from him.

Andas took the teapot full of wine and produced a goblet, creating the vessel out of thin air as Sigella did with her teacups.

"You drink of your own accord," Andas said as he poured the goblet so full the dark red wine spilled over the edge. "Every last fucking drop."

I didn't trust Keefe, not one bit. I stepped forward to grab Orlaith's hand and pull her from his lap. I could have used magic, though I was occupied with containing Orlaith's essence. Besides, there was some satisfaction in seeing the back of her skirts drag in the mud.

I could almost hear her sniff at me in irritation.

Slowly, ever so slowly, I threaded her essence back together and carefully lowered it into her body. The soul of who she was felt...not greasy, not dark, but exactly what I'd expect a trickster to feel like. Surprising, she felt surprising. Like every time I looked at her, she was someone slightly different, playing the part she thought I wanted or needed. Ultimately, she wanted power. Because in the darkest part of her life, she'd had none, and she'd sworn to herself that she'd never be in that position again.

Keefe cared far more about Orlaith than she did about him, if I'd guessed right, but she was smart enough to never let him discover it.

With one last push, I shoved the last of her into her body and sent a spark of lightning from my fingertips to her heart.

Orlaith jerked and sat up, gasping. "What...what happened?"

Keefe sighed. "You led them right to us, my Orlaith. Your connection to Silver goes between your hearts, so she followed that path as only she could have. It gives her much power over you. You weren't supposed to love her, Orlaith."

"But I did," she replied to him. "And I do in the capacity I still can."

My jaw ticked as I stared down at Orlaith. I did not want her to know how much it pained me to see her as an enemy, battling me instead of standing at my side.

Orlaith's eyes were wide and watery. "And you didn't kill me?"

"Almost." I bit the word out. "Keefe is right. We are bound. Things are more complicated now you have returned to this form, but there was a love that was family found and chosen when you were a bat. We did share friendship then. What we share now will be different, but I do not believe we are done with each other yet."

Her throat bobbed, and she lowered her head, a sob ripping through her. "I cannot help what I am, Silver. Any more than you can throw down the mantle of Underhill, I hold the title of Traitor, do I not? That is my calling in this life, and the next, much as it is my father's title to trick."

I hated how much my heart ached with her words—understanding and sadness were a terrible beast to deal with when I needed to be strong. "Keefe. We're done with this. Say your goodbye."

He stood as if to move toward Orlaith.

"No," I said. "You can see her. You can hear her voice. It's more than I was given. Take the gift you don't deserve."

Keefe swallowed, staring at Orlaith. "You'll be fine; I've taught you well. I was never meant to find a daughter. You were a surprise, even to me. The most wonderful surprise."

Orlaith trembled, her eyes locked on him. "Thank you for becoming my father. For showing me my strength."

Was I the only one who'd forgotten their history? I glanced at Andas, whose face was screwed up.

Not the only one.

I waited, but that was all they were going to say apparently. I'd have made an endless speech if it had meant gaining one more second with those I loved. "One more thing, Keefe. Where's the cutting?"

Keefe smiled then; a slow-burning smile that made me want to smash his face in. "So you figured that out too. My, but I *did* underestimate the pair of you. You have underestimated me as well. Now you want two things from me, but only offer one in return. Which is it? Do you wish me to drink the wine or give you the sapling cutting for Orlaith's life?"

Another time I would have fought like a mountain cat, trying to secure both, but a soft nudge in the middle of my back turned me toward Peggy, who stood behind me. What was she telling me with her nudge this time? Which was the better choice?

Her gentle eyes were dark and sad.

"A soul that is all trick and no loyalty for one that is all loyalty and no trick. That would be a trade, would it not?" the pegasus whispered.

A chill swept through me. "No." I wouldn't lose Peggy. Not for me, and Kik…"It would break Kik's heart. There's no way."

"This serves your best interest," Peggy told me.

Her eyes weren't sad because she wondered what I would choose…

She *wanted* me to trade her life for his?

Keefe laughed. "Oh, this I like. Yes, I see what you are offering, Pegasus. I see, and I accept on Orlaith's behalf if I am no longer present to benefit from this deal."

Peggy tipped her head.

"Peggy, stop!" I cried out. "You're with foal."

But one of her feathers had already fallen to the ground. And my magic failed to grasp it as it floated on unseen currents to Keefe. He scooped it up and held it high as the feather darkened to a mottled black and white. "Lovely. Yes. I accept indeed."

"That wasn't the deal," I boomed. "Her foal wasn't in the deal. You *will* release the child."

"I disagree," Keefe said, peering past me to Peggy.

Andas shook his head, but I saw the sorrow in him—not for Peggy, but for me.

Keefe pulled the cutting out from behind him. But I knew it had not been there moments before.

He set it on the ground at his feet. The leaves were more black than silver, as the tree of life had been when he'd yanked it free.

"Drink the wine," I snapped. As soon as he did so, I'd rip the foal from Peggy's body. I had no idea how it would survive outside of her, or if I could find a mare strong enough to carry and birth the foal, but I'd figure it out. I had to.

I'd lost Peggy.

Kik…Kik would break on this news. He'd defied death to get back to her. I reached for Peggy and tangled my fingers in her silken mane. "This was not the way," I whispered. "Why did you do this?"

"It is the path, Underhill. I saw it clearly, even if you

could not," she said unsteadily. "Worry not. This is what is best."

"You said that I had a choice about what was best for me. You took that from me." My words were angry. Hurt. Bereft of hope.

"Yes, because you should not have to bear the weight of some choices."

Furious tears stole down my cheeks as Andas handed Keefe the drink. "Wayward trickster of mine, drink up and say goodnight. Forever. Some fucking help you were."

Keefe looked to Orlaith, then lifted the goblet in a salute and brought it to his lips. There was a moment, a pause, when his eyes met mine. As if he were trying to see if I were serious about this. Like perhaps it was all a joke on my part.

But I wasn't the trickster.

Gaia's touch rippled through me.

Balance is more than balance, child. Think of how the fae looked to their last queen, and now their new queen in a different time. There is a need for light and dark. Look how a common threat has united two forces that have always been opposed. Time is a predator you have not yet observed.

I frowned. What did she mean?

Keefe had been granted power to balance the alliance and relationship between Andas and I. Then, we'd united more and more to oppose Keefe after our individual efforts failed.

If Keefe was asleep, Andas and I would continue to *be*.

Surely.

I was missing something. Something big.

Time is a predator you have not yet observed.

"There's a need for light and dark in different times," I said aloud.

Andas shot me a look, but I could feel a truth pleading with me to find it, one that he couldn't find. Because the instability of this situation called to him.

The instability called to *me* to fix it.

"Cheers, Underhill, Balance and Unbalance. You've won. Also, fuck you, Gaia. You condescending bitch." Keefe tipped the goblet and began to drink, his throat working as he swallowed the wine down.

No. The word reverberated through me. We needed Keefe!

Without thinking beyond my instincts, I leaped toward Keefe and knocked the half empty goblet from his hand.

"What are you doing?" Andas roared. "He won't sleep if he doesn't drink it all!"

I stared at him, panting hard. But what could I say? I still had no idea why I'd just done that.

"You…damn it, Silver." He shook his head at the tea pot in his hand. "That was all of it. That will only weaken him."

He won't drink more now. I blinked. No, he wouldn't.

He shouldn't. He'd had enough to loosen his power. I straightened as the answer blinked into my mind and warmth and peace trailed after it. My lips curved. "He won't drink more."

Andas studied me intently.

"Trust me," I told him.

Keefe wobbled in his seat. "Tricky, tricky. You caught me, Underhill. Not for the first time, but perhaps this was the most important time. Going to sleep for a while would have been worth destroying the love between the two of you."

"What does he mean?" Andas muttered. "That was a trick?"

I nodded. My error was in thinking we could put him in an endless sleep to control him with no repercussions. The whole point of Keefe's existence was that he couldn't be controlled. He was a third player. His power had to be awake and alive for the love between me and Andas to be awake and alive.

The only remaining solution to the pain in the ass that was Keefe was that we had to *regulate* his power; trimming it when needed while knowing that he would always be a nuisance. That would be the price of love between Balance and Unbalance.

He wasn't the only one we'd need to manage.

Orlaith was part of his team. While Keefe might lean more toward Andas, Orlaith leaned more toward me, but they were a father-daughter team.

I motioned to Orlaith. "Take him and go. You two will have the prison realm. We concede it, knowing that you must anchor your powers, but none of us have a claim on the scale realm any longer. That realm is without a ruler, and its time in this war is done."

Andas growled but didn't interject further.

I looked at Peggy, my heart breaking, knowing I'd not only lost her, but Kik as well. "Kik will come to you." I gathered my power, setting my intention on the feather she'd drifted to Keefe.

I was getting that foal.

"Stop, please." Peggy shook her head, her white mane catching the light of the realm. "I did not give him myself, Underhill, but the foal that I carry. Only once he is old enough."

My jaw dropped and I spluttered my outrage. "You paid Keefe with your *child*?" The child they'd thought impossible. The child Kik didn't even know about.

Nausea swam in my stomach. "Peggy—"

She said in undertones. "He was always meant to be more like his father than me. My foal will walk in darkness, Underhill, and I saw that path clearly when the conversation turned toward the cutting. If I do not do this now, then Keefe will still introduce my child to darkness, but Kik and I will die, and our foal will not meet his true rider in life. Though dark, he will be a force of unity and exist in great joy with his true rider if I make this choice."

My stomach swooped because I'd seen some of this too. I'd seen that the foal would walk a dark path.

Keefe clapped his hands and took a wobbling step back. "Orlaith, you help me. I need to sleep for a good while. This has been the most exhilarating...fun times...I'll be seeing you both." He gave an overexaggerated wink toward me and Andas.

Orlaith ran to his side and caught him around the waist. Then she looked my way. "Thank you. You...you could have taken him from me forever, and you didn't. You could have killed me, and you didn't."

She cared about one of those things far more than the other, but I had to commend her forethought in including Keefe in her tearful thanks.

"Remember that," I said quietly. "When you stand against me again."

"I won't stand against you."

I laughed, my heart strangely light considering the weight of my awareness of Orlaith's shortcomings. "You will. It is what it is."

She frowned, and I knew she didn't understand. Maybe she never would fully. But it was enough that I could see what we needed to do.

Finally, *finally*, I could see what the future would be.

A twisted, unprecedented future.

A painful, joyful future.

My path with Andas had cleared, and now I was finally strong enough to walk it.

Orlaith and Keefe slid away, and Peggy walked away a distance as Andas whirled to face me.

"What in the actual fuck was that?" He grabbed at his own head. "We could have been rid of him forever, Silver!"

I scooped up the cutting and handed it to him. "You have a tree to plant, my love."

He stared at me, jaw clenching. "You know something that I don't."

I smiled. "Nothing new. But yes, I may have figured a few things out. Peggy, go to Kik. We must close this realm without delay."

I opened a portal for her and without a backward glance, she left me there, alone with Unbalance.

The scale realm had been used by my mother, her counterpart, and their predecessors for all time. Doing without it would be difficult, and yet we'd managed well enough so far. If we couldn't access it, then neither would Keefe and Orlaith. Everyone would be at the same disadvantage.

Andas frowned. I lifted a hand and smoothed it down the side of his face. "You'll give yourself wrinkles if you keep doing that."

That only deepened his frown. "I don't age. I'm immortal."

We both were. And our common enemy was immortal too.

I'd explain everything to Andas, but first…"Take me

to your realm, Master of Unbalance. Let us close the realm we leave forever and give you a home."

I leaned into him, and his arms wrapped around me as he fell backward through a portal and into the realm that had once been my home and now would be his.

There is a way for us.

CHAPTER 20

"Is it done?" Andas asked from where he'd crouched behind me for the last ten minutes.

I'd drawn on his power and twisted our essences together to seal off the scale realm, much as I'd sealed away the cave holding the tree of life, though without the naga or health of trees to consider, I hadn't left any holes in the seal.

Not for Keefe or Orlaith.

Not for Andas.

Not even for me.

And now an entire realm would exist for the rest of time without anyone to witness its evolution. It saddened me that I would no longer walk where all the Balances before me had ventured, but leaving it open was too risky even if neither me, Andas, or Keefe and Orlaith were anchored to it. "I would have collapsed the realm, but I couldn't be sure of the cost. Likely, it would have gone your way."

Andas smirked. "Likely."

Andas stood and dusted the black dirt from the base of Dragonsmount off his pants. "Are you going to tell me everything yet?"

"Not until the cutting is in the ground. Have you picked a place for it?"

He rolled the black cutting between his fingers. It had synced with his essence upon our arrival in Underhill. "Home. An anchor. The thought is a foreign one."

I inhaled slowly. "I'm going to have a one-hundred-year tantrum if you've decided not to plant that."

Andas cracked a grin, which faded. "I plan to. I'm just not sure how to go about it." He extended the cutting to me. "You know what a home is. Do this for me."

While scanning his serious expression, I took the cutting from him.

Home.

I never could have envisioned a day when this realm wouldn't be *my* home. For me, home had always depended on who surrounded me. My creatures were on Earth, therefore Earth was my home now.

Andas was solitary. He didn't view his creatures in the same way I viewed mine. His home was his power.

And his power was endless and dark, mysterious and unexplored.

"Keep up if you can," I told him.

Breaking into a sprint, I blurred from the base of Dragonsmount toward the plains. Creatures that used to be mine dove for me, their eyes blood-streaked and rabid now that Andas had made his claim.

None of them could harm me.

Andas matched my strides until I stopped abruptly, my toes curling over the edge of the ground.

"You are a sight to behold when you run in that silver dress," he told me. "Like moonlight."

I extended the cutting back to him.

He took it, a question in his gaze. I lifted my finger and pointed down, and Andas tore his focus from me to peer down into the ravine. I'd been down there once with my mother's most trusted servant, a blood fae named Lilivani, but thinking back, I wasn't sure whether she had taken me to the very bottom. It might be the only place in this realm I hadn't fully explored.

An echoing groan rose from the ravine, and Andas's breath hitched.

"This is it," he breathed out.

I nodded. "I'll wait here. This place is yours."

Andas stepped off the edge, and I kept him in my sight until the blackness swallowed him whole. My ears tracked him for another minute, but after that, Unbalance disappeared from my senses.

I definitely hadn't been to the bottom before. I would have remembered a drop like that.

I sat cross-legged, trying to gather my thoughts and theories. What I'd done with Keefe, knocking the wine out of his hands, was just that...a theory. My whole existence ran on theories. Perhaps I'd learn more with a few centuries of experience, but I could finally admit that my mother had prepared me for what she'd seen I would become.

I'd grown up with constant unpredictability.

I'd grown up with peril.

I'd grown up without anyone to depend on but myself.

But she hadn't counted on the love in my future. As powerful as mother had been, she'd been overly rigid in what she'd defined as the boundaries of balance. And I could *feel* those same boundaries trying to assert themselves within me, in the tug on my feet and the warmth in my chest when balance reigned.

But I was willing to forgo some of that warmth in my chest and to ignore somewhat the tugging at my feet. For love. For a different path through this eternal rift between Balance and Unbalance.

I had to wonder...

Had every Balance and Unbalance been designed for one another? Had each couple failed to see past what they thought they were meant to be?

I could be wrong.

I could be right.

I was willing to find out.

Pitiful screams echoed up from the ravine. When the sides began to collapse inward, I pushed my essence under me until I hovered a distance above the imploding ravine. So I had a perfect view as the ground continued to crumple and then smoothed over, the definition between plain and the volcanic territory of Dragonsmount was lost.

The ravine was gone.

A portal opened, and I floated through it to join Andas back at the top of Dragonsmount. He stood on a jutting rock, taking gulping breaths that expanded his chest. His face was pale, his eyes wide with shock. He clutched at his heart, driven to one knee as he continued gulping breaths down.

"Give in," I told him, resting a hand on his shoulder. "That is the tie between you and your creatures, between you and this place. That is the feeling of home."

A great shudder vibrated through him as he heeded my advice.

The only other option was to cut all ties, and I doubted the cutting he'd planted would allow that.

Sweat dripped from his jawline as he rested forward on his closed fists.

I perched on the edge of the rock, letting my feet dangle. There was a fang bat looking at my feet, but it quickly decided against the risk of lunging in to snack on my toes.

Andas, still panting, lay down on his side next to me, propped up on an elbow. "So. A cutting. Spilled wine. A foal. And freeing the most powerful being—

one who's more powerful than each of us individually. Talk."

"It was simple really," I said.

Andas snorted.

I continued, "Keefe was granted power to balance us when I bound to you, so killing him would have destroyed our bond. Removing his power by placing him in endless sleep would either have created a new power to balance us—which might not have been possible considering he is a god and such vessels aren't easy to find."

Andas snorted again. Perhaps he was remembering that he was two people forged together by a tree and a bond to Underhill.

"Or..." I hedged. "If another power was not born, then the bond between us would have broken or put into sleep also. Considering Keefe's reaction when I knocked the wine from his hands, I assume we would have returned to mere enemies as Balance and Unbalance have always been."

"He was going to take us down with him," Andas said grimly. "That's a lot to put together on the spot. I'm glad you did."

As was I. "Gaia had a few words for me."

Unbalance pursed his lips, glancing out over his realm. Screams and groans had replaced the birdsong and roar of dragons. He seemed to enjoy it. "I need to get a Gaia."

"You might get one when our power balance shifts

to me again," I told him. "Until then, I get goddess help. And the coolest team."

Andas's lips curved. "Don't hold your breath. You know I've got at least fifty years of a lovely war between fae and humans to enjoy."

I did. The future had become clearer and clearer since I'd bonded with Andas, especially since I'd figured out Keefe and Orlaith's roles in the realms—and since they'd figured out how they would use their powers.

I wasn't sure how to feel or think about the certainty of war yet—that Andas would strive for battle, and that I'd strive against it, and that we were supposed to still love each other at the same time. How did I find peace about such a thing? I hoped that time would make these things even clearer. "And I'll do everything I can to stop it." Not that it would change anything. The war *would* last for fifty years. After that, I'd reign again. For a time.

Gaia had said there was a need for light and dark, and I believed her. Time really was a predator that I had yet to learn.

But I'd learn it like any other.

"If we're constantly opposing each other, then I don't see how a relationship between us can work," he said quietly, his eyes searching my face. "You'll hate me, Silver. How can I stand that when I've felt how it is to have your love?"

"It's simple really," I repeated.

Unbalance rolled his eyes, then rolled onto his back. "This should be good."

I joined him, and we both stared up at the black, sooty sky of his realm.

"The bond was crucial," I said. "Keefe had to live, but he couldn't be given access to the scale realm. Which means none of us could have it. And yet without the scale realm, you and I would constantly be clashing in the realms, each trying to best the other. Like you, I didn't see how that could end in us having a future together." I took a breath. "So the scale realm had to close, yet the purpose of that realm, the information it provided, needed to be preserved."

Andas turned his face to me, and from his ajar jaw I could tell he'd finally put the rest of it together.

I smiled. "Keefe and Orlaith. Keefe drank just enough wine to loosen his power. He is weaker than us again. For now."

"I feel him, yes. I'd planned to torture him for a time."

"That he's anyone's creature again will be torture aplenty for him, my love. We must focus on maintaining power over them, while also using them. They have a Gaia-given purpose. Keefe is your creature, and Orlaith is mine. Orlaith has a little darkness in her, and Keefe has a sliver of love for Orlaith that prevents him from embracing darkness completely. They exist somewhere between us, and they can be used to keep the balance between us over centuries and millennia."

I could already feel how many lives we would save by doing so—and that relieved a deep guilt of mine that had originated when loving Andas started to claim so many lives. Keefe's power was only given to him to balance us, after all. But our love wouldn't be selfish. I wouldn't need to choose between my duty and my love as centuries went by.

Andas looked up at the tumultuous sky again. "Keefe knows what his role will be. He will work against us."

"And Orlaith will learn very soon. Keefe will be telling her right now. We will have to watch them carefully."

"Neither can be trusted."

I shook my head, then admitted the hardest thing yet. "No, they can't. Because both will need to betray us often to play their role of dealing out just enough balance or just enough unbalance."

Sometimes Orlaith would need to hurt me and my plans to swing power between Andas and I. Sometimes Keefe would need to do the same to Andas. The darkness in Orlaith would allow her to betray me where the bat version of her never could have stomached doing so. I couldn't be friends with Orlaith any longer, but I could respect her role. And I could love her for what she would do, in that it would allow me to share love with my enemy.

Really, Orlaith and Keefe had walked a perfect path to this day. Orlaith, with her networking ability and the way she made the rich and powerful her puppets. Keefe, with his trickery. And, most of all, the strange loyalty and love that existed between them. They belonged to us, but with the amount of wine Keefe had taken in, I felt sure he'd never thwart us on this level again. If he did, it would take him a millennium.

"We will wear the crowns and they will be our general. They'll navigate the acts and deeds that switch the realms between light and dark over the decades and centuries to come, but we will give the orders and be responsible for unleashing our power."

"Along with watching the greater path," I replied. "They will give us distance between fighting each other and loving each other. In time, I believe they will grow skilled at identifying acts of balance and unbalance for us."

I didn't say so to Andas, but I believed a time might eventually come where we could exist in a nearly equal power state. Not for a long, long time though.

"Middle men," Andas mused. "I see the future now —the way has cleared. This path will have its challenges, Silver."

"Nothing between us will ever be without challenge. The question is…are we willing to meet it head on and accept that what we share won't ever be as unconditional and pure as the love of others can be?"

Andas rolled to face me and cupped my cheek in his hand, resting on his bent elbow. "I cannot exist without you. We cannot exist without Keefe and Orlaith. Our life together may have challenges, my love, but for as long as I can see, I will choose to love you through all of them."

"And I you," I whispered, a lump rising in my throat. "Is this really it then? Is the worst done?"

He kissed my forehead. "Not nearly, Silver. Yet the path is clear, and you've made *us* possible. I can't fathom how the hell you did any of it. But you did."

Andas tilted my chin, and I pressed my lips to his.

As long as we could keep doing that—as long as we chose each other every single day—then Balance and Unbalance might love each other until the end of time.

Without half of the suffering I'd feared.

CHAPTER 21

One Year Later

The tiny nose and tips of hooves was all I could see at first, mottled black and white. Crouched behind Peggy, a hand settled on her hip, I reached out and touched the foal's nose, feeling a pulse of magic from him. "I can see him, Peggy, keep pushing. You're almost there."

Peggy lay flat on her side, breathing hard, wings and legs stretched taut as she strained. Sweat slicked her white hide and made her appear more gray than white. Her nostrils were flared and her eyes were wide as she stared at the far side of the oversized stall. Because no one had ever seen a land kelpie-pegasus hybrid, we'd all thought it best for Peggy to foal at the Alaskan court, closest to the best healers in the realm.

Contractions rippled through Peggy's body and

flexed and squeezed her middle, and she groaned. "Him and his big fat head did this to me. Put it back, I've changed my mind. I don't want to do this anymore."

My jaw dropped. "It's…it's too late for that, Peggy."

"I fucking well know it's too fucking late." She roared as she bore down on a spasm. "That fucking land kelpie did this to me!"

Sounded like Peggy was being reborn…

Was it possible that she'd take up Kik's old mantle?

She sagged and her whole body heaved with her labored breathing. I shook my head. This wasn't like with people—Peggy had told me that much—she'd said birthing would be quick once the nose and feet had presented.

But this…wasn't going well. Thirty minutes had passed.

A hand on my shoulder tugged me from Peggy, and Sigella took my place. "Peg, we all know males are terrible. This future one you carry is so stubborn that he got lost somewhere inside of you. Now we need to pull him out. Agreed?"

Peggy let out a sob. "Agreed. I…I can't do this alone."

Somewhere outside the barn Kik was yelling at people. Demanding to know what was going on. Because he knew what we did— we were running out of time.

Please, Gaia, don't let my friend lose her foal to death. No matter how troublesome he will be, and no matter what the future holds for him with Keefe, Peggy needs her child to live.

There was no answer from Gaia. She'd been quiet on many matters I could have used her help with over the last year, and I suspected that she'd largely left me to figure out balance now that everything had settled down.

"Are you ready?" Sigella asked.

"I need to stand." Peggy whispered.

"No—"

Too late. Peggy was on her feet, head down, sides heaving. Two tiny hooves waiting to be grabbed. I wrapped my hands on the skinny legs just above them and looked at Sigella.

"With the contractions," she told me.

Peggy groaned and swayed, and as the contraction came on, I pulled downward. I could have ripped him free, I was strong enough, but that surely would have hurt Peggy.

"Again," Peggy groaned.

Another contraction, another tug, and this time the little—or not-so-little—colt's head and neck appeared. I didn't have time to look at coloring.

Peggy screamed with the next contraction, and I pulled again, but his shoulders were sticking...I didn't want to pull too hard—

"Pull him out!" Peggy yelled.

I connected to the earth below me as an anchor and

pulled downward with as smooth and steady a motion as I could manage.

His shoulders popped free, and he fell toward me, forcing me to catch him before he hit the ground.

"I got him, I got him," I blurted, and then looked up.

Blood. There was too much blood. "Sigella!"

"I'm on it," she said, her movements quick but calm. "A simple thing, hardly anything to worry about."

I didn't look down at the foal in my arms. I couldn't look away from Peggy as she swayed on her feet. Sigella's magic wove around her, sealing off the torn flesh, soothing the damage the oversized colt had caused.

"Thank you," Peggy whispered as she buckled to her knees in the thick straw and collapsed onto her side.

I could barely hang onto the squirming, wet foal. "Peggy!"

"She sleeps." Sigella turned to me. "She needs it. It has been three days since she was able to rest."

I peered down at the colt. He blinked up at me, eyes as mottled as his coat, swirling with black and white.

"Hello." I lowered him to the straw and brushed some slime off with a wave of my hand. The tiniest pair of wings sprouted from his back, and I didn't know if they would grow with him or if they were token wings. He was thick from head to toe, built far more like a land kelpie than the finer-boned Pegasus.

I ran my hand over his face, marveling. I'd seen much death over the last year, as the war raged between the humans and fae.

Seeing life, even one destined to be trouble, was...

He reached out, sniffed at my leg, and then, striking with the speed of a naga, he bit my calf with enough force that I fell backward.

"What the hell?"

He whinnied and showed me a set of teeth in a mocking smile.

Little fucker!

"They should not be born with teeth," Peggy said softly. "I think perhaps we should use the bottles you suggested, Sigella."

Sigella grunted. "I agree with you, my friend."

"Should I let Kik in?" I reeled away as the colt tried to stand, his long gangly legs going in all directions. "Or should I tell him to go away?"

"Go away?" Peggy tipped her head. "Why would you tell him to go away?"

"Because you said this was all his fault, you...you *swore* at him, Peggy," I said. "You said—"

She rolled so that she was still lying down, but in a more upright position. "Childbirth will do that, Silver. And it is his fault. Bring Kik in to meet his son."

I was confused, but I was used to that. It seemed like I was confused by something nearly every damn day of my life. So I strode across the barn.

Opening the door, I peeked out. "Kik? All is well, you can—"

He nearly ran me over as he bolted inside. I stepped back and slowly walked up to join the family.

"Oh wow, Peggy, look at him," Kik said. "You did great, amazing. He's awfully big, isn't he? Fricky dicky, he's huge. How did you push him out? Will you be the same down there?"

I winced. Probably not the best thing to ask...

"Hey, fff—."

I froze. Who'd said that? Such a little voice...

It couldn't be.

I ran the rest of the way to the stall to find Sigella shaking with laughter.

"He...he...oh my gods. He has your mouth, Kelpie." She snorted.

"I was an early talker too," Kik said proudly, drawing himself tall.

The foal gave a full body shudder, then bobbed his head with each word. "Hey, fucker. Fuck. Fuck. Fuck."

Was this foal an early talker? Or an immediate talker?

Kik shook his head. "I don't talk like that! Now. That's not...Peggy, what have you been saying around our son?"

I laughed with Sigella as the new parents squabbled over who'd done what. Even as they did so, Kik nuzzled against the foal—which didn't bite his father as he'd done with me. Kik already knew that while they'd share a joyous two decades with their child, Keefe would then claim the foal for the thirty years after. I was sure that he and Peggy were desperately trying not to think about that time right now.

Beings with power like ours had to learn to appreciate these happy occasions without giving our fear of future days too much space.

I let my heart fill at the sight of them together. One thing had worked out. Peggy was alive, the foal was alive, and they'd already agreed to name him Pik, a mix of their two names.

One crisis averted, but another awaited me.

I walked toward the palace, using my magic to pull the birthing fluids off me. A flick of my fingers cast them aside.

As it was nearing three in the morning, the palace was quiet with only a few fae hurrying about. Sheathed weapons were strapped to their hips and thighs and the fae wore the weapons like they were used to the weight of them—and used to wielding them. The Alaskan Court was far different to how I'd first seen it, and while I knew that some of the changes were due to the effect of my power on this realm, my sister had changed many things in the last year too—for the better, I thought. The glitter was gone, and Kallik expected every fae to sharpen their skills in an area that benefited fae in the war against humans. Fae dressed for function now instead of flare. Opulence had been exchanged for necessity and practicality.

The constant presence of my power was connecting fae and humans to their innate urge to survive. Each day both races remembered and respected more of their primal natures. One day, all creatures would exist on Earth as I had when growing up in the previous Underhill. We would return to the simple cycle of life and death and predator and prey. Because with everything else removed, all creatures understood their place and the risks. That made my job easier.

I knocked on Kallik's door.

"Sister. Come in."

I smiled and opened the door. Kallik sat on her bed, maps and papers strewn over her lap.

"Come. Sit with me." She patted the small clear spot beside her. "I'd assumed you were coming."

I scanned the room until I found the black rose hovering over her breakfast table. My smile grew wider, though my heart ached. I crossed to the rose and gently took it between my fingers.

"He keeps close tabs on you," Kallik said.

Andas left me black roses everywhere, a reminder of our thorned beginnings, his darkness, and the challenging path we'd chosen to walk together.

"Where's Lan?" I asked her, walking over to the bed.

"He's in Louisiana. Working with the new regent. She's young and terrified, but determined to salvage as much of her court as she can." Her eyes narrowed. "As for those who attacked her. Well, that's another story."

I sunk into the soft mattress beside her, saying nothing about the path I'd seen for the young regent with the dark brown hair and softer brown eyes. *Lisella.* She was brave and smart, but...she wouldn't live long. "Have Faolan look to Remy."

Kallik's sharp gaze swung to me. "Remy is third in line for regency in Louisiana."

I shrugged and leaned back, closing my eyes. "So he is…for the time being. Will Faolan return soon?"

"Soon," she muttered. "Not soon enough. You should rest for a while. You look worn out."

So did the queen.

So did everyone fighting the war for balance. We'd look like this for a long time yet.

Like me, Kallik had spent a great deal of time away from her mate. General Faolan was invaluable to the war effort. She saw him far more regularly than I saw Andas, however. A year. Already a year had passed since I'd last seen him, since I'd been able to do more than curse his name or rage at the rampant unbalance spread by his actions.

I picked up the black rose and rolled it between my fingers, listening to Kallik rummage through papers as I stared at the flower.

When I'd left Andas in his new realm to check on my friends and family, I'd never expected so much time would pass before I would see him again. I should have checked our fate before leaving him that day. When I'd finally thought to do so weeks later, our immediate path had driven me to my knees.

Ten years.

I wouldn't see him for another nine years.

We could just portal to one another if we chose to, of course. I'd nearly broken and done so many times. If

I did so, however, then balance would take a serious blow that would hurt thousands of my creatures. I'd gathered that if Andas did so, then his current hold over the realms would take a similar hit. Gaia's silent message was clear enough to interpret.

But ten years...

I couldn't fathom what would become of us after so long apart. Perhaps, given a few centuries, ten years would feel like a blink.

Gaia had warned me that time was a predator I didn't yet know.

I'd assumed that Andas and I would come and go from each other's lives as we pleased. I'd been so fixated on peering farther down our path that I'd failed to look at the hours, days, and weeks of the immediate future of *us*.

There would be times when we could come and go as we pleased—times when our powers were well balanced. The time between those patches was a terrible fate to behold. But maybe, just maybe Andas and I would figure that out as we'd figured out the rest.

Surprisingly, I slept in my sister's bed, though my dreams were bits and pieces of the war we'd fought so far. The deaths, the fighting, the unreasonable fear from my children. My fae children understood this was an era that would pass. They trusted in me to fight that battle. The humans were also mine, but they did not listen or trust well. Their decisions to take realm-sized decisions upon themselves led to disaster more often than not.

I woke only when I heard Kallik's voice rise with excitement. "That's good news indeed. A temporary ceasefire. One week. Agreed."

I jerked upright. "Ceasefire?" The war wasn't over by any means. I could see far too many incidents coming down the line for it to be over. But I'd never considered the possibility of a ceasefire.

Kallik paced the room. "Yes, one week, starting tonight at midnight. A respite to get food and supplies to various camps."

"How? Who suggested it?"

Kallik's eyes went to mine. "A friend of yours. One you saw not too long ago?"

I was up and running, already knowing who'd made this happen. Orlaith. I'd seen her a week before and... she'd seemed sad.

I bolted from the palace, portaling toward the cave where the naga and the tree of life resided. This was always where I met with my Traitor, and I was assuming Andas met with his Trickster at *his* tree of life.

And there was Orlaith, standing as if she'd waited for the sun to rise. Even in the dark, glimmers of silver showed in her skirts as she moved. She was more mine than Andas's, for whatever her slight allegiance was worth. Still, she'd fallen into her role—and Keefe into his—with an ease that had confirmed I'd put everyone on the right path.

From whispers around the realm, I'd gleaned that fae saw the father and daughter as great powers who did the dirty work of Balance and Unbalance. Which was right in a sense.

"Hello, Silver."

"Orlaith." I stared. "Why did you do it?"

Her smile was...not that of a friend, but it was the smile of a person who'd been with me through hard times. "You miss him. You need to see him, and he needs to see you. Plus, you charged me with walking the line of 'enough' balance, not perfect balance. If you won't make this choice for yourself, then I'm willing to do so."

My heart did a double thump. "That's not why."

Her smile slid a little. "I miss you." Her words were quiet and small. "I know our friendship will never be what it was, Silver. I know that, and that just is what it is. But I do hold you in my heart, and believe it or not, I do want to make your life less sad when I can. This is one of those times."

My eyebrows arched. "So Keefe's sleeping, huh?"

Her smile was wide, and light flashed in her eyes. "Yes. He has no idea that one of my people spoke in his stead at the summit. I have a week to play with the French fae I just met—oh, he is luscious and has such a connection to the president of France and to the King of England if you can believe it. He'll be a good addition to our side." Her wink said it all. She had plans up her sleeve.

Orlaith loved the game she played. She *thrived* at it, and while I had to curb her darkness now and again, she was a fast learner and had crossed the line of balance less and less in recent months. This was the first time she'd done so by choice, and she'd done it for me. I couldn't find it in me to deal out any consequences.

"A week," I whispered. A whole week?

She dipped her head, then curtsied. "You're welcome."

I stepped toward her, and she flinched.

I grabbed her and pulled her into a tight hug.

She hesitated, then hugged me back. For just a moment, we were Silver and Orlaith. While I'd never be able to fully trust her, she played a part that allowed me to love Andas. Orlaith had never asked for this, just as I'd never asked to be Underhill. We shared that, and so—yes—I cared about Orlaith in a different way than when she was a bat.

"Thank you," I said.

"Do you need me to get a message to him?"

I shook my head and put distance between us again as our roles settled over us once more.

"No, he'll know where to find me." I smiled and turned from Orlaith, portaling to a place only Andas and I knew.

The cave where we had first chosen ourselves—the

cave where we'd first explored one another. It hovered between realms and was dark enough for Andas to occupy, but its location on Earth meant I could maintain my connection to Underhill.

The cave didn't look like it once had, dark and dank. I'd expanded it and created space for a large bed. Because being bent over a rock while we made love didn't appeal long term. I'd looped strings of light to hang from the ceiling like stars. An ever-present fire burned in an alcove, combatting the dark and the moisture. And I'd grown a thick layer of moss on the rocks so that every step was easy on my bare feet.

How long would it take him to find me? Should I have let him know or—

"So this is what you've been up to," he drawled. "You must've had some spare time."

I answered, "I needed a distraction. I waged war and made our nest more comfortable. It's not my fault *you* can't do multiple things at once."

I spun to see Andas lounging in a chair I hadn't brought here. He'd set it down by the bed.

"You didn't wait till midnight." My words were breathless because the sight of him—powerful, dark, and *here*—stole the air from my body. He hadn't changed at all aside from the new layer of pain in his gaze. I held the same pain. It was the pain of being away from the other half of you, forced apart by circumstances and duty.

A wicked smile curved his lips. "Neither did you."

My stomach fluttered. I hadn't touched him in a year, and I wasn't sure how to break the strange awkwardness that had fallen between us. Did he still want me? I'd yearned for him in every waking hour and sleeping hours too. The year that had passed had felt like ten, all of it riddled with a growing uncertainty of whether he would still be the same at the end of our time apart—and whether I would still feel the same.

"How do we do this?" I whispered. I wanted to leap on him and tear his clothes off, but so much had happened in the last twelve months…so much pain and damage. He'd caused it all, and I'd been a constant pain in his side. I'd yearned for him at every moment. I'd been horrified by his acts time and again in the last year too. I'd raged at him and cursed his name.

And now we were here…

In his eyes, I saw the same uncertainty. Maybe we'd been foolishly hopeless to believe this could ever work.

"In this cave," Andas said. "Nothing exists except us. That's how we do this. We accept that what's outside remains outside and is inevitable—that we are mere vessels for the work of greater beings. But whenever we're here, we leave that at the door."

Could I switch all my thoughts off?

I let my focus roam over him and felt my body warm. The cave suddenly felt very hot. "I have an idea of what might help."

"Fuck and talk later?" he asked.

I stared at him, at every line of his body that I'd longed for and wished to touch, then nodded. "Fuck first. Talk later."

CHAPTER 22

As soon as Andas trailed his fingers up my thighs, my uncertainty flittered away like the useless thing it was.

His attention remained on my face from where he still sat in the armchair, and I cupped his face, peering down at him.

Our shared look held so much—an entire year of figuring out how *this* might work. Worrying about it. Missing each other.

My exhale shuddered from my body, and he sucked in a sharp breath at the same time, as though drawing in the very air I'd held in me.

"I'm sorry, my love," he said, his voice pitched low.

I swallowed. "I'm sorry too."

He trailed his fingers over the laces at the front of my top. "This is new. I like it." A hint of growl entered his voice.

I hummed. "Do you?"

Andas smirked and sat back. His magic replaced his hands—and more. I let him pin my arms to my sides, and when his essence slowly began to unlace my leather tunic from the middle of the low neckline, I smiled.

The two sides of my tunic slowly parted to reveal my breasts, and though Andas's magic held me still, the power at work was all mine. He went rigid in the armchair and the rise and fall of his chest halted.

His expression was robbed of humor as the flat of my stomach was exposed. The tunic had held onto my breasts, but it pooled around my hips now, the last lace remaining threaded in place.

I straddled Andas on the armchair, and his hands replaced his essence. He gripped my elbows and pushed them together behind my back to arch my breasts toward him.

Our shared groans when his mouth closed around my nipple shook the realms. For a brief second, I imagined Orlaith's knowing smirk before Andas circled his tongue, and then all thoughts of anything but him were thrown outside the cave again.

"I won't last long," I told him.

This was nearly causing me to combust.

Andas chuckled, still kissing and sucking his way across my breasts. "My love, that's my line."

I didn't know what he meant. "I'll just need to be

quick the first time, then I'll last longer for the rest of the week."

His rich laughter filled the cave, and I frowned, waiting for him to share the joke—but I never got the chance to hear it before my pants disappeared.

He'd left the tunic pooled around my hips.

Andas stilled as I unfastened his tunic and pushed it over his head.

I peered down. "A zipper?"

"Humans have some useful creations."

They did, and I could barely name one I didn't dislike. In this, Andas was far more accepting of my creatures, ironically.

I ran my fingers over the zipper of his pants, more curious than anything, but when Andas choked, I peeked up at him through my lashes.

"Did you like that?" I repeated the movement.

His hips jerked. "You're not going to get a chance to be quicker than me if you keep that up."

Just like that, a wash of frantic need hit us both.

"I fucking need you, Andas." I drew the zipper down, forgetting entirely that I could've just banished his trousers on the spot.

He steadied my hips, his breaths rapid as I gripped his length and positioned it where we both wanted it.

There was no more build up. I sank down onto him until our thighs touched. My head craned back as joy and the start of hot pleasure filled me.

And desperation.

There wasn't any time to waste. I gripped his shoulder and rocked my hips hard and fast. A blur. He pushed and pulled me, seemingly furious as he drank in my reactions.

He gripped the back of my neck, and I—needing a better hold—gripped the back of his with one hand.

Forehead to forehead, we stared at each other as we chased our climax.

I'd warned him.

My movements grew erratic as the climax hit too easily and out of nowhere. It wouldn't satiate me—I could already feel that. I had a feeling that a week of Andas could barely achieve that.

As languidness spread through me, Andas kept rocking me to milk the pleasure from our love making.

I panted. "I can go again."

"You can," he replied. "I'll need a minute or two."

I peered down. "You finished too?"

His words were dry. "About a minute before you."

"We only fucked for a minute."

"Exactly."

With him still inside of me, I collapsed against him, and our bodies shook with quiet laughter.

"You're exquisite," he whispered in my ear. "I've missed you so damned much, Silver. I've longed to see you each moment of being apart."

I kissed the base of his neck. "Everything feels right again. I'd worried about a lot of things. I'd worried about how things might be...if they might have changed."

He nodded. "I flattened an entire city when Keefe told me you'd slept with the new Irish Ríchashaoir."

I stiffened. "I did no such thing."

Andas took a breath. "No. Keefe got the better of me that time. Orlaith sent a message through an urchin to inform me that there was no truth to the matter. Then my jealous rage cleared enough that I recalled our bond would have fractured at the betrayal."

It would have. "Our bond has helped me a lot. And so have the black roses. Thank you. I've carried each of them with me."

And dried the petals to save too.

"Thank you for the pulses through our bond," he said. "I received all of them, and to my surprise, your love remained with me long after."

"Did it store in your wings as well? The first time I came back to a black rose, my raven feathers soaked up what I felt, and I could feel your love for three days after. I hoped your crow feathers would do the same with the pulses I sent." Turned out there was a deeper reason for the painted wings we'd both received.

"They did, and the slow release of your love kept hope alive in me," he said. "We will need to explore them more to see how they might help us."

He began to absently trace over the painted raven wings on my back, and I shivered.

Andas spoke again. "Promise me that for every

week we are apart, you'll send a pulse through our bond."

"One long pulse for 'I'm okay,' and two short pulses for 'I love you.'" I paused, then added. "An extra-long pulse for when I'm pleasuring myself?"

Andas hissed an exhale as he swelled within me. He scooped under my ass to lift me slightly, then began to gently slide in and out of me again.

I stuttered on whatever I'd been about to say, then asked, "I heard what you called your realm."

"What's that?"

"Your realm."

"What realm?" He picked up his pace.

I groaned. "Eldritch."

Andas portaled us to the bed, and I shrieked at the change of angle as he sheathed his cock completely within me.

"What Eldritch?" he demanded, slamming into me.

"What Eldritch?" I gasped, though the words came out garbled.

I met his thrusts, relishing in the harsh slap of our skin—the sweat, the clash of our magic. The anger. We were both venting a year of frustration and rage.

I flipped him and pinned his shoulders with my power as I rode him hard, grinding down with every pass

Andas reached a hand down and circled my clit without mercy.

I screamed my outrage and gripped his hair.

I was tossed onto my back, then batted onto my front before I could think. Andas pressed a hand in my lower back to keep me still, then spread my ass. His magic slid up between my folds, toward my lower back, but paused halfway.

He said tightly. "Before this week is up, I'll be exploring this."

My body clenched in response. I hadn't known that was possible. I didn't get a chance to reply before he was in me again, shoving me into the mattress with each savage burst.

The covers muffled my screamed encouragement and fury.

I dislodged his hold and kicked onto my back. He was sitting on his haunches when I straddled him again, shoving his length into my entrance.

Intertwined in sitting, we thrust together with an impossible and wild tempo. It was brutal. It was needed.

It was our outlet.

This was our cave. Nothing but us existed in this cave. But there had to be room for us to acknowledge everything we felt. Without words sometimes, and maybe with words eventually.

For now, this felt right.

I felt Andas swell in me this time.

I choked on a breath as his climax spurred my own. His roar filled my ears, and a sigh rose to my lips.

One of acceptance.

One of gratitude.

We could do this.

Andas guided me flat, and I felt him pull on essence to harden himself again. We locked gazes as he slowly moved in and out of me, cradling me in his arms as if I were the most precious thing in all the realms.

The way I cradled his black roses.

I clutched at his back, wrapping my legs around him to help him move as deeply as possible.

The desperation.

The frustration.

The love. This round was *us*.

We rocked together lazily, knowing the climax would come and in no hurry to attain it—so sure were we of its imminent arrival. Our bond was open and shining. My worries were gone, as was my pain.

Surety blazed between us.

And we had another six days.

This climax was a quieter affair.

"Silver," he hushed, bowing his forehead against my shoulder.

I held him to me as I trembled my way through the waves of pleasure. They went on and on in a way the first two hadn't, and I allowed them to catch me up and carry me for the duration.

When the aftershocks stopped, we were both left breathing hard.

I stroked up and down his back as he slipped from me at last.

Andas gripped my chin and kissed me softly. He searched my expression.

I smiled. "I enjoyed every moment."

He relaxed and grinned. "Enjoy is an understatement. You're worth the wait, my love. You'll always be worth the wait."

I curled in front of him under the blanket. War—and the several hours or more of our love-making—had taken its toll. Andas's kisses on the back of my neck grew further apart and fewer between, and eventually, his breathing evened out.

I couldn't help myself.

Opening to the paths, I peeked at the week ahead. A week of us. And of healing from the intensity of war and strife.

This week would renew us and our realms, and we could thank Orlaith for that. And Keefe's timely sleep.

An added glimmer caught my eye from ahead. *Gold.*

The path I shared with Andas was a shimmer of silver and black, but ahead the path shone with the color my mother's essence had been.

And yet not.

The color was vibrant and bursting with life. The color was complex. Not just light and balanced as my mother's essence had been but carrying the undertones of ancient knowledge. An awareness of darkness and unbalance.

I drifted up our pathway until I stood upon the vibrating golden hue.

The gold mixed with our paths for a time.

I studied it more closely. The color mixed with the silver in the path predominately. Particularly for around nine months, and thereafter, the golden linked to Andas's darker essence too. After a time, the gold ventured off...

Onto its own path.

I blinked as the hairs over my body lifted. Every one of them.

My breaths grew shallow, and I could do nothing but stare at my future. Andas's future.

Our child.

We'd have a child. Just one—I could sense that was so from the finality of our gold child.

From the finality of our gold queen, who would replace Kallik.

She would become the Queen of all Fae in truth, not just of light creatures, but both balanced *and* unbalanced beings.

She was the missing piece. The completion to the war always faced by these realms.

Our daughter would ride a land kelpie-pegasus hybrid that matched her unique mixed essence.

Yes, we'd have a daughter. Not any time soon—Kallik would reign for longer than she wanted to, and then she and Faolan would stay on as my daughter's trusted advisors. But when the tide started to shift back to balance in thirty years or so, my child would be born. And she would be the catalyst to finally end the war twenty years later when she was crowned as the gold queen.

Joy filled me. Joy—and pain and hope. Perhaps only Gaia had a word for the enormity of what I felt.

"What is it?" Andas said from sleep, tightening his hold around my middle.

Tears slipped over my face in the dark.

My love was at my back.

We rested in the home of our hearts, where our daughter would be born and grow strong.

My life was perfect. Disastrous, of course, but utterly perfect for me.

Andas would discover the truth for himself soon enough. I couldn't wait to see his face when he did.

"Sleep, my love," I whispered. "We're together and safe."

His breaths were already even again, and my smile softened.

I closed my eyes and matched my inhales and exhales to his, along with the beating of our hearts. I let the shining of our bond cloak us and safeguard us from the wearying emotions and actions of what must lay ahead.

And together, we slept.

Sign up for future updates by visiting the authors' websites.

www.shannonmayer.com
www.kellystclare.com

ABOUT THE AUTHORS

Kelly St. Clare is the USA Today and WSJ Bestselling author of fantasy romance books, including *The Tainted Accords, Supernatural Battle, Magical Dating Agency,* and *Honey & Ice Trilogy.*

Shannon Mayer lives in the southwestern tip of Canada with her husband and son, on a farm full of animals. She has a tendency to write stories that blend action, unexpected twists, and humor with a touch of romance that leaves readers on the edges of their seats. If you can't handle a bit of salty language and heart pounding moments that leave you gripping your kindle or book, you should probably leave now. #NoWiltingFlowersAllowed

She is the Wall Street Journal, and USA Today, and New York Times Bestselling author of numerous urban fantasy, paranormal romance

Made in United States
Troutdale, OR
10/17/2024